**Look out for the link at another book absolutely free.**

© 2019 by Michael Christopher Carter.

This is a work of fiction. Any similarities between events, places and characters in this book and real life are purely coincidental

## Contents

# An Extraordinary Haunting

**Glossary of Welsh from the story:**

**Cariad** – Darling, love
**Bach** – term of endearment. Lit. 'small'
**Hwyl -** Used as goodbye. Lit. 'fun'
**Cwtch** – Cuddle. (can mean cubbyhole)
           **Prynhawn Da** – Good Afternoon

# Chapter One

White knuckles gripped the rusty gate. The bottom hinge had corroded, causing a struggle to lever it open; an effort Neil Hedges couldn't bring himself to make. The tarnished metal provided a barrier against having to go inside the house.

Flakes of faded red paint, clinging desperately to the swollen wooden door a few feet away, stuck out like tongues poking their contempt. Neil shrank back, feeling it. He was being a fool.

Biting too hard at a quick on his finger, he flinched and shook his hand.

"Come on, Neil. Go in. There's nothing to be afraid of," his timid voice fell unconvincingly from his dry, chapped lips, his own words of encouragement lost in the winter air, barely reaching his ears and falling far short of his resolve.

His bladder joined in persuading him to try, and he silently cursed himself for not using the toilet back on campus. Still gripping the rusting green gate, he hauled it to the open position.

Before taking a step onto the weed infested cracked path, Neil's gaze drew slowly to three small windows. Lifeless rooms beyond shed no light from behind dirty glass. The emptiness peered out at him through the inky black eyes of a spider, with him fused to the streetlamp like an encumbered moth.

Cuffing a dewdrop from the frozen tip of his nose, he forced his foot forwards. The impetus carried him, step by tentative step, to the door. Fumbling in his pockets, he grasped for the key and offered it, in trembling fingers, to the lock.

He paused, took a deep breath, and plunged it into the depths of no-return. As the barrel turned, his heart flipped, pounding in his ears. The latch free, the door had only to receive a gentle shove to swing open. Neil looked up and offered a silent prayer as it creaked back on its hinges. Light from the streetlamp shone dimly inside illuminating the stairs and partway down the hallway.

Taking a cautious step over the threshold, nothing happened; which is exactly what the logical part of his mind expected. Eyes flicking in every direction, his racing heart finally slowed at the confirmation of stillness. Sighing with relief, he almost laughed.

Shaking his head, he bent to pick up the daily pile of junk mail accumulating behind the door, placing it carefully on the nearby chair in case any of his fellow student housemates might be tempted by the offers of two-for-one pizza deals, or loft insulation.

Reaching above the chair to the switch, he turned on both the hall and landing lights together to give greater illumination. Keen for the brightness, but nervous of what it might show, he flinched back a step, then snorted at his silliness.

Stepping down the hallway leading to the communal lounge, and beyond that, the horrible, dirty little kitchen the housemates took turns risking their lives from salmonella to cook in, he smiled, pleased with himself. He was inside. And he was fine. If one of the others had returned to find him trembling under the streetlight, he would have died of embarrassment.

Reaching the lounge, he opened the door quickly and thrust his hand to the light switch. With the room lit, Neil was almost sure everything was as it had been this morning. But then, with a sickening realisation, he glanced back to the table, aware of something not quite right.

Without going in, the scene made him gasp. Another timid step, and he was certain. The revolting plates of congealing food, which he was positive were there earlier (it had been the deciding factor in choosing a McMuffin for breakfast) had been swept from the table and lay strewn and broken on the floor, the food debris seeping onto the thankfully hard floor. Neil stared, shaking in reluctant disbelief.

His heart jumped to his throat at a noise from the kitchen. Was that footsteps? He should never have come inside. This was too much. And then, from the corner of his eye, the giant tower of week-old dirty washing up toppled spectacularly to the floor.

The crash, as splinters of broken plates shattered against every surface, exploded in Neil's ears. Too much for his jangled nerves, his full bladder betrayed him, its contents leaking profusely down both legs.

He fled soggily (albeit slightly warmer from the hot stinging urine) back along the hallway and out through the front door, knocking the chair and its stack of post over and back onto the floor.

Slamming the door behind him and leaving his key protruding from the lock, he passed the streetlamp and kept on running, tears streaming down his face. Reaching the end of the street, he squealed as his tiny build collided forcefully with the rotund bulk of Matthew and Lurch-like Josh—two fellow housemates walking back from the pub.

"Whoa! What's your hurry, Neil? Slow down," cried Matthew. He noticed the smell, and Neil's wet trousers. "Have you wet yourself?" he sneered, a look of utter disgust on his ruddy face.

Neil's quick mind realised his little accident at least gave him an excuse why he'd been in such a hurry.

"I lost my door key," he lied. "I was rushing to the toilet back at Uni. And now… Crashing into you two…" Neil could hold their stares no longer.

Nothing more needed saying. It made sense. Neil struck Matthew as exactly the kind of person who wouldn't think of using the toilet before leaving for home. The software-engineering bunch were not the most practical of people in Matthew's opinion. If Google didn't tell them to do it then it wouldn't be done.

As a drama student, he was a lot more confident than his compatriots. At least, he had the skills to act that way.

"Come on then," he said. "We can let you in. Maybe you left your key in the house. Let's hope so! We don't want to have to cut you another one! The landlord's getting sick of us asking for more keys."

Shuffling from foot to foot, weighing up his options, Neil knew he had to go back with them. He couldn't go anywhere else in this state.

"Come on. Don't dawdle," Matthew badgered.

When they arrived together past the lamp post and up the path to the front door, Neil's key was soon apparent sticking out from the lock.

"There's your key isn't it, Neil?" Matthew queried with a frown. Neil nodded, staring at the floor.

Matthew exchanged a knowing look with Josh. They said nothing, but shook their heads. Their opinion of Neil as an oddball had gathered significant new evidence. Even for a geek he was strange, spending most of his time locked away in his room. The brief exchange about wetting himself was the most they'd spoken in months.

They walked into the house as far as they could before the obstacle of Neil's hurried exit prevented further progress. Mumbling a few expletives, Josh set about picking up the chair and strewn post from the floor.

Neil tip-toed past up the stairs to change his clothes. Exclamations from downstairs forced their way through the floorboards as Matthew and Josh discovered the mess in the kitchen.

"Bloody Hell!" Josh roared, joined by a whine of "What the f…" from Matthew.

Neil was just pleased they were here to deal with it now. It was more than he could cope with.

"That sodding cat must have been in again. I keep telling everyone- do the washing up, or the cat finds a way in to lick the plates... We'll have bloody rats before long!" Matthew tutted.

Josh swore profanities under his breath as he struggled to clear up the disgusting mess of coagulating food and sharp broken crockery. He glared unnoticed at Matthew, who instead of helping, watched contentedly whilst declaring the necessity of a house meeting ASAP to make sure this sort of thing didn't happen again.

Josh had almost finished clearing up when Bronwyn, the only girl in the house, and her boyfriend and room-mate Aeron, arrived home from their own night of pub fun. With four fifths of the tenants present, Matthew tried to air his concerns.

"Me and Josh have been forced to clear up a disgusting mess in the kitchen. The bloody cat's been in again cos of all the food left on plates." Josh looked skywards, shaking his head at Matthew's inclusion of himself in the tidying.

"Okay. Okay!" placated the newly arrived couple in Welsh accented unison. "Can we talk about this another time?" Bronwyn slurred. "I'm not feeling my best right now."

"Fine," Matthew had no choice but to agree. The couple left to sleep off their inebriation. Matthew, noticing the good job Josh had done, disappeared too. Josh tutted, any chance of help now absconded.

Being last to leave the kitchen and lounge, he checked as he left that all windows were closed to prevent further feline intrusion. Feeling around the frame to the handle, his eyebrows furrowed in confusion. The window was already locked. Why would anyone open it in such cold weather anyway?

But if they were closed, how did the cat get in? Still puzzled, he pulled the curtains shut to conserve any warmth. Walking across the room, frowning and drumming his leg, he reached the lounge door and paused. With his finger poised near the switch, a reluctance to plunge into darkness prevented him pressing it.

Glancing around, his eyes darted to every corner. Hairs on the back of his neck stood on end as a wave of nausea crashed over him. But his nervous glances revealed only that everything seemed to be in order.

His gaze returned to the light switch as clammy sweat trickled down his forehead. With gritted teeth, he forced himself to move his hand to the switch. From the corner of his eye, the curtain flapped over the window. It couldn't be wind. He'd just checked it was locked

Thump, thump, his pulse drummed in his ear. The hairs on his body joined those on his neck, sending a violent shudder down his spine. His wide eyes stared at the wall. Knowing someone was watching him but certain no-one was there, he couldn't bring himself to check. Muscles rigid with fear simply wouldn't be coaxed to move that way again.

Instead, he flapped at the switch, fumbling the light off after several failed attempts. He didn't turn to look further into the room. Slamming the door behind him, he sprinted up the creaky stairs to his bedroom.

Halfway up, a loud bang almost made him trip and fall. He couldn't help but steal a look back towards the lounge but immediately wished he hadn't. The light he had struggled so to turn off glowed from the crack under the door.

Teetering on the edge to glean any noise which might offer a clue to who was there, Josh slipped with a painful thud onto the step below. His heart leapt to his throat, the sound of it blocking all else. He didn't know what he expected, but someone, or something had turned the light back on. And if they heard him on the stairs…?

He ran, lurching up the last three steps, skidding around the half landing towards his room. Rattling the door handle which usually gave no trouble but now seemed contrarily determined to torment him further, he finally (more through luck than any moderation of technique)

managed to shake it open. He leapt inside, snagging his sweater pocket on the handle, catapulting him back onto the landing.

Untangling himself, he slammed the door shut, then reacting to the total darkness he'd rushed into in his panic, he batted his hands on the wall hunting for the light, knocking a few empty cans and DVD cases to the floor.

At last he found the switch. Thankful for the light, he leaped the room to his bed in a single bound, hauling his covers over his head. He knew it wasn't a good idea to sleep in his clothes, but there was no way he was moving again until daylight.

# Chapter Two

Neil's ears pricked. Fitful sleep had succeeded by him leaving the light on and stuffing a feather pillow over his head, but something now penetrated his defences and woke him. Identifying a source over the pounding in his chest was hard. Pulling away the pillow, he reluctantly gave it his full attention.

He fought the urge to call out. Part of him wanted to—a reply from Josh or Matthew would put his mind at ease—but responding to the impulse, his hand clasped over his mouth. What if someone else, or something else answered instead?

Too late. He had already spoken.

"Hello? Who's there?" His heart banged harder on his chest, desperate to escape. "Why did I do that?" Neil berated himself. No answer came from Josh, or Matthew, or anyone. But there was still the sound.

With the pillow in his hands, the impulse to throw it back over his head was hard to fight. Realising sleep would be impossible until he knew what had woken him, he had to be brave and investigate.

"You're gonna regret this," he warned as he pushed the duvet aside and placed his feet on the carpet, hard with encrusted stains from coke and food.

Pushing himself to stand, he steadied himself on a chest of drawers when his sleepy legs failed in their solidity. Walking towards the door, he shook his head. He had a bad feeling about this.

The sound became louder as he moved, a whooshing noise he recognised but couldn't place. With his hand on the doorknob, he froze. His sweating palms struggled with grip and he seemed to have the strength of a baby.

Pulling his pyjama top down to hold the knob with more friction, this time he threw it open with an unwelcome force. He stood in the doorway, breathing heavily, anxious the source of the noise might be alerted to his presence.

And then, with a laugh of incredulity at his edginess, he recognised what had woken him. The muffling thickness of the door must have disguised the sound. Someone was running a bath.

The wall caught him as he leant back, a hand on his shaking head. Bath taps. That's all it was. Turning to his room, he chuckled again and grabbed the door to close it, but something wasn't right. Glancing back down the hallway, then staring fully, Neil's sleepy head tried to work out what it was.

The sound of running water was unmistakeable, so what was wrong? Darkness. There was no light in the bathroom. Someone must have turned on the taps and

17

forgotten about them. He walked with purpose to turn them off. Who would do that? A flood would cause so much damage. He tutted, flinging the door open with annoyance.

His hand outstretched, he shuddered. Looking at his bare arm, watching detached, almost as if it were a nature documentary, all the hairs moved thirty degrees up, their follicles protruding in little mounds. He smiled in fascination as though witnessing a sunflower grow from seed to ten feet high in rapid time-lapse film. Then the fear which goes along with this biological reaction gripped him as the light faded and the bathroom door creaked closed.

"What!" Neil leaped towards the diminishing slither of light, terrified of being alone in the dark. Why hadn't he just switched the light on? Stumbling over something on the floor, his arm flailed as he fell, grasping for support, his arm tangled in the grubby pull chord with its little china cat on the end. The force of him falling with it in his hand propelled the small blue feline at speed toward the ceiling where it smashed into a hundred pieces.

The noise reverberated around the room, but soon a reason for the darkness blocked the memory when the grating motor of the extraction fan ground into life. Filling the air with its hideous noise, juddering and shaking the entire house.

Neil disentangled himself from whatever he had tripped on and pulled the chord again. In the split second it took for the light to fade, his heart leapt to his throat at what he glimpsed. Long hair floated on the surface of the bath water concealing naked female flesh beneath.

"Oh my God. I'm so sorry. So, so sorry," Neil uttered, hurriedly closing the door behind him. Running the few steps back to his room, he slammed the door and leaned against it.

"Shit!" Bronwyn would be so mad with him. How would he explain that to Aeron? "You perving on my girlfriend?" he could almost hear him yell. He pulled at the collar of his T-shirt imagining his large hands around his neck.

He forced a laugh. "They'll see the funny side, I'm sure," he said, muffled by his pillow which he'd returned to its comforting position over his head. He lay, trying desperately to push images of the nakedness from his thoughts and steal some sleep.

Morning brought relief. Neil lay staring at the ceiling and contemplated moving. A knot in his stomach tightened and his face glowed hot. The redness came before the memory.

"Oh, God," he sighed, his hand over his eyes. He allowed his feet to swing around and contact the floor. "I hope I don't have to deal with them yet," he said to the empty room, knowing he probably wouldn't. Most mornings, he was last out of the house, apart from Josh who slept through the day, venturing out only for lectures and Starbucks.

Going downstairs, he was pleased to find the kitchen tidier than usual—a benefit of the depleted crockery being washed out of necessity, he supposed.

The bread bin hunched on the worktop, ready to assault his senses. Neil squinted, and opened the sliding plastic door with a spoon to avoid touching the butter smeared surface. A packet of bread inside looked happy to be released from its grimy incarceration and rewarded him by being relatively mould free. He carefully picked the few green flecks from the crusts and toasted two slices under the grill satisfied the heat would kill any germs.

Next, a search for something to spread on it. There was butter, still in its packet, but so contaminated with jam and marmite and goodness knows what else that he was indisposed to use it. Solidified honey stood forlorn at the back of the cupboard. A quick run under the hot tap would render it usable again and clean the stickiness from the bottle.

Wiping away clutter from the table in the lounge, Neil landed his toast and honey, and a steaming cup of sweet tea, and sat down. This wasn't what he had expected from life in a student house, he considered, whilst chewing his first bite of toast.

His own room was a mess, but it was an organised mess. He could find most things he needed right away. And it was clean; apart from the assortment of cups, glasses and food plates from when he snacked in his room, which was most days. Okay, so it wasn't clean at all, he realised. But it was his mess. He took more care in communal areas.

When he had first learned of the available room, Matthew had even warned him that Bronwyn, was 'a bit of a neat-freak.' But apart from her occasional nagging, and insisting on having the downstairs bathroom all to herself, there had been little evidence of it.

He took comfort in knowing the Christmas holidays were coming up. To be back with his family in a lovely clean house, with his mum's cooking... heaven. This term had been so long. And so much harder than last year.

But beyond the mess, it was all the weird stuff he was most keen to leave behind, and he was damned sure it wasn't the cat. The large furry beast had been a nuisance when they first took over the tenure, due to the previous occupants feeding it. After weeks of shooing it away, it learned it was no longer welcome.

Yowls of disdain were still heard occasionally outside Josh's window (no mean feat, as it involved the scruffy thing climbing to the second storey of the high ceilinged Victorian house to a precarious perch on the sill), but a well-aimed empty beer-can made enough noise to chastise it away. No, Neil was certain none of the weirdness could be blamed on any cat.

He almost choked, recalling again with horror, the excruciating embarrassment of last night's bathroom blunder. Gripping the table and perching forwards, he dislodged the wayward toast crumb, washing down any remains with tea, ignoring the globules of fat from the on-the-turn milk.

But Aeron and Bronwyn's disapproval was the least of his worries. As he stuffed the last crust into his mouth, dribbling honey down his chin. If anything, it was a useful distraction from his constant nagging fear. He was smart. He knew that. But how could logic explain everything that had happened? And it wasn't just the things he could identify either. It was more... a feeling.

How did he feel? Unwelcome? Yes, that was it.

Someone, or *something*, wanted him out.

# Chapter Three

"That's it!" screamed Bronwyn. "We're having a house meeting!"

Her hysteria was caused by the discovery of her clothes, which she had left in the tumble dryer, strewn all around the lounge.

"If someone needed to dry their own washing, they could have folded mine, or waited, or at the very least piled them in one sodding place!" she fumed. "This little temper tantrum one of you has had is pathetic."

Flouncing around the room, she collected clothes from their unusual resting places. Knickers on top of the telly, a bra behind the sofa, and all number of once crease-free items crumpled in heaps like rags on the dirty floor.

"This is sooo disrespectful!" she shrieked. No-one came forward to own up. She didn't even know who was in. She should find out, because whoever was home would be the culprit.

Folding her creased clothes, she left them in a pile on a chair, then presuming to uncover the offender, she marched into the hallway and shouted up the stairs. "Hello? Hello?" No-one answered. She couldn't be doing with this. She had enough work to do without this hassle.

A long hot shower in her nice clean bathroom, her own little sanctuary with no boy mess, would calm her temper. But before that, she scrawled a note on an old envelope:

*'House meeting tomorrow (Saturday) as soon as everyone is up! We need to talk!!!'*

Scribbling her signature, she pinned it to the noticeboard in the hallway and headed off to enjoy her shower.

She heard no-one return to the lounge and toss her things around again because she was under the hot flow of water. Nor did she hear the crash of washing up, smashing once again on the kitchen floor.

Aeron had been oblivious to most of the goings on. His bar job took up his spare time. When home, he usually locked himself away in his room catching up with his desperately lacking course-work.

Bronwyn supported her boyfriend by bringing him drinks and snacks and keeping on top of his laundry, so he had little reason to visit the shared areas of the house.

Today though, he had thoughtfully brought back some kitchen surplus from the bar-food leftovers, and planned to put it away. Hearing Bronwyn's shower flowing, he called out 'hi', but she didn't answer.

When he found the mess of scattered clothes, he wondered if they'd had a row he couldn't remember; that she'd kicked off, chucking her stuff about in a temper. Tutting to himself, he decided to placate her displeasure at whatever he'd done by picking them up and re-folding them.

He forgot about his food in carrier bags beside the lounge door and went off with Bronwyn's freshly boy-folded garments to put lovingly on her bed.

She returned dripping wet, wrapped in just a towel, and was touched that Aeron had been thoughtful enough to bring her clothes in. She called out her thanks, from which he deduced she wasn't cross with him anymore, and smiled to himself. "Good job!" he said, and raised his hand for a self-high-five.

He popped his head around the threshold with a boyish grin. Bronwyn's towel fell seductively to the floor. Aeron stepped inside, closed and bolted the door and the pair prepared to enjoy some closeness. Matthew's discovery of the chaos in the kitchen ruined that.

"Oh no! Not again?!" he screeched. "We can't afford to buy more crockery just because some idle so-and-so's too lazy to wash up!"

He was as guilty as anyone else, but the particular plates laying like unhygienic crazy paving on the lino, he was fairly sure were nothing to do with him.

"This is f'ing ridiculous!" he persisted. "I'm not clearing this up. It's not my mess. And now I can't even have a cup of coffee!" He marched into the hallway so that whoever was home and responsible for the mess could hear his ranting and deal with it.

"Hello? Hellooow!?" he hollered.

A dishevelled and sweaty Aeron opened Bronwyn's door and stuck his head out.

"What's up, Matthew, mun?" he barked. Intimidated by Aeron's superior physique, Matthew calmed his tone to a more respectful whine.

"Someone has left dirty plates again and the cat's knocked them all over the bloody floor," he said. Aeron looked thoughtful before replying.

"Wasn' me mate. I ate at work." He turned back into the room. "You leave any washing up, cariad?" he asked, already certain of the answer.

"No. But while you're moaning, Matty boy, I'd like to know who threw my clothes out of the tumble drier and chucked them all round the lounge," she squealed from the bed. "Someone's having a laugh aren't they? Well it's not bloody funny!"

"I wondered what happened to your clothes," Aeron commented, but Bronwyn didn't know it had happened again since her own discovery and clear up.

"I've put up a notice. House Meeting. First thing tomorrow we're going to put a stop to this nonsense!"

Matthew had nothing to add apart from his nervous nodding in ready agreement. Aeron closed the door and went back to cheering up his girlfriend. Matthew went out again to buy a coffee, at an expense he could ill afford, from Starbucks. At least it would taste better than the crap they bought from the Cash and Carry.

Once again, it was left to a cursing Josh to clear up the broken plates when he arrived home. He observed the

'House Meeting' notice approvingly and went upstairs for a well-deserved rest.

Neil arrived shortly afterwards and gratefully noted the tell-tale signs of life within: voices coming from Bronwyn's room, and the buzz of Josh's computer vibrating through the wall to the landing. He almost went into the kitchen to attempt to find more food fit for human consumption, but when he saw Bronwyn's handwriting pinned up, he changed his mind. Something else must have happened.

Instead, going straight upstairs, he retired to his room, listening out for when he might latch onto someone else's meal plan. He would probably end up just going to the chippy on the corner.


After their post lecture naps, the housemates' all roused themselves for food. Them all being determined to avoid the kitchen entailed leaving the house intermittently to go to the various and plentiful takeaway establishments nearby.

It all meant that by the time Matthew returned from his Starbucks coffee (and whilst he was there, a slice of cake, and whilst in town he may as well save himself the bother of coming out again by grabbing a burger, or two), he was alone.

All was quiet. Nothing unusual to report. He didn't hold with the supernatural explanations Neil had been hinting at. Everything had a logical explanation, even if it was admittedly a little odd.

The House Meeting tomorrow would hopefully clear things up. He didn't expect anyone to own up to anything because it was probably down to all of them being a bit thoughtless. A few well-conceived ground rules, and it should be a much nicer place to live.

He sat in the lounge watching telly, then remembering some washing he'd been trying for days to get done, he got up and checked the machine. It was empty now, and the dryer, so it seemed like the perfect time.

He brought his laundry basket down from his room in the front corner of the house. He separated the loads of appropriate colour. When he had made several piles of little loads that would take forever to get done, he abandoned laundry protocol and bundled them all into the machine together, taking care only to remove the couple of white things.

Goodness knows when he'd have enough items to complete a reasonable load of whites. Maybe he could share with someone else, but he hated the idea of his clothes mingling with the others' pants and stinky socks. He shuddered.

"Damn!" he exclaimed as the tiny amount of washing powder in the box clung damply to the sides like soapy concrete. "I'm not going out again now," he declared to the empty space. "At least I've bagsied the machine."

He ventured back to his room to update his Facebook friends of his annoying laundry experience, and to play his X-box until dawn.

Saturday morning arrived to a houseful of sleepers. The meeting wouldn't happen until well after lunch (or breakfast as Josh would insist on calling it, no matter what of time of day. If he lay in bed and didn't eat until evening, for him it would be breakfast because breakfast is the first meal of the day; even if it's roast beef.)

Bronwyn, first up and remembering the washing powder had run out, took some money from the petty cash (that everyone was supposed to contribute to, but she was sure not everyone did). She braced herself against the cold and made her way across the couple of cross-roads to the local convenience store.

Buying the cheapest washing and fabric softener combination in the shops own brand, she sauntered back to the house. Pausing at her room to collect her basket, she balanced the detergent atop of the dirty clothes. She almost dropped the lot when she entered the kitchen, such was her rage at the sight.

Someone's stinky washing (she was sure she recognised that lard-arse Matty's T-shirts) were tipped all over the lino. She could just picture him finding no powder and chucking the clothes on the floor in a ridiculous sulk. Well, she wasn't about to go anywhere near his putrid pants.

Using her basket, she cleared a path to the machine without having to physically touch any of Matthew's pongy clothes. She would probably wipe it with disinfectant afterwards.

She placed her dirty washing, and the freshly purchased powder into the machine and set it to wash. This bloody meeting couldn't happen soon enough. Aeron might punch Matthew's lights out for being such a twat if she didn't stop him. Maybe she wouldn't, she smirked.

Neil hadn't slept too well. Noises had infiltrated his feather-stuffed fortification. He wasn't about to suffer the excruciating embarrassment of the bathroom light incident again, so he persuaded himself it was a cat and doubled his pillow protection. Roll on Christmas holidays. Only a week to go now.

In the calm silence afforded by his bedding, Neil pondered what to expect from the house meeting. Moaning, definitely. And everyone agreeing to whatever rota of chores Bronwyn or Matthew cooked up.

He wasn't planning to mention any supernatural explanations, convinced they thought him silly and wouldn't listen anyway; but more that talking might make it real. He would just sit and listen and agree to everything until it was over.

Creeping down the stairs to the kitchen, he noticed (he could hardly fail to do otherwise) Matthew's clothes littering the floor. Ignoring them, and the smell, he grabbed himself a bowl from the shelf.

It was his turn to go shopping with Josh this week, according to the unofficial but regular arrangement the household had come to. Aeron and Bronwyn would shop one week, and he and Josh the next. Matthew would join either pair every week. It was imperative for him to have his say on food buying.

Whilst Neil wasn't as concerned as Matthew, he was no big fan of the healthy eating Quorn and Tofu crap which made up a lot of the food supplies on a Bronwyn shop. She wasn't vegetarian, but she was obsessed with low fat.

He also didn't enjoy her choice of breakfast cereals. Granola and muesli were a boring way to wake up in Neil's opinion. Give him Coco-Pops or Golden Nuggets any day of the week. That might be worth a mention at the meeting.

He jumped out of his skin when a loud voice behind him bellowed,

"Are those your clothes in there, Neil?" a furious Matthew challenged. Neil shook his head and quietly suggested they were probably Bronwyn's, as she was the only one who wore a pink bra.

Matthew, ignorant to Neil's sarcasm, studied the machine more carefully and watched, wondering how to play it, as Bronwyn's enormous bra tumbled soapily round and round the glass in the washing machine door.

"Did you see her chuck my clothes on the floor?" Matthew demanded again. Neil shook his head once more. "Well, I'll have something to say about this at the meeting!"

"Say about what?" Aeron's deep voice inquired from the doorway.

Matthew, careful not to name names said, "Someone's thrown all my clothes out of the washing machine so they can do their own!" in a far more respectful tone than he'd used towards pint-sized Neil.

Aeron could see Bronwyn's bra. He shrugged, suggesting he didn't know who could have treated Matthew's clothes this way. The similarity to yesterday's mess creased his brow.

He supposed Bronwyn had known about her strewn stuff and throwing Matthew's around the room was her revenge. Well-deserved, if not a little childish. He'd wait to hear what both of them had to say before taking Bronwyn's side.

"Is Josh up yet?" Aeron asked, keen to start the meeting and see Matthew squirm at the accusations.

"No, but I could wake him," offered Neil. He was still hungry, having been unable to find a cereal to his taste. After the meeting he could get something he liked.

"Okay," said Aeron. "I'll get Bronnie, and we can start. We'll all need strong coffees," he directed at Matthew. "You can make those. Three sugars for me." He didn't bother adding please.

Matthew gathered the eclectic assortment of cups which had survived the washing up attacks, and added instant coffee granules and three sugar's to all but Neil and Bronwyn's.

The housemates, with varying degrees of blurry eyes, sat clutching their hot mugs to them for warmth.

"Right, let's begin," announced Matthew as self-appointed spokesperson.

"I need time to wake up a bit first," Josh growled from under heavy hooded eyelids. They all waited, taking occasional sips of their coffees for the best part of half an hour before they noticed that Josh, far from waking up, was falling back to sleep.

"Wake up! We can't wait any longer," Bronwyn shrieked. "There's stuff we need to sort out." Josh gulped down the last of the now cold coffee, and slapped himself in the face a few times before announcing he was ready.

Bronwyn, not Matthew, introduced the agenda; which she deemed only fair as it was her who had called for the meeting. Neil stared down at the floor, unwilling to meet her eye. It was the first time they'd been in the same room since the bathroom incident. His mind searched for words to explain, and to apologise, but Bronwyn spoke before any came.

"We all know what's been going on, but I think a re-cap would be in order… I'll begin. Yesterday, I arrived home to find my clean washing removed from the tumble-dryer in a most disrespectful fashion. I don't know which one of you boys thinks it's okay to throw a girls private property around, including some very intimate items of clothing, because it isn't!"

"Bang out of order," Aeron added supportively.

"Well don't look at me!" objected Matthew as the entire group looked at him. "I'd never do that! And besides, if you go in the kitchen, you'll find *my* clothes all over the floor now."

"That's because you threw them there in a temper when you realised we'd run out of washing powder. I bought more while you were still asleep. I washed my own clothes then—fair enough? I wasn't going to pick up your pongy pants, was I?" Bronwyn almost shouted.

"You liar!" Matthew shrieked. "I put my dirty washing in the machine. You must have taken them out to wash yours. It makes perfect sense."

"Well I didn't," asserted Bronwyn.

"Liar!"

"Oi! Watch it, tubby," Aeron warned.

"She must be lying," Matthew protested.

"Well, I'm not! I never touched your bloody stinkin' clothes."

"Alright, alright," Aeron placated. "This is getting us nowhere. JOSH! Wake UP!" Josh sat bolt upright and apologised. "What do you think has been going on? If you've even been listening?"

"I have been listening," an indignant Josh mumbled under his breath. And then a little louder he said "I don't know what's been happening to Matt and Bronnie, but twice I've had to clear up broken crockery that no-one's washed up. We all need to chip in and make sure we leave it clean. Or the cat comes in and knocks it over trying to get to scraps of food."

"It's not the cat!" blurted Neil to an awkward silence. Glances of disdain were shared by the others before Josh decided to confess his own fear.

"The windows *were* all closed the other night when we got back and found the mess," he began, before logic fought its way back into his mind and he amended his anxiety, wondering if one of his fellow housemates might be going insane and throwing clothes and plates around.

"Well, rats then," suggested Aeron. "Rats can get in anywhere. They don't need a window open and with all this leftover food…"

"And I suppose they threw my clothes on the floor too!" Bronwyn added sarcastically, objecting somewhat to the idea of rats in the house. "No. Someone's playing silly buggers and it's got to stop," she concluded.

Neil suspected he was the only one considering a supernatural cause, and he wasn't prepared to make a fool of himself arguing his point. Instead, hoping fervently that the others were right, he made another suggestion.

"Obviously no-one's going to own up to throwing the clothes. Maybe it was one of us sleep-walking or something," he submitted sensibly. "But it could easily be rats coming in and knocking the washing-up over. Why don't we have a really good clear-up today? We can look for signs of entry and block them, and discourage them from entering the house in the first place by keeping it really clean."

Everyone agreed. They all hated housework, but they hated rats more. They decided having it spotless for when their respective parents collected them next week for the Christmas holidays would be a nice surprise too.

Full of relative enthusiasm, they also discussed the shopping arrangements and agreed to separate shelves of the cupboard each, so they could have food to their own taste.

The others taking up Neil's suggestions so readily buoyed him to tackle the elephant between him and Bronwyn. For the first time, he looked her in the eye.

"Sorry about the other night, Bron," he said in as friendly and confident manner as he could muster. Her eyes flashed with curiosity, shrouded by a frown.

"What are you on about, Neil?"

"Turning the lights on when you were in the bath. I didn't see anything improper. Promise," he answered with a weak smile.

"I don't know what you're talking about," she said with a dismissive shrug, her scowl sharp enough to cut paper. "I've never used that bath! Your bathroom's a disgusting, piss-reeking mess for starters. And I only ever have showers. Laying in your own filth for an hour getting cold is not for me."

"But... I saw you. Well, your hair anyway, when I turned on the lights—just for a second. I thought someone had left the taps running. I didn't want it to flood through the ceiling into your room or the lounge."

They were all silent. A vision of a girl in the bath, combined with the other weirdness was compelling and terrifying.

"For goodness sake, Neil. You obviously dreamt it all. Don't bring your wet dreams of Bronwyn in the bath—

pardon the pun—to this meeting and bother the rest of us with your nonsense," Matthew harangued unkindly.

Despite the unfair rebuke, Neil grasped onto the rational description. It must have been a dream. It was the only explanation which gave any comfort.

# Chapter Four

The morning cleaning regime occurred elsewhere too. The Railway Tavern was getting its usual pre-opening-time spit and polish. They would open late today after a rowdy Friday night.

"Aww, shit!" exclaimed Jon, the live-in manager, upon his discovery of a pile of vomit which hadn't quite made it all the way to the Gent's.

"Efa!" he called. "I need you to clean up here, please."

The young and pretty girl who did the cleaning in the pub at the weekends to help pay her way through a photography degree course almost wretched at the sight. Cleaning wasn't exactly a calling, and she felt a little delicate after drinking herself silly at the same bar the night before.

She managed to gulp down her disgust and not add to the mess on the floor as she slopped hot soapy water over it and scraped it up. Afterwards, she continued diligently cleaning, collecting glasses, and mopping floors. She even cleaned the toilets.

"Come here, Efa" Jon invited. She wiped her hands on her apron and walked over to her boss.

"I might have to put a little extra in your wage packet for your dedication!" he encouraged. "And don't think I failed to notice you adding to the profits here last night. I didn't expect you in today, or late at the very least. But here you are, bright and on time and doing a fantastic job. Thank you. I really appreciate it."

Efa was pleased about the extra, well-needed money, but she wasn't sure how much of Jon's demeanour was gratitude and how much was just smarmy charm. His presence gave her the creeps. She didn't know why he had joined her in the usually solitary cleaning of the bar.

He didn't scare her. She knew she could handle herself if he became a problem, but she didn't like him. With the pub being so close to her digs and college, she had been grateful to him for giving her the job, but she hoped his creepy company wouldn't become the norm.

Jon patted the stool next to him at the bar.

"I've made you a coffee. You look like you could do with it," he said. Efa debated refusing his invitation, but his interest in her had not been evidenced. It was just a feeling. She decided she had no justifiable grounds to decline. And she could certainly do with the caffeine. She sat at the bar with her boss.

"There you go," he said. "You're becoming quite a valuable fixture here." She raised her eyebrows whilst simultaneously sipping the hot coffee. "You are very, very pretty, Efa. A very attractive girl."

Efa stiffened. This is exactly what she didn't want to happen. She glugged down her coffee too fast, burning her lips and throat, keen to finish and be away before he said anything else they would both regret.

"If you ever want some bar work as well as the cleaning, just say the word. I'm sure I could use a pretty barmaid like you."

She softened. His comments made more sense in the context of being offered more work. She was calculating whether she could spare the time and what she would do with the extra money when she became aware of his hand on her thigh.

It took a couple of seconds to come out of her musings and react. She pushed it respectfully away and said, "No. You mustn't do that."

"Aw, come on…" he grinned at her. "What's wrong with a little fun? You scratch my back…"

He placed his hand back on her thigh but slightly higher.

"No!" she said, sterner this time. She shoved his hand purposefully away and jumped down from the barstool. Jon grabbed her wrist and thrust his hand up her skirt.

"Let's just have a little fun," he insisted. Efa swung her arm and smacked him hard around the face. Jon's fingers pressed into her delicate forearm. "You fucking little cock tease!" he screamed.

Efa scowled. Opening her mouth, her white teeth parted and drew closer to Jon's fleshy cheek. Opening wide, her eyes rolled in her head like a white shark as she thrust her mouth forward. Feeling the meat in her mouth, she forced her teeth together. Winding her head, Jon's screaming made her almost frenzied.

Yelping, he let go of her arm to clutch his savaged face as Efa spat blood on the floor walking away.

"You fucking little bitch!" he whimpered, rocking on the spot. Efa had reached the door and was opening it. She wouldn't let him get away with it. Stepping outside, the muffled cursing of her boss made it out to the street.

"You're fired," he squealed.

Efa's steely eyes pierced the closing door as it swung on its hinges. "I don't think so," she vowed under her breath.


No evidence of a rat infestation, or even that any rats had ever been inside number twenty-four, Rhondda Street became apparent. The cleaning efforts had discovered no rodent entry points, or faeces, or signs of nibbling. The only suggestion of their presence remained the fallen crockery, and that was no indication at all by itself.

No-one bothered commenting upon these facts. They all knew that if the washing up was done and put away, it couldn't possibly fall over again no matter what the original cause had been.

The stairs were vacuumed and floors were mopped. The tidying didn't go so far as to deal with the mess in their rooms. That would be a day or more's work on its own. So after a tentative start was made on them anyway they decided they'd done enough for today and declared it time to eat.

Bronwyn cooked soup from everything they had in the fridge she deemed healthy. She served it with toasted, gluten-free bread and everyone enjoyed it. Nothing like physical activity to boost your appetite.

After a post lunch nap, Aeron jumped up remembering his scheduled pub stint. He showered, changed and bid the rest of the group farewell. It was a short walk to The Railway Tavern. He burst through the door, a smile already in place, and jogged behind the bar.

"Welcome, welcome, young Aeron" bubbled a pseudo-buoyant Jon. He attempted to hide his left cheek from his staff but the plaster was too obvious to miss. Noticing Aeron's gaze he pre-empted any question with a quick explanation.

"I cut myself shaving" he said. Aeron couldn't help but raise an eyebrow at the unlikely account. "It's a bloody cut-throat one," Jon defended. "Could have been worse," he added with a wink. Aeron wasn't that interested, so he happily dropped it. A customer needing serving soon took his attention and he got to work. Jon disappeared out to the back and Aeron, along with another student barman and an older barmaid ran the busy bar.

He'd miss his wages when he went home for Christmas. Especially with the increased opening hours and double-time he could have earned. Jon said he was welcome back when he returned from his family, which Aeron considered could be soon. He loved them, of course, but he really enjoyed the money and independence here in Swansea.

If Bronnie would join him, it would be a lovely quiet time together. He daydreamed his way through his shift and the night's end soon approached. His colleagues beat a hasty exit, leaving him alone with his manager.

"Do you fancy staying behind and doing a bit of cleaning?" Jon asked. Aeron agreed without question, but Jon explained anyway. "That young girl, Efa? She came in very late this morning, so I had to let her go."

Something in the reddening of Jon's uncovered cheek told Aeron there was more to it than he was being told. Efa had given a good account of herself, he could tell, and he smiled knowingly. Negotiating double-pay, he set to work.

As the evening turned to midnight, Jon, staggering slightly, re-joined him in the bar just as he was finished and preparing to leave.

"Stay and have a drink," Jon slurred, the high pitch to his voice belying an anxiety Aeron didn't understand. "On the house," he assured.

Aeron couldn't account for Jon's generosity, apart from his obvious inebriation, but a free drink was a free drink, and he was not about to refuse without a good reason.

"Okay. Thanks," he said.

"What'll you have?"

Aeron wanted his freebie, but didn't want to be nursing a pint for the next half an hour, chatting with this person he was none too fond of. "I'll have a Penderyn," he said, testing his boss's intentions by asking for the expensive Welsh single malt whiskey. When he didn't bat an eyelid,

Aeron tested his cheek further by adding, "make it a double."

Jon smiled, knowing his desperation for company must be all too apparent to his barman. He decided an explanation rather than appearing too weird and creepy would be a good idea.

"I'm not too keen on being alone here after closing time," he indicated the room with a wobbly waft of his arm. Aeron feigned interest with a questioning arch of his eyebrow. He didn't care much, but a reason for his boss's odd behaviour wouldn't go amiss.

"Since about a year from when I started here…" Aeron sipped at the strong liquor, Jon bit his lip, reluctant to continue, but before Aeron's interest faded completely, he blurted, "It's haunted."

Aeron took another sip, looking less than impressed by this revelation. "In fact," Jon continued, "You are sitting on the haunted bar-stool." As soon as the words departed Jon's lips, a shiver ran down Aeron's spine.

Suddenly, the crash of glass smashing on hard floor shattered the previous quiet of the empty pub. The whiskey did little to calm Aeron's nerve and he struggled not to drop it as Jon turned ashen, the colour dissolved from his face. The broken bottle of Penderyn glugged its contents behind the bar.

Without stopping to clear up the mess, Jon rushed through the door. Aeron followed, pausing to finish his generous free drink in one shuddersome glug first. When he stepped outside, Jon was leaning against the pub wall, bracing himself against his terror.

Obviously waiting for Aeron, as soon as he appeared, Jon blurted out, "Can I stay at yours tonight?" Aeron couldn't hide his reluctant grimace before it had been witnessed.

"You do have a cushy job here that I'm sure you want to keep," Jon sneered in a barely concealed threat. Aeron didn't appreciate those sorts of methods, but his mind after the excitement and rushed double measure strained to find an excuse.

"Maybe," he began, "but I gotta tell you…We've had our own share of poltergeist activity too." He surprised himself. It wasn't true, of course. He'd thought of the perfect excuse. That was all. Jon vomited.

"Shit," muttered Aeron. He couldn't just leave his boss puking in the street. He wracked his brain for some idea of what to do. Before he had the chance to come up with a plan, an ideal solution materialised from nowhere.

"Are you okay, Jon?" a pretty female tone broke through the retching sound. Aeron recognised Efa standing beside them. She turned towards him.

"You can go. Don't worry. I'll look after him," she said sweetly. Aeron hesitated, but Efa's stern assurance left him no choice but to agree.

Relieved of his burden, he thought to check with his boss that it was an okay plan. He didn't care, but he thought asking might appear thoughtful. Jon looked up gratefully at Efa. Despite his fear, his loins stirred, and he readily agreed.

"Of course," he said, gesturing Aeron on his way. He didn't need telling twice. As he disappeared around the corner he heard Efa's soft tones through the darkness. "Come on. Let's take care of you, shall we?"

Happy to be off the hook, he walked on to his student digs hoping he wasn't too late to enjoy some midnight Bronwyn loving.

When Aeron was well out of sight, Efa made good on her promise. From the alleyway beside the pub a figure appeared. A large, threatening individual with a face that could kill if his massive fists wanted a night off.

"Jon." Efa said calmly, gesturing towards the hulking man. "This is my brother, Gareth."

Gareth stepped menacingly forward and gripped Jon hard on both shoulders. The force left him gasping for air. The enormous man carried his sister's abuser to the alleyway he had emerged from moments before. And then, just as Efa had promised, he took care of him.

# Chapter Five

The peculiar activity causing such anxiety and distress calmed noticeably after the clean-up at number twenty-four. Occasional, strange, unsubstantiated occurrences still bothered them: the curtains flapped when there was no breeze, but maybe it was just a trick of the light. Noises of someone moving around downstairs could be heard with everybody in their rooms. But it could be the cat, or the very tidy, non-defecating rats. And a few things not being left where they'd been put. But that was no reason to be afraid.

They ignored these signs uneasily, despite there being no logical explanation to satisfy any of them. The Christmas holidays were fast approaching, and they were reluctant to broach the subject and spoil the peace. Soon they'd be home, away from their silly fears.

Matthew's parents had already collected him as one of his lecturers was off sick, and he had nothing of any importance to do. Josh was due to hop on a train tomorrow, leaving only Neil, Aeron and Bronwyn who would be gone by the weekend.

Aeron had a couple more shifts left at The Railway before going home. On his way to help with the Wednesday mid-week rush, he was agitated at the thought of seeing Jon. He hoped he wouldn't expect him to stay late again. Luck smiled on him last time with Efa turning up at just the right moment, but he doubted such luck would befall him again.

He reached the pub envisioning an unbearably smug Jon, having enjoyed the attention of pretty Efa for the night, welcoming him with boorish good humour. When, instead, he was met, not by Jon, but by a large imposing man, it was with open-mouthed surprise and gratitude that the fearsome face looking down at him from the man's great height was smiling. If it had not been pleased to see him, he dreaded to imagine what menace might show on those brutish features.

Evolutionary instinct made him look away as a sign of submission. But compelled by curiosity, he glanced back to try to make sense of those startling features. The man's nose hooked alarmingly to one side and seemed to point to an old and deep scar running the entire length of the slab of meat which was his cheek and around to a weirdly deformed cauliflower ear.

He wished never to meet whoever had given this monster his war wounds. It would have to have been King Kong at the very least.

The brute offered a hand of such vast proportions he felt as a toddler about to be led across the road. He had a handshake of surprising gentleness, aware as he must be that he could easily crush him, like a bear being kind to a butterfly. He introduced himself as Gareth.

Efa entered the heaving bar from the rear staff quarters and explained. "This is my brother. He's agreed to help out while Jon's recovering. He took quite a turn for the worse last night." Aeron was shocked and guilty.

"Sorry," he uttered. "I shouldn't have left you to cope with him... I thought he was just a bit drunk, that's all...sorry," he said again.

Efa let out a little laugh. "He'll be fine. He *was* just a bit drunk. But maybe a bit more drunk than we realised! He fell and caused himself quite a mischief, mind. Don't you worry. There was nothing you could have done."

Aeron wasn't sure about that. If he'd been there to carry Jon in, it would have been safer. Efa continued her assurances, hesitant to mention Gareth in case Aeron put two and two together and realised a fall might not be the whole truth. Although, she didn't imagine him doing anything about it if he did. People did tend not to want to upset her brother. He had a certain *Je ne se quoi* that was most persuasive.

Not desperate to feel guilty, Aeron gave up asking before learning something he shouldn't.

"We've agreed to manage here until he recovers," gesturing towards herself and Gareth, she added, "I'm sure it won't be for long."

"You must be pleased. Jon said he'd fired you for being late." Efa smiled.

"He couldn't refuse, could he? Not after I took care of him so well." Aeron shrugged. He supposed it made sense.

"I'll be leaving for the Christmas break at the weekend. Probably only for a week. I might be back for New Year. Will I be able to get some shifts?"

"I'm sure that'll be fine," Efa encouraged. "I expect Jon behind the bar again soon. It wasn't such a bad a fall."

The shift proved exceptionally hectic. They talked in bursts whilst working the busy bar which was at least four deep all night. Closing time seemed a distant prospect, but Aeron didn't mind. The temporary management were a refreshing change.

Buzzing and sweating, the bell rang for last orders, and twenty minutes later Gareth ushered out the remaining laggards.

"I don't normally stay late," Aeron said, "I'm bloody knackered!"

He helped wipe the bar awhile before announcing he must go home to bed.

"Not worried about the pub's ghost at all are you?" Efa teased.

"What? You know about that?" Aeron asked in surprise. Efa nodded. "Jon was petrified about it last night," he resumed. "A bottle of whiskey slid off the bar and smashed on the floor. He nearly shit! He wanted to come and stay at my house until you turned up!"

"I reckoned it was a publicity stunt to attract more business," Efa said with a frown. "I didn't know he actually believed it!" Brother and sister sniggered.

"Silly sod!" Gareth's gravel tone added when he'd finished laughing.

"I'll be off then," re-stated Aeron, not sure what he believed. He headed purposefully towards the door.

"Seeya, mate," Gareth called, his deep voice echoing in the empty bar. And then, after a loud thud, he yelled alarmingly, "What the fuck?"

Aeron turned to look at what had caused the outburst. A barstool, *the haunted barstool*, was lying on the floor.

"That bloody thing moved by itself and fell!" exclaimed Gareth. The three of them stared where the barstool lay on the floor.

"Don't be daft," Efa scoffed.

"That's the stool Jon was afraid of!" Aeron hissed from behind fingers which had shot to his mouth in disbelief. "He called it 'the haunted barstool!'"

The large bulk of Gareth, tense at the unknown threat, gave a chilling poignancy. Efa sighed and shook her head. "You two! It's just a wonky stool! If it's prone to falling, that's obviously why the idiot thinks it's haunted." The boys shrugged it off, happy to let Efa's logic win them over.

Aeron bade his goodbyes and almost made it to the door again before the deafening cacophony of smashing glass exploded in their ears. Another spirit bottle lay shattered on the hard floor. This time it appeared to have fallen from the optics. Aeron and Gareth shared a look of bewildered terror. Efa tutted.

"This place is falling apart," she declared, apparently un-phased, and giving no credence to a paranormal explanation. The men bucked themselves up. Falling apart it certainly seemed to be. Efa said it would be a good idea to assess in daylight what needed fixing.

They mopped up and left without further incident. It was with relief Aeron watched the door slamming shut in Gareth's firm grasp. He turned with a smile, keys jangling to indicate it was locked up for the night, and they went their separate ways.

Roll on Christmas, Aeron muttered as he walked home.

# Chapter Six

Aeron's return was noticed by both the remaining occupants of number twenty-four. In Bronwyn's case it was intentional. The two of them keen to make the most of their time together before their families cleaved them apart for the brief Christmas break.

Neil roused to the sound of the enthusiastic Lothario closing the front door with a flourish and then talking in loud whispers to his awaiting lover. He found the hushed tone even more piercing than if they'd spoken at normal volume

He was fully awake when the impossible to ignore sounds of a banging headboard made him realise he would remain conscious in cringing embarrassment for a while yet. He hated that he was embarrassed. If he had a girlfriend (or if he'd ever had), maybe he would accept the disturbance with a knowing smile. Maybe he'd laugh, instead of lying here squirming, desperate to block it out.

The concentration on the floor directly below allowed him to detect the acoustic anomaly he became aware of next. He really wished he was asleep and hadn't heard it.

At first he thought he must have got it wrong. That he had assumed incorrectly the couple's activity. That in fact, Aeron had brought a friend home instead. Because there was definitely someone in the lounge, he could hear their shuffling footsteps.

But, the knock-knocking of fervent copulation was unmistakable, and Neil knew that whoever he could hear couldn't be there from Aeron's invitation. The hairs on the back of his neck pricked to the dread. Removing the pillow from his ears to discern the noise, he left the cover over him for the illusory protection it proffered.

There would be no help from his housemates. He would have to deal with this alone. If it was a ghost, what could he be expected to do? But it wouldn't be a ghost, would it? It was someone else—an intruder.

The telly, the X-box, and other things of value would be easy to steal. Bronwyn had wrapped a few presents. He didn't know who for, but he was certain she'd be gutted to lose them. The student purse was tight.

He couldn't pretend he'd heard nothing and go back to sleep. He couldn't allow himself to be such a coward. Careful not to make a sound, he pulled his door ajar. It creaked alarmingly, forcing him to scurry to the stairs. Creeping gingerly, he lowered himself onto the edge of each step whilst taking some of the strain by gripping the banister.

He had almost reached the bottom when he realised he hadn't a clue what he should do next and was mere feet away from whatever was making noises in the lounge. He could call Aeron for help but he would be none too pleased if it turned out to be simply a cat or something.

Reaching Bronwyn's door, he heard the insufferable final throws of passion. Creeping past, his attention was momentarily taken with the notion they might catch him in the hallway and get completely the wrong idea.

His concentration snapped back to his original endeavour when the unmistakable sound of a chair scraping against the floor-board effect vinyl hit his ears like a bee sting. He flushed with a new wave of fear, his legs turned to jelly and a whimper escaped his lips betraying his hiding place.

What should he do? He knew he had to look before someone made off with their stuff, but his shaking limbs commanded by his stiff, unyielding brain, would struggle to accomplish that.

He spotted something in the door he had never given much thought to. Its lack of function made it almost invisible. A large keyhole, for which they had no key, was the ideal covert viewpoint. He knelt down and put his eye to the small hole.

It took a moment to recognise things. The light was on and his view unobstructed, but the hole was too small to give the panorama needed to see the entire room.

There was the couch against the wall, and the wires of various consoles tangling around one another. And the chair, which moments before must have been dragged across the floor, sitting curiously in the middle of the lounge. The rug, normally covering the vinyl, rucked up against the leg.

Neil's eye widened, his forehead pained by a much painted-over screw from the keyhole as he pressed his face against it, straining for a better view. He gasped, flinching back before forcing himself to resume his gaze. The empty chair which filled his view tipped back, all by itself, balancing mid-air as though someone was sitting, rocking backwards.

The confirmation of the glanced aberration escaped from Neil as an involuntary yelp and he shot away from the door. His eye, still focussed on the ever shrinking image, just caught sight of the chair tipping forward again.

Scrambling to his feet, he scurried to the staircase, almost tripping over himself but never taking his eyes from the door. The sound the chair made, skidding back along the floor and banging hard into the table, echoed up the hallway. For the second time in recent memory, Neil wet himself. He ran crying up the stairs just as Aeron and Bronwyn's door flew open.

"You alright, Neil?" asked a half-naked Aeron, looking towards the lounge as he spoke—the noisy crashing of the chair made him expect that's where he'd see Neil. Spotting him trembling on the stairs, he did a double-take. Neil wanted to put it behind him. He needed answers but he couldn't face going back to the lounge to describe what had happened. So he just nodded.

Relief that the burden of hearing supernatural shenanigans was now the duty of Aeron and Bronwyn, he made his way gratefully back to bed. Laying, quivering in a tight ball with the covers over his head, as the darkness of the night gave way to the light of dawn, he finally fell into fitful sleep.

# Chapter Seven

He woke to the grating drone of his alarm at half-past seven. Surprising himself, despite his tiredness, he leapt straight out of bed. The opportunity to leave the house was reason enough to be efficient.

His dad was due to collect him and take him back home today and he was desperate to see his loving family and be away from this place. Soon he would be back in the happy town of Bishops Stortford, where he had lived his whole life.

His family: himself, his parents and his little sister Emma, had moved house once in his lifetime, but only from one big fifties semi to an even larger detached house on a new estate in the same town. He loved it. Large enough to have all the shops, pubs and nightlife he liked without being at all sprawling.

Swansea's small size for a city had been one of its attractions when making his choice of University, hoping it would be a home from home. Crossing the vast stretch of water of the Severn estuary made it feel further away. But the hills brought back comforting memories of family holidays in the Brecon Beacons.

Standing outside campus for the first time, he had been finally seduced by a high panoramic view of the gorgeous sweep of Swansea Bay. But he hadn't considered how he would have to walk down that bloody hill every time he wanted to go into the city centre, and more significantly, walk back up it again. Nice, flat Bishop's Stortford was going to be great.

Sitting alone in the canteen, eating sausage beans and chips, picturing his home at Christmas, he grinned. Four large trees adorned the house every year. Three were artificial, but they always had a real tree in the lounge, and it would always be huge. For the authentic smell, his mum always said.

Gifts inclined to the generous side. He was really hoping this year for a car to compliment last year's gift, among other things, many other things, of a long course of driving lessons. Swansea hills wouldn't bother him then, would they? He sat, half a sausage midway between plate and mouth, daydreaming about offering lifts home from pubs and clubs to pretty girls, and maybe, if it was a nice car, getting a girlfriend, or a kiss, at least.

He couldn't wait to be away from dreary Rhondda Street. Three or four weeks not worrying about food in the cupboards would be bliss. Three or four weeks without being petrified in his bed at night, listening to sounds of goodness only knows from below his room would be even better.

He only had one more, short lecture, then he'd rush back and finish packing. The thought made him almost giggle out loud but he was thankful he didn't. He returned his empty plate helpfully to the canteen service counter and headed to his last lecture of twenty-fourteen.

"I'm gonna miss you so much, presh!" Bronwyn purred in her strong Welsh accent, nuzzling Aeron's neck. "Why can't we just stay yere for Christmas?"

The lure of young love tempted them away from their families, but they knew how much they were missed at home and wouldn't really deny them their company. They also knew that once ensconced in their comfy family homes, they'd be quite reluctant to come back to Swansea again anyway. For now though, it felt like a poignant goodbye.

"I know, babes. I'd love to," Aeron agreed. "It'll fly by though, I'm sure," he reassured, squeezing her hand as they sat watching TV in the lounge. Pleased with the time together, they occasionally looked away from the screen to gaze into one another's adoring eyes.

The sound of footsteps on the stone front steps disturbed their peace. Keys rattled the lock, and then they were no longer alone. Neil flew through the door full of excitement. Hearing Aeron and Bronwyn in the lounge, he called out an embarrassed greeting after last night's weirdness before heading straight upstairs to finish packing his bags.

He had just reached his bedroom and was fumbling with his key when his phone vibrated, Bohemian

Rhapsody floating up from his pocket. Plucking it deftly out, 'Home' flashed on the screen.

"Hello," he greeted cheerily.

"Hello, Son," his dad's voice emitted from his phone's tinny speaker. "Listen. I've got a bit of work to do, and I wondered if it would be alright to come and get you tomorrow instead?"

Neil felt stupid, but he struggled to answer through the treacle of emotion. "Mm hmm," he mumbled. Collin Hedges knew his son well enough to gauge his distress.

"If you're desperate to get back," he said, "I could probably sort something out. But it would be late, not until about ten or eleven. We wouldn't get back home before two or three in the morning."

Aware he was being selfish and unreasonable expecting his dad to drive all this way after working late, he couldn't help himself.

"I would prefer to come home tonight..." he sniffed, choking back tears of homesickness and hopelessness. "If that's okay?" Neil cringed at his own feebleness. Acknowledging his son's disappointment, Collin agreed to come tonight and ended the call after confirming he would see him later.

The guilt dampened his spirits, but not for long. His dad was probably chuffed at how keen he was to get home. Parents liked to feel needed, Neil nodded to himself.

Completing his packing only took a few minutes. Laying back on his bed, he looked around the room. It wasn't so bad he supposed. It was roomy. And its location—up a separate little staircase from the landing—made him feel private from the others. But what had been great for keeping himself to himself had added to his anxiety with all the goings on of late.

With that in mind, and with a long wait for his dad in front of him, he decided to be uncharacteristically sociable and join his two lingering housemates in the lounge. When he got to the door he pushed down a flush of apprehension and made himself go in and be with his friends.

Aeron and Bronwyn disentangled and sat up.

"Come in, Neil," Bronwyn invited, patting the spare place on the sofa. Not wanting to feel a complete gooseberry he opted to sit on the chair instead.

The three of them enjoyed a couple of beers together. After which mild inebriation, Aeron decided to share with the others his experiences at The Railway. Neil looked as though he might cry.

"So, it's not just us with a poltergeist then!" he declared triumphantly. "Did you hear the noises in here last night?"

"Poltergeist?" Bronwyn snorted, spraying a fine mist of Double Dragon bitter into the air. "Steady on Neil. I'm sure there's a more rational explanation than that."

Aeron, remembering how afraid Neil had been last night, couldn't help but blurt out, "Jon at the Railway seemed pretty terrified of it. A proper old state, he was in." Embarrassed at his outburst, he coughed to clear his dry throat and carried on. "He's got staff covering for him because he's apparently had a drunken fall. But I think he's really too frightened to come back."

"He's a right creep that one," Bronwyn said, ignoring the crux of Aeron's statement. "He's always looking at my tits."

Aeron smiled, thankful his unease seemed to have gone unnoticed.

"You alright, Neil?" he asked, leaning forwards and placing a comforting hand on his knee. Neil nodded, but he was visibly trembling.

"I don't like it," he said solemnly. "We need to get a priest or something. I can't live like this."

"Oh, for heaven's sake, Neil!" Bronwyn protested. "What exactly is it you're so terrified of? Eh?"

"Don't you hear the noises late at night?" he whined. "Not just last night though. And then there's the washing all over the floor, and the broken plates and stuff!"

"Noises in the night! That'll be that fat fucker upstairs! You don't get to be Matthew's size without some serious midnight grazing. And I've caught Josh cooking up all sorts in the early hours of the morning, so that's what that is," argued Bronwyn.

Neil baulked at the word 'caught' in reference to anyone using the kitchen whenever they wanted to, but he didn't have the courage to voice his dismay. He pointed out that he would have known if either of them had walked past his room to the creaky stairs, and it didn't sound like cooking noise anyway. And, neither of them were even in the house last night!

Bronwyn gave a look which concisely conveyed her contempt of Neil's credibility.

"Well I didn't hear anything, Neil. And my room is much closer than yours."

"But I'm right above it!" Neil almost yelled. "And it was not cooking noises. Who would cook with no-one here anyway?"

"Oh, and what does cooking sound like then, Neil?" Bronwyn challenged, unnecessarily aggressively, deliberately missing the point. "I'm sure there's plenty to eat that doesn't need cooking anyway. I just said I caught Josh cooking once, that's all!" Neil could hold his temper no longer.

"What do you mean, 'caught'?" he shrieked. "You don't bloody own this house, you know! We all pay rent. You've already got your own bathroom. That's not fair."

Aeron roused himself to keep the peace. "Come on you two," he soothed. "Calm down. It's nearly Christmas!"

Bronwyn's face softened and her mouth opened and closed a few times as she considered the point. "It is the time for good will to all," she agreed and added warmth to a forced smile. She said a heartfelt 'sorry' and Neil returned the sentiment. He was pleased he'd asserted himself.

They settled down with another can of beer each and watched Will Ferrell's 'Elf', in Neil's opinion the greatest movie of all time. It was part of the television schedule counting down the nights until Christmas. They were soon all laughing so loud they barely heard the knocking on the door from Neil's father. Bronwyn noticed eventually.

"Is that your dad?" she prompted. Neil leaped up and skipped down the hallway to answer the door.

"Hello, hello," Collin greeted, stepping into the house from the cold outside. "I thought you must be asleep!"

"No, just watching 'Elf'" Neil explained.

"It's definitely Christmas!" Collin declared. "You love that film don't you?" Neil grinned, and grinned doubly when his little sister leaped from her hiding place behind their dad's legs.

"Boo!" she cried and giggled.

"Emma! What are you doing up?"

"I'd promised her she could come before I realised it would be so late. She was so keen to see her big brother at University. And there's no school tomorrow."

Neil was thrilled. He lifted her up and carried her through to the lounge.

"Emma! You're up late," declared Bronwyn. She rushed into the kitchen and returned, having robbed some of the Christmas supplies she'd collected over the last couple of weeks, and thrust a chocolate Father Christmas and snowman into her hands.

Emma's eyes widened with joy. "Thank you," she said before frantically ripping off the foil and chomping Santa's head off. She chuckled a chocolate toothed laugh when Bronwyn pointed out that her callous behaviour might mean less presents from the newly decapitated Father Christmas.

"Hello, Mr Hedges," Bronwyn greeted politely as Neil's dad entered the room.

"Please, call me Colin," he replied.

"Cuppa, Dad?" asked Neil, including Aeron and Bronwyn in the invitation by way of facial contortions. They nodded enthusiastically. Collin, usually reluctant to partake due to the questionable hygiene in the grubby student abode, reassured by the relative cleanliness, gratefully accepted. Neil set about it.

"Come on, titch. You can help," he invited, planning to spoil his little sister with biscuits and fizzy drinks when they were out of sight. He was also pleased to have someone he could call 'titch'. There weren't many.

After negotiating Emma down to a more reasonable two or three of each type of biscuit in the cupboard (Bourbon, Penguin and fun-sized Kit-Kat), instead of the five she had tried to insist would be a good amount, Neil returned to the lounge with the respective teas and coffees.

"Wow. You're being rather spoiled, young lady!" commented Collin. He didn't really mind.

Aeron sat in silence as he usually did in the company of other people's parents. He was used to not really being approved of. He wasn't sure why. Bronwyn, conversely, was a parents' dream. She charmed and chatted easily, putting Collin right at ease.

After sufficient recuperation, the time for the Hedges family to begin the long journey back to East Hertfordshire, beckoned. Aeron and Bronwyn helped by carrying some of Neil's things to the car, and entertaining Emma with peek-a-boo and silly faces.

Ensconced in Collin's large Jaguar, the horn was tooted, waves of goodbye given, and wishes of Merry Christmas and Happy New Year echoed down the street until the car disappeared around the corner.

Aeron and Bronwyn waved until they were out of sight, then walked arm in arm back to the house for some long anticipated alone time before they too would be whisked back to their home towns by eager families.


The Hedges' travelled down the hill from Neil's campus, heading out of the city. Emma piped up from the back of the car,

"Who was that girl?" she asked innocently. Neil was confused because she'd met Bronwyn several times before. Maybe she'd lost weight or changed her hair and make-up. Neil hadn't noticed, but that didn't surprise him.

"That's Bronwyn, you silly," he said. "You've seen her loads of times." Emma looked surprised.

"No. Not Bronnie. I do know her. The other girl. The blonde one, standing by the window."

# Chapter Eight

The colour drained from Neil's face before Emma even finished her sentence.

"Wha...what blonde girl?" he mumbled.

"She was pretty. But I don't think she was very pleased with you! She looked cross. I thought she might be your girlfriend or something, and you'd upset her 'cause you didn't introduce us. I would have said when we were in the house, but she wasn't there for long." She paused in thought. "And then I had the chocolate Santa and all the biscuits and I forgot... Sorry."

"That's okay," Neil sighed hoarsely, staring resolutely ahead, anxious to disguise his terror from his little sister.

He looked across at his dad, who through many years of not getting involved in sibling squabbles, appeared oblivious to the odd conversation his two children were having. Neil didn't know what explanation to offer, other than that he hadn't seen the girl she was talking about.

"You must have!" she insisted. "She was right there!" Neil floundered for an answer.

"Look, Em. I'm too tired now. Can we talk about this another time? I want to relax for Christmas. What have you put on your list?" Emma babbled on and the crisis averted for now.

Collin tapped the steering wheel and smiled along to the radio, unaware of the disquiet growing in the seat beside him. He turned to his son and grinned as one of his favourite 'golden oldies' was selected by the incessantly upbeat midnight DJ. Neil removed a chewed fingernail from his teeth and smiled back as best he could. Collin noticed nothing untoward and let the road regain his full attention.

The relief of speeding away from Wales' second city and the phantom girl in his lounge, was countered with terror of his return. Could he ever face coming back?

He had seen films about ghosts, and poltergeists in particular stayed around because they wanted something. So, who was she? And what did she want? If he could find out, could everything return to normal again?

A sigh eased the strain. It was something he could actually do. A little Google research and things might look a lot more promising. Maybe he'd find a girl who died in the house who had what she saw as 'unfinished business.'

A surge of anticipation raised him in his seat and he shuffled from cheek to cheek at the prospect of detective work. Picturing the girl grateful for his help in whatever it was she needed, he blushed as he recognised he was partly pleased because Emma had said she was pretty. How pathetic. How desperate *am* I?

Saving a damsel in distress sounded appealing though. His unexpected bravery surprised him. The increasing distance from Swansea must be playing with his psyche. He suspected he was all talk (or all thought, anyway). If the girl were to manifest before him in the lounge of number twenty-four, he would probably faint.

If he found a solution from a distance (which a country and a dozen counties gave him), he need never worry. The feasibility of that goal was something he preferred not to dwell on, for now at least.

His thoughts bouncing around his skull like balls in a lottery gave him a headache.

"You okay driving, Dad?" he asked with a yawn. "Is it okay if I get some shut-eye?" Collin nodded, still dashboard dancing to his tunes. Neil leant on his arm against the window. Filled with distress and alternate relief as his thoughts insisted on ruminating the possibilities of a resolution, he fell asleep. The many nights of disturbed sleep back in Swansea clearly taking their toll.

His consciousness roused to acknowledge passing over the long bridge into England. He stirred briefly again when they stopped for Collin to stretch his legs at the motorway services. By the time they reached the M25 he was sound asleep again and didn't wake until he was nudged by his dad on the driveway of the family home

"That was quick," Neil commented, rubbing some feeling back into his arm, numb from contorting against the window. Collin snorted in amusement

"Four hours and twenty minutes, including breaks!"

Neil sheepishly realised the effort his dad had put into collecting him tonight. "Sorry. Thanks Dad. I'm really glad to be home."

"Glad to have you," Collin said, reaching over and ruffling his son's hair.

Neil carried Emma in, whilst Collin lugged a couple of his bags. He was thrilled and surprised that his mum was still up, albeit snoozing, with the telly threatening to go into standby.

"Hello, angel!" she greeted blearily. Hooded eyes smiled and she pushed herself up from the couch to enwrap her son in a tight hug. Neil noted with regret that he still wasn't as tall as his mum. He didn't even seem to be catching her up.

They chatted briefly about nothing of significance before the entire family retired for a long needed good night's sleep.


"It's nice to 'av the place to ourselves, babes," Bronwyn said to what she could see of Aeron's chin as she lay on the couch with her head on his lap. He stroked her head in response.

"Oh, that's lovely," she encouraged. "Give us a scalp massage. One of them Indian ones would be just the job".

Aeron picked up strands of hair uninspiringly whilst he nodded off to sleep. Bronwyn nudged him awake a couple of times before giving up and leaving him to his slumber. The film on television had gained her attention with an intriguing plot that her somnolent mind struggled to keep up with.

She gave into fatigue for brief, spasmodic periods, enough to make the storyline unfathomable. She continued to kid herself that fathom it she could indeed accomplish, but proved herself incorrect when she awoke to a different film which had come on afterwards.

In her delirium, it took a while to recognise it wasn't the same one. When she realised, she debated if she should rouse Aeron and go to bed, but felt so comfy, she allowed herself to drift off again where she was.

Squinting for a moment, she peered about, unsure what had woken her. When she saw, she froze as her saucer eyes comprehended her surroundings, grabbed her consciousness and shook it hard. She was wide awake now, but didn't trust her senses. Impulsively pushing herself further into Aeron's thick arms, she hissed his name in a near-silent whisper.

She patted him, uncertain if he was awake and petrified like herself, or if he was still fast asleep. Wanting desperately to steal a glance at him, she just couldn't take her eyes from the unfathomable apparition before her.

Tapping frantically at her boyfriend's hand, willing him to wake up but loath to make a sound, she shed a tear from her trembling lids when a loud snore signified she'd deal with whatever this was, alone.

 The girl, about her own age, seemed unaware of her as she stood in front of the window, gazing out. The vision was there for only a second before disappearing back into the ether. When Bronwyn shook her head to dispel sleep, and the notion this was a dream, the girl had disappeared.

Had it just been a dream? What else could it have been? But she had seemed so real; like she could reach out and touch her.

"Aeron!" she shouted, and louder again, "Aeron!!"

He woke with a start, instantly picking up a lock of Bronwyn's hair and continuing with the feeble head massage he'd been performing before he fell asleep. "Sorry, babe," he muttered, assuming that was why she had woken him.

"There was someone there!" she hissed, pointing towards the window. Aeron sat up and roused himself to the threat of whoever Bronwyn was alerting him to.

"Were they in the garden?"

"No! Not in the garden. In the lounge, three feet away from us staring through the window. Then she just disappeared!"

Aeron didn't know what to make of it. He'd half believed Jon when he had been afraid, but now Bronwyn? She was so smart and clever. She should definitely be trusted.

"We have drunk quite a bit. Do you think you just had some sort of hallucination?"

Certain he believed her and was only trying to be helpful, Bronwyn gave serious consideration to his suggestion. She supposed it had to be the answer. What was the alternative? A ghost? "I suppose it must have been. I don't even believe in ghosts, so that's the only answer isn't it?" she admitted.

He nodded, but something wasn't right. He'd never given any thought to whether he believed in ghosts. Now the question assaulted his mind daily.

"Is there any possibility it might be a ghost?" Aeron couldn't help but ask. Bronwyn frowned and shook her head.

"I don't think so. I did when I saw it," she confessed, careful to objectify what she'd seen as an 'it,' and not 'her.' "But, I'm sure you're right. A hallucination makes a lot more sense. We have drunk a lot, as you say, and I'm super-tired."

Unconvinced, they said no more.

"Find something light-hearted on the telly," Aeron suggested. "I'll go and make us some nice strong coffee." They were already wide awake, but sobering up suddenly seemed like a really good idea.

# Chapter Nine

The pretty market town of Llandovery, nearly forty miles north of Swansea, and the other side of the Black Mountain massif of the Brecon Beacons National Park, looked resplendent in its Christmas glory. The colourful lights on the guild hall were the centre piece. In partnership with an absolutely enormous tree, they gave the town a magical ambience.

Elin Treharne was usually much more enamoured with the display than she was today. She just felt too ill to enjoy it. Well behind with her Christmas shopping, she had forced herself from the comfort of her parents' house, where she had been recuperating, to do at least a bit before the big day. No-one would expect very much from her this year, but she wanted to get something.

Having completed her degree from Swansea University, she'd been far too poorly to begin her career. Financially, it hadn't been the disaster it could have, ironically, due to her illness. Since her glandular fever had taken its toll and left her virtually bed-ridden, she had been living back with her parents for convalescence. An all-inclusive deal for the sum of zero rent.

Today, she was shopping with what little money she did have, perusing the array of stores in the town with an apathetic disposition. Picking up the occasional item and trying to imagine her mum, or her dad, or her sister with it, and immediately feeling unimpressed and putting it straight back.

Meandering through Llandovery's cobbled streets, fatigue ate away at her doggedness with the biting cold adding shivers to her trembling frail frame. She pulled her coat about her, even though it was already closed as much as it could.

She didn't want to walk too far in the wintry air and soon found herself in the warm comfort of a familiar shop, the one closest to her heart—the town's bookshop—and quickly became engrossed.

She wasn't sure books were gifts her family wanted, but couldn't help feeling excited. Her heart skipped at the very sight of a book. Confronted with shelves and shelves full of every sort, Elin was in her element.

At home she boasted a stack of titles so high she didn't have a hope of reading them all. Particularly as she continued to buy more and more before she read even a tenth of those she already owned. She didn't care. She just couldn't resist.

After a good time flicking through a dozen or more possibilities, she settled on a few ideal(ish) presents. A couple of romantic novels—a historic one for her mum, and a far more adult choice for her sister. Her dad's present was a pictorial history of the area. He didn't have the patience for novels. She hoped he didn't own it already as he was quite a collector of anything local. She felt fairly sure it wasn't on any of his overflowing shelves.

It struck her that home was perhaps not what she should call her parents' house, as she hadn't lived there before Uni. It was her mum and dad's hard earned retirement treat. Her mum, Glenda, had worked for years as a nurse and her dad, Emyr, a successful architect.

Due to their respective careers, they'd had children relatively late in life. Glenda, in her thirties when she and her sister, Alis, were born two years apart, and Emyr had been in his forties.

Alis, now in her second year of a B.A. in Film and English; and much to Elin's chagrin, in the rather more prestigious Bristol University, was a whirlwind. Elin couldn't wait to see her, but worried her lethargy would get in the way of their fun. She was back for the Christmas holidays today. Her train due in at seven.

Elin paid for the three books (and a couple more for herself to add to her collection) and left the shop, quietly pleased.

Seeing advertised on a chalk board outside a quaint café: mince pies and mulled wine, she stopped and sniffed the air. Studying her purse, there was about enough change for a seasonal treat, but she didn't go in. Shrugging, she turned away, her concerns of spreading germs to the good people in town getting the better of her. Being out at all had been risky. She probably wasn't contagious anymore, but if there was a chance, then sharing crockery, glasses, and cutlery would be a definite no-no. Glandular Fever would be an awful gift to give.

She called into the news-agents and bought festive patterned wrapping paper, and bows, then called a taxi for the short trip back to her parents' new home. The three pounds to pay because she felt too rough to walk less than a mile, she resented, but there was no choice. Glenda had dropped her off earlier so she hadn't had to pay twice at least.

The taxi pulled into the impressive driveway of Erw Lon (which translated into 'Quiet Acre'). Elin grabbed her couple of bags and paid. The driver seemed to be waiting for a tip, the Christmas season and the large house growing his expectations. Embarrassed that one would not be forthcoming, Elin walked up the path from the gravel drive, pausing only to give a dismissive wave before opening the door and disappearing indoors.

Inside the large grey Victorian house, the cold, square hallway leered in sombrely. Christmas adornments did little to lift the oppressiveness. A holly wreath hanging on the mirror made Elin think more of a funeral parlour than a family home at Christmas.

Rising like two mighty serpents, the staircase forked left and right from a half-landing and hung sinisterly above her head like the impenetrable blackness of an angry storm cloud. Shadows cast by various ornaments on shelves and in alcoves projected eerie images on the chequered red and white tiled floor and white-washed walls.

It was a strange way to feel about her parents' beloved new home, but being alone here gave her a queasy uneasiness. Trying to shake off her absurdity, she couldn't help rushing a little on her way into the lounge. The warmth of the red walls and pretty pine tree with its strings of fairy lights welcomed her as though stepping into a different house. She sighed in relief.

Taking the chance of her time alone, she wrapped the few presents and put them under the tree. When she'd placed them jauntily with the others, she was dismayed to feel completely wiped out and had to lie down on the sofa.

Her reluctance was not only due to all the time wasted away to her unconsciousness, but more because her unconsciousness had not been a very pleasant place to reside.

Intolerable visions had plagued her dreams more and more. Her recollection was patchy, but frequently she awoke, heart pounding, racked with desperate emotions she couldn't place.

Sleep had improved for the last few nights, but she didn't know when the next terrible nightmare would torment her. Despite her reluctance, she had no choice but to give in to exhaustion and rest.

"Elin?" the soft voice permeated her slumber as Glenda shook her gently awake. "How are you feeling, cariad?"

"Exhausted," she admitted.

"I told you, you didn't need to go out and get us presents. We all would have understood," her mum scolded with a shade of sympathy.

"How do you know I got you anything?" Elin teased. Glenda nodded her head toward the tree. "Ah." Elin smiled.

A steaming cup of tea greeted her from its place on one of the nest of tables by the fireplace. Glenda smoothed her skirt as she sat down beside her. Her neat bob of brown hair shone in odd waves, reflecting opaque lights from the tree as they flickered on and off and on again.

She placed her cup, on its matching saucer on her lap before bringing it up to her lips to take dainty sips. Elin slid around from laying down so she could grab her tea in her favourite large mug. She always joked she only kept it in the cupboard in case they had any tradesmen in.

Elin sat cross-legged on the sofa, hugging the cupped warmth to her chest with both hands.

"Aah!" she exhaled contentedly as she took her first satisfyingly hot sip of the sweet infusion. "I'm glad you're back mum," she said.

"Why's that, cariad?"

Elin, realising the truth that she had been a little afraid would make her appear foolish, shrugged and said, "Just am, that's all…"

The pair sat in gratified, tea slurping silence for a moment before Elin's mum broke the contentment with her next question.

"You weren't scared, were you?" she asked, taking another sip of tea, "being alone in the house?"

Elin's legs shot to the floor from their folded position and stared open-mouthed at her mother. "Don't be silly!" she protested. "Why would you say that?" She too sipped her tea to cover her apprehension.

"Well," began Glenda. "I have to admit to feeling a mite uncomfortable myself when your father's out and I'm here on my own," she said in a matter-of-fact tone. "I especially don't like the hallway."

Elin struggled to keep a grip of her mug of tea dregs without dropping it.

"The hallway!" she exclaimed, surprising herself.

"You've noticed it too, haven't you?" her mum stated. "I've seen your reluctance to leave this room. And it isn't all down to your glandular fever and feeling tired, I'm sure," she proclaimed.

Elin, taken aback that her dread had been detected, coughed, covering her true feelings. But at the same time, there was relief she was not alone in her fear. She decided to probe further.

"It is a bit oppressive, I suppose," she admitted, immediately regretting the harshness. "I think it's because in here it's so welcoming with the red walls," she tried to recover. "Like a cosy womb!"

"It's more than that", Glenda said firmly. "It is okay in here but I have never liked that hallway." She put her teacup and saucer gently down on the table and placed her hands neatly back in her lap.

"Your father found the house and fell in love with the place. Well you can understand it, can't you? The views are phenomenal." Elin nodded. "The pictures the estate agents sent to our old house in Bridgend were great. The room dimensions were most impressive. As you know, our reconnaissance missions to the area left us almost breathless with excitement. It's a lovely town."

She took a deep breath before continuing. "I had an awful feeling when I first walked into this place. Your dad seemed not to notice, and I put it down to the rather gruff greeting we got from the vendor. I don't think he really wanted to sell the house, explaining that his wife had recently died, and he was struggling to manage the place by himself."

She had Elin's full attention. "By the time we looked around everywhere and were chatting in this room, I felt completely different. I had fallen in love with it too. As we left I noticed the hall still felt strange, but I was on a high by then and couldn't wait to move in. Since we have moved in, I get the shivers every time I'm there."

"Did the man's wife die in the house?"

"I never asked, and he didn't say."

Mother and daughter sat in uncomfortable silence, imagining the seller's wife coming to her death, and her sticky end befalling her in the hallway. Glenda announced that more tea would be a lovely idea in an effort to change the subject and lighten the mood again. They spent the rest of the afternoon playing chess, with Elin losing most every game

# Chapter Ten

Neil woke late. The three hours of bumpy sleep in the car had done little to satisfy his requirement. He opened his eyes and realised where he was. A huge grin bisected his face as the thrill and relief of being back home consumed him.

He could hear Emma's shrill voice coming from downstairs. Not what she was saying, but from her tone she was asking Mum something. The gorgeous aroma of baking wafting through the crack under his door signalled a lovely family Christmas scene unfolding.

He threw on his dressing gown and stretched and yawned, then made his way downstairs to join them. As he walked into the large oak kitchen with its impressive feature island, his mum looked up from tapping some pies.

"Hello sleepy-head," she greeted lovingly, ruffling his bed hair the while. "Want to taste one of these fresh mince pies for your breakfast?" She then corrected after a glance at the wall clock, "lunch?"

Neil oohed and ahhed as he threw the hot pie from one hand to the other, snapping at the unfeasibly fiery mincemeat with his goofy bucked teeth to try and avoid burning himself.

"Be careful," his mum warned with a rueful shake of her head, "They have only just come out of the oven."

"Delicious!" Neil declared, a finger of triumph pointing in the air.

"Good! You can help with the next batch if you like."

Neil loved crumbing the flour and butter to make the pastry. He joked that nothing got his hands clean quite like making pastry (but of course he had washed them meticulously first).

Emma looked as though something on her mind was troubling her. Neil could guess what before she spoke. He wouldn't try to stop her. If she was curious, she deserved a grown-up answer he supposed.

"Mum?" she began, glancing at Neil, she took solace in his compliant expression. "Mum?" she said again, a little firmer to make sure she had her full attention. "There was a girl in Neil's lounge last night. Not Bronwyn, a different girl." Neil's mum gave him a knowing look, as if to suggest 'at last, my son has a girlfriend.'

"Yes?" she said with a smirk. Emma was oblivious to the hopeful undertones.

"She was as close as I am to you now, but Neil didn't see her!"

Neil exhaled slowly, releasing some of his tension. For the first time, the subject would be broached by people he respected and loved, Neil looked up to heaven and offered a silent 'thank you.'

"I think she was a ghost!" Emma hissed, wide eyed.

Their mum stared at Neil, lips crinkled to counter the twinkle in her eye.

Neil decided to tell all. "I didn't see the girl, but there have been weird things going on at that house". He explained all the bizarreness, and when he was finished, his mum wore pursed lips and a frown.

"I think you may well have a ghost."

Neil's shoulders slumped in both relief and dismay. He had known there was no rational explanation, and his mum's readiness to agree frightened him, but at least now he could have her support.

"You should have a séance," she suggested.

A flush of nerves caused Neil to sweat. That sounded too up close and personal. His plan of helping at a distance was exciting. But actually contacting spirit… No. He couldn't.

"What's wrong, Neil? There's nothing to be afraid of."

"You're an expert, are you, Mum?"

"Not really. But Auntie Sylvie is. She's psychic. Didn't you know?" Neil did not know. "When you go back after Christmas we could ask Sylvie to conduct the séance, if you like," she said rhetorically. "She'll soon tell you what's what. She's coming over on Boxing Day. You can probe her then."

Neil opened and closed his mouth but no words came. His mind assimilated possible responses: Terror? Gratitude? If Auntie Sylvie was an expert, maybe it would be okay. It was not knowing how to deal with it that was distressing, wasn't it?

Neil had until Boxing Day to do whatever he could from the safety of his computer. Perhaps Auntie Sylvie wouldn't have to bother. And if she did, Neil hoped he could count himself out and leave the self-proclaimed experts to it.


Aeron and Bronwyn were leaving together. Their bags in their respective parents' cars, they were going for a last drink, mums and dads too, before heading home for Christmas. They didn't mention the strangeness at number twenty-four, but both of them, despite the prospect of missing one another, were secretly pleased to be leaving.

The two sets of parents greeted one another warmly. Bronwyn and Aeron's relationship was no secret, and they were all aware they would see each other a lot more when their offspring finished university. Marriage had been talked of, and although anything could happen in the year left, it was definitely on the cards.

Bronwyn had always been super-confident in front of her possible future in-laws, but Aeron suspected he wasn't liked by Bronnie's parents. He was large and tattooed, and he didn't speak as eloquently as his cultured girlfriend.

He was wrong. Bronwyn's mum and dad thought him perfect for their daughter. Quiet and respectful and never gave them a moment's worry in his treatment of her. No philandering or fibbing ever was brought to their attention. And Bronwyn had never seemed happier.

But as they sat for their lunch in the magnificent heights of The Tower at Meridian Quay, the two sets of parents became aware of a vague undercurrent of anxiety between the pair of lovebirds. The two gazed not at one another, but at the vast sweep of sand of Swansea Bay, three hundred and fifty feet below them.

"Is everything okay, you two?" Bronwyn's mother, Natasha felt compelled to ask. With their attention brought to their odd behaviour, Bronwyn and Aeron looked at one another and immediately squashed closer on the bench seat. Aeron took Bronnie's hand to appease her mother and plastered a smile on his rugged face.

Bronwyn answered for the two of them.

"Yes mum. We're fine." She reached over and placed her free hand on her mum's leg and gave a reassuring little squeeze. "It's been a little odd at the house for a few weeks that's all," she explained.

"Odd?" replied Natasha in concern. "What do you mean?"

Aeron and Bronwyn glanced at one another in brief conference before Bronwyn explained it was nothing. That it had just been a long term at uni and they were all tired.

Natasha wasn't entirely satisfied but was reassured that whatever squabbles had gone on in Swansea hadn't been between her favourite couple, so she let it go and did her best to lift the mood. She did a sterling job, and they were soon as far removed from the strange troubles at Rhondda Street as the lofty height their lunchtime venue could provide.

After lunch they bid fond farewells and hugged before getting in their cars and making the drive to their not-too-distant homes. Bronwyn's family lived in the rugged interior of Carmarthenshire, whilst Aeron's lived even closer in the valley's community of The Rhondda. It wasn't far, but it felt far enough for the pair of them to immerse themselves into Christmas family life, untroubled by the spooky uneasiness they were escaping in Swansea.

The Hedge's family home was beginning to look a lot more Christmassy. Neil and Emma were always in charge of decorating the tree in the lounge. It was a tradition they enjoyed greatly, despite some fairly childish, lop-sided attempts in Christmases past.

It had looked classier the last couple of years due to Emma being old enough to take a bit more care, and Neil being especially keen to do a good job after the relative squalor of his Swansea accommodation.

Seeing the tree nearly done, and spending time with his jolly little sister caused a spring of delight to bubble up within him he could scarcely contain. He felt a bit silly at how excited he felt. It wasn't the presents. Although, who wouldn't be thrilled about getting a car? But it was more than that. It was the whole feeling of Christmas. Of family.

He had even asked not to be told what Emma was getting so he could enjoy the thrill of her surprises too. His mum and dad always said what a great big brother, he was. Last year he stayed up late on Christmas Eve building a bright pink bike with stabilisers whilst his mum and dad wrapped all her other little gifts. Festive music filled the room from one of many Christmas CD's in their collection while mulled wine and one or two chocolates from the tree sustained them.

The tunes put them in good Christmas cheer, but also made them nervous they wouldn't hear little footsteps coming down the stairs. So Neil's other job was to keep leaping up and checking every few minutes in between tightening nuts and bolts on her bike.

He smiled down upon her angelic blonde head knowing she must be even more excited than him. He gave her a quick squeeze and she looked up at him with adoration as she put another sparkly bauble on the tree.

It soon looked magnificent. Proudly showing their doting parents, who made all the right noises, they continued with seasonal adornments to the rest of the room. Once completed, Neil had nothing left but to relax and wait for permission to start on the Quality Street and Roses chocolates. That, and find out what he could about previous pretty girl occupants of number twenty-four, Rhondda Street, Swansea.

# Chapter Eleven

N eil's hands hovered over his laptop keyboard, unsure what to type. He began by entering the address. Zoopla informed him of its purchase price, and the average of other houses in the street compared to the national average. No interest to Neil.

He added 'death', 'died' and 'obituary' to the search. No-one came up as being listed present at the address at the time they had passed away. He was getting nowhere. If he couldn't find out who the girl was, how could he learn what she wanted?

He changed tack and typed in her description, wondering if whatever had happened to her might be newsworthy enough to get a hit. Quite a few as it turned out. From the 1940's right up to a few years ago. He decided the most recent might be the most likely.

There was no direct link to the girl on his screen and the house. But maybe a boyfriend had lived there, or possibly a best friend, or somebody at least. He tapped the keys in furious excitement, opening tabs with pictures of all the girls fitting the description Emma had given. He thought she might recognise one of them as the same girl.

"Emma," he called. She skipped in expectantly.

"Yes?"

"Come here and see if any of these pictures look like the girl you saw," Neil invited. Emma gazed long and hard at the images on the display. Neil moved from screen to screen showing the various photos, but none seemed to be familiar to her. He tried brightening the image. Then he tried pre-empting his own suspicions by clicking on further pictures of the most likely candidate.

Emma peered unconvincingly at the images that meant nothing to her on her brother's laptop. She really wanted to be helpful. It was exciting. Neil could tell she was struggling to come up with something of any use.

He let out a huge sigh and lifted his hands away from the keyboard at a loss what else he could do.

"I suppose that one might be her." Emma volunteered in response to Neil's despondency. "I didn't see her for very long. It doesn't look that much like her though."

Neil took what he could get, encouraged the image was at least from the most recent obituary. And it was undeniably an 'unfinished business' sort of story. The poor girl had been murdered by her boyfriend. He put aside Emma's uncertainty, attributing any error to her young age. This could be it, Neil concluded.

"Thanks, Emma," he said, going back to the display and blocking her view.

"Who is she, then?"

"I'm just reading about it now. I'll tell you later."

"Let me see!" she shrilled.

Not wanting to squabble and attract attention, he let Emma get to the screen.

She perused the content as though she understood every word. "Ah," she said, then "Hmmm." Taking in precisely none of it, she was satisfied that reading about this girl was completely boring. She decided to leave her brother in peace and go and play something fun.

Neil carried on reading everything about the murdered blonde girl.

Her father had disapproved of the union. Born of resentment, her lover killed her in a 'if I can't have her, no-one can' fit of jealous rage.

It struck Neil as entirely possible that someone involved with the victim may have lived at number twenty-four, Rhondda Street. How could he find out? He noted the girl's name, 'Jacqui Lloyd'. A Google search produced much the same result as the description of her had with only a few additions. Still no mention of number twenty-four.

The boyfriend, convicted of her murder and presently serving consecutive life sentences at Bridgend was named as one Ryan Evans. Accusations flew of him being a gold digger whose main interest in Jacqui was her connection to her father's empire of pubs and clubs in the area.

A search of his name and the address achieved nothing either. Neil wouldn't believe he wasn't onto something. Even if he didn't understand quite what it was yet.

His fingers poised for action above the keys were failed by a mind which could think of no other research to perform. And even if he did come up with a plausible theory of what Jacqui might want, he wouldn't know how to go about achieving it. That's if he even had the stomach for it. He had tried, but he was slowly coming to the conclusion he was going to need Auntie Sylvie's help after all.

# Chapter Twelve

"What time is Dad picking Alis up from the station?" Elin asked after her fourth mind-numbing trouncing from her mother at chess.

"Seven or eight, I think, cariad," she answered. "Your dad's going to pick up a takeaway on the way home. It'll be far too late to cook, and I'll be doing enough of that over Christmas."

"Chinese, or Indian?" Elin inquired.

"He'll probably let Alis choose after her journey. Any preference?" Elin shrugged. Her appetite was so poor at the moment it would be unfair to give an opinion.

"Another game?" Glenda offered. Elin shook her head with as much vigour as her incredible fatigue would allow.

"Sorry mum," she said. "I'm far too shattered to engage my brain again. What about finding a soppy Christmas film on the telly? Get us in the mood," she suggested.

Glenda was plainly happy with the proposal because she immediately switched the television on and searched the listings for something suitable. One of the many family friendly films on offer was selected, then the two Treharne women proceeded to talk through it.

"So, do you regret moving here, Mum?" Elin asked.

"No," Glenda answered with convincing firmness, but then again softer, "no, not really". The moistness of her eyes betrayed a deeper emotion.

"You do! You're actually afraid, aren't you, Mum?"

Glenda galvanised her stiff upper lip and blustered her assurances that she was fine. Elin thought it unlikely to be just the odd vibe in the hallway causing her mother to be this upset.

"Has something happened?" she asked, trying to be sensitive but sounding interrogational. Glenda gathered the hem of her skirt and put it down again. With pursed lips, she glanced to the corners of the room, then to the floor before raising her head and meeting Elin's gaze with the same steely stare.

"No, of course not, cariad!"

Elin wasn't convinced, but before she had the chance to pursue her line of inquiry, Glenda leapt up briskly from the couch and announced she could hear Emyr home from the station with Alis. She left the room on the pretext of setting the table for dinner.

When the tell-tale footsteps on shingle and the thump of the front door didn't follow, Elin realised Alis and her dad weren't home after all, and it was far too early.

She didn't have the energy to follow her mum and continue the interrogation, and she wouldn't want to anyway. Noticing her own furrowed brow, she made an effort to relax her face, rubbing her temples to diffuse the tension. What could be going on? Glenda was such a strong minded woman. Elin shuddered. Whatever was troubling her, Elin hadn't the strength to deal with.

Struggling to get into the film they had talked through the start of, she found herself gazing into the blurring images on the screen, the sound washing meaninglessly over her. She fell asleep again into odd dreams that, on reflection, were heavily influenced by the background noise of the television.

She awoke to the genuine return of her dad and sister, and the delicious smell of curry. She was surprised that after the unnerving conversation with her mother, on top of her glandular fever, she had an appetite to appreciate it. It must be the thrill of seeing her sister again after three months at university.

The aroma of spices wafted down the hallway, past the lounge door on their journey to the dining room adjacent to the lounge. Her dad called out 'hi,' whilst Alis charged into the room, stopping from bowling her delicate sister over just in time. The pair threw their arms around one another, Alis with considerably more energy.

"How are you?" she gushed. "Any better from that pesky glandular fever?" a sympathetic frown on her ruddy face. She'd always been a lot more robust than Elin. It was hard to tell they were sisters. Elin the far prettier of the two, but Alis attractive in a completely different way. She'd never had any trouble finding boyfriends, whereas Elin endured perpetually alone.

"Meh..," Elin shrugged. A distant call to come to the table was answered zealously by the incredible volume Alis could command from her mighty lungs.

She aided her sister by taking her arm, but was more of a hindrance than a help.

"Thanks, Alis, but I can walk! I even went into town and bought some Christmas presents today."

"Oh. Sorry, sis," she said, letting go of her arm and skipping off through the door. I can't imagine any oppressive ambience bothering her, Elin thought, curling her lip. Alis had a lot to be envious of, not least her robust health.

Elin ran the gauntlet of the hall to get to the food. Having people home helped, but she still didn't like it. When she slouched pitiably into the dining room, her mum and Alis were already seated and her dad stood serving the various dishes to their appropriate plates.

"I got you a Korma again, bach. Is that okay?" It was a bit late to be worried as it already sat congealing on her plate next to a pile of colourful pilau rice, and a torn corner of peshwari naan. She smiled wanly and nodded as she heaved her chair out to sit down.

As she looked across at Glenda, she gasped and shot a look to the other two, wondering if they'd noticed how awful she was looking. The robust colour gone from her cheeks, she appeared almost grey in the dim light of the dining room. Something must have happened to affect her so much.

Maybe with her sister's help (or maybe not!) she could make sensitive inquiries in the coming days. That's if her own temperament could afford the patience of being subtle. Perhaps her dad might know.

Over the course of the meal, Glenda thawed. It was impossible to remain trapped inside personal thoughts in the company of Alis. By the time she'd recounted every intricate detail of her courses, and how the lecturers all loved her, and how she was sure that one even fancied her, and how she did this amusing thing, and that amusing thing, and countless other amusing things, the quieter members of the Treharne family had no option but to enjoy the exuberance.

When everyone finished eating, Alis demonstrated her usefulness by scraping the plates and carrying them through to the kitchen where Emyr loaded the dishwasher, leaving Elin and Glenda in uncomfortable silence.

Glenda forced a smile, which Elin gratefully returned.

"That film was rubbish," she announced, attempting to start a non-threatening conversation. She wondered how long her mum had been so troubled. She hadn't noticed, but then she'd been in no fit state.

Guilt at the care she had demanded over the last few months pricked her. She knew her mum didn't mind. She was probably grateful for the diversion, doing what she had trained her entire working life to do.

She vowed to keep an eye on her mum, and Christmas was a great distraction. Close family time together was to be cherished. Her own poor health had taught her that.

"Shall we go and warm up the telly," Glenda invited. Not entirely serious; the television would function at full capacity straight away, but she couldn't help but reference days of yore. Elin smiled and nodded, pushing her chair back and standing up.

Before they'd chosen what to watch, Alis and Emyr rejoined them after their kitchen chores, Alis announcing she didn't want to watch dreary television. Instead, she was keen on a game of charades. When that was universally declined, she suggested a variety of board and card games before declaring the rest of the family boring and then laughing the loudest at Christmas TV specials.

Sometime early in the evening, Elin predictably fell back asleep. When she awoke with a stiff neck, she reluctantly bid her sister and her mum and dad goodnight and ventured into the cold dark hallway.

She stood at the foot of the stairs, towering, foreboding and abrupt to her state of exhaustion. But the cloud of ire which daunted her arrival at the house earlier, appeared lighter now. Even that, it seemed, had succumbed to Alis's vociferousness.

Hauling herself up the first step beyond her reluctance, her bed awaited. She sighed. All she ever seemed to do was sleep. For weeks, she slept on the large couch in the lounge with a duvet, but it had been decided now she was improving, she should try to introduce more normality.

Ignoring her discomfort on the eerie staircase she took another leaden-footed step. A heaviness sat on her shoulders dispersing as a violent shudder. Tears pricked her eyes as thoughts of her own fears combined with images of her mother's wrought face prevented her carrying on.

Not even halfway, she was unable to take another step. Turning round, she mooched back down to the lounge.

"I'm feeling a lot more awake now," she lied. "What are we doing?"

What they were doing was listening with ever-waning interest to Alis's university exploits. It wasn't long before Glenda and Emyr declared bedtime and even Alis seemed happy enough to call it a night.

With them all going upstairs, Elin managed to join them. Wresting back her duvet and crawling into bed, her head barely grazed the pillow before she fell into a deep, deep sleep.

She woke late. The clock beside her bed pronounced the time to be one thirty. Breakfast and lunch had been slept through. A cold cup of tea on the bedside table showed someone had checked on her at least once. She smiled.

The smile was short lived as memories of the gloomy hallway and last night's dread came back like a slap in the face. Reaching out for the cold tea, she took a glug and considered moving.

A stark recollection —not of the hallway, nor the anxious wringing hands of her mother—something else, just a flash. It was herself, standing beneath the streetlamp outside her old student house in Swansea. The image jolted her, and she spilled half the mug of tea on her lap. "Shit." Relief she wasn't burning was tempered by frustration. She swore again with a sigh. "Shit! The nightmares are back."

Frowning, she shook her head, dabbing away the spill with a wad of Kleenex. After several nights free of them, what had caused their return?

Her thoughts were interrupted by a rap on the door. Then, a fresh steaming hot cup of tea arrived, carried by her boisterous little sister.

"You're awake! At last," she grinned. "You better not sleep in like this tomorrow or I'm opening your presents!" Elin came out of her reverie enough to muster a smile.

"You okay, Sis?" Alis asked, her brow puckered in concern. Elin shook herself back to reality.

"Yes. I'm fine. Just a bad dream. A nightmare. I was trying to piece it together when you barged in."

"Sorry!" Alis decried with mock indignation. "I'll take your lovely cup of tea away, shall I?"

Elin giggled, grasping the hot mug and taking what she anticipated being a satisfying sip. It tasted awful. How anyone could get the simple art of pouring boiling water on a teabag so wrong was a mystery. Her eyes watered in her attempt to disguise wincing, whilst falsely proclaiming "delicious" with a grimacing smile on her face.

"What was the nightmare about?"

Elin shrugged, "I don't rememeber."

With a grateful nod, Alis dropped the subject, glad she wouldn't have to endure the absurd ramblings of someone else's dream.

Elin placed the revolting mug of tea on her bedside table beside the cold half-mug from earlier with an assured expression conveying her intention to drink it in a minute, so as not to cause offence.

"Alis, what do you think of it here?" and added in response to Alis's confused pout, "in this house?" Alis still didn't get it. "I keep feeling really…" she paused to find the right word, "uncomfortable," she settled on. "In the hall especially. And coming upstairs. Mum seems really bothered by it."

Alis's expression shifted to one of seriousness at the mention of Glenda. "Mum's bothered? About what?"

"She hasn't actually said. Just that she's always hated the hallway, ever since her and Dad first looked around the house before they bought it."

"Really?" Alis protested. "She's never said anything to me."

"She doesn't see you much. I've been here for months and she only mentioned it yesterday. Since she has, the hallway is even more terrifying to me." Alis's face contorted into a disbelieving sneer. "I know you don't believe in anything out of the ordinary, but that doesn't change the fact I'm worried about Mum." Alis nodded.

"Maybe you should ask Dad if something strange has happened," Elin continued. "He's more likely to listen to you than me. You're so level-headed."

Alis couldn't disagree with the compliment. "Sure. I'll ask. I doubt if Mum's told him anything, but, if you're worried…"

Elin got dressed for her thrilling trip downstairs to flop unenergetically on the sofa yet again. She spent the day giving her sister present ideas.

"Why have you left it so late?" Alis glared at her. "Sorry. I don't mean to criticise… I just thought Bristol would have been a better bet than sleepy Llandovery!"

"Yes. I'm sure you're right," she glowered. "But I didn't, because I was too busy partaaaying." She flicked her fingers rapidly, her contorted face breaking into a wide grin.

"I could get you a book!" she gasped in excitement. Elin was as easy to read as a traffic sign. "Oh. I see. Maybe not. I don't want to get one you've already bought for yourself!" They laughed together until Alis slapped her knee and stood up. "Well, this isn't getting the baby bathed." She grabbed her cardigan from the back of a chair and walked to the door.

"See ya. Wouldn't wanna be ya."

Elin watched through the window as her sister disappeared from view. "I'm sure it's coat weather," she tutted with a rueful smile.  When moments later, Emyr burst in and panted, "Any idea what your mother might like for Christmas?" she burst out laughing.

Venturing into the kitchen to ask Glenda if she needed help with the last minute baking, she choked at the flour cloud in the air. Her mother had decided perhaps they didn't have quite adequate supply of mince pies after all. Who she expected to eat them wasn't apparent. They hadn't made many friends locally, especially those close enough to call in at Christmas.

Careful to keep the conversation cheerful, she mentioned nothing about the house, or about her nightmares.

When they finished baking and tidied away, they retired to the lounge with a traditional Christmas Eve glass of mulled wine. Footsteps crunched the shingle drive. Alis and Emyr popped their heads round the door and ordered them not to go into the study where the art of secret present wrapping would obviously be taking place.

After Emyr came back with anxious requests for sellotape, gift tags and pens, the disorganised pair returned, grinning, with armfuls of untidy looking presents which they proceeded to place proudly beneath the Christmas tree.

Glenda served, then replenished, mulled wine and mince pies to her clan slumped on the couch. Flopping in her favourite chair, she sighed, and finally relaxed. Christmas was here at last. They were all, the two sisters especially, ridiculously excited about tomorrow morning.

"Do you think he'll come?" Emyr asked.

"Not if we don't go to bed," Glenda smiled.

They hugged good night and retired to their rooms. Glenda had one more job to do. When the girls left, she snuck back to the lounge and filled the stockings on the mantle with sweets and little gifts procured since early September. Some were even January sales bargains!

Emyr glugged down brandy and ate another mince pie in homage to years gone by when they used to leave the same out for Sion Corn/Santa Clause. He stopped short of nibbling a carrot.


Unlike any Christmas before, Alis wasn't first to wake. When she had been four years old, the family caught her with her own and Elin's presents, all unwrapped, with her sitting in the middle of a huge pile of colourful paper!

Whilst she had calmed with maturity, she still roused the rest of the household at an ungodly hour most years. Her absence in shaking her with excitement confirmed to Elin that she must be the only one awake.

She'd woken in a panic having had what she was becoming aware was a recurring nightmare. It hadn't been a particularly frightening dream. Much like her experience in her mum and dad's hallway, it was more a feeling of anxiety. Something not right.

The uncomfortable sensation in Erw Lon was ultimately her mum's problem. It was for her to decide the cause and if there was anything she could do. Elin would find her own place to live as soon as she was well enough and it would all be behind her.

This nightmare she kept having felt personal, but still no reason it should be anything to trouble her in her waking life. She hoped as she got better the nightmares would stop again. They didn't make any sense.

Whilst musing resentfully, her door burst open to an excited Alis bounding through in an Eyore dressing gown and Piglet slippers.

"Let's wake Mum and Dad!" she hissed. Elin looked scathingly at her as she swung her legs from her bed and placed her feet in some equally comical monster feet slippers.

"You are nineteen years old, Alis Treharne!"

Alis shrugged and pulled a face. "And your point is..?"

Elin giggled as she pulled her boring, unadorned, pink flannelette dressing gown around her. "Nothing. Come on."

The two sisters skipped to their mum and dad's bedroom across the landing, Elin with noticeably less energy than Alis, but she was sure she was getting better. Alis flung the door open to the bleary eyed couple sitting up in bed.

"Six forty seven!" Emyr declared. "Quite reasonable for you two!"

The family crept down the creaky stairs to the lounge with Alis leading the way.

"He's been," she yelled upon seeing the bulging bounty hanging on the mantelpiece.

They loved the thoughtful and intriguing little gifts their stockings bestowed. Puzzles, bookmarks and chocolate coins were thrilled at, then put aside so that presents to one another could be opened. Alis was particularly enamoured with her raunchy romance novel. Elin hoped it wouldn't encourage in her sister any behaviour she would regret.

A typical Christmas day with traditional Christmas Fayre finished with a full and sated family slumped in front of Christmas specials, wearing ridiculous paper hats. Before going to bed, Alis insisted on them playing some family favourite board games, which ended in the traditional huff as she failed to win every game. For someone so jolly, Alis could be quite the petulant brat if everything didn't go her way.

After the early start and rich food, the atmosphere at the Treharne's suffered and it was decided to call it a day and go to bed.


"Wake up Elin. Wake up!" She became dimly aware of her mum's voice, and the sensation of her legs being shaken. Alis's voice came next, and she was vigorously tapping her shoulder.

"Wake up, Sis! You're having a nightmare! Wake up!"

Elin finally jolted awake to a pounding heart and a cold sweat. She flung her arms around her mum and burst into huge sobbing tears.

As she racked with her distress, Glenda stroked her hand. "Come, come, cariad. You're safe now. There, Elin bach. You let it all out." She glanced at Alis. "Go and fetch some tea, please, bach."

Elin let out a further wail, which probably in this instance, was unrelated to the fear of the putrid brew she would have to endure. But the promise of hell's swill being imminent roused Elin back to reality and subdued her snivelling. She pulled back, rubbing her eyes and apologised for her outburst.

"That's okay, cariad. What was it all about?"

Elin stumbled for words, unwilling to get into it, but with the emotion she'd revealed, she didn't think she would get away with saying she couldn't remember. "I keep having nightmares about Swansea." A tear tracked her cheek.

"Really!" Glenda exclaimed. And then a realisation. She knew something nightmarish had happened to her daughter. She'd become very subdued. Compared to her sister, she was always quiet, of course, but she hadn't been herself. A mother knows.

And then she'd succumbed to the fever. Glenda wondered for the first time if whatever had unsettled her in Swansea had brought on her illness. With pointed concern piercing into her daughter's eyes, Glenda asked, "What *did* happen to you there, cariad?"

# Chapter Thirteen

Christmas day for the Hedges was the quiet family time they always enjoyed together. Taking it in turns, opening their stockings, then their Santa sacks in appreciation at what clever Father Christmas had thoughtfully got for each of them.

In Neil's case, his wish for a car (albeit a very cheap car) had been answered. He was now the proud(ish) owner of a Daewoo Matiz, apparently the cheapest car ever to insure. Well, there had to be a reason they bothered making the ugly, faded red jalopy, Neil supposed.

He liked it really. It wasn't the babe-magnet he'd secretly dreamed of, but he'd known that wasn't likely. As soon as he passed his driving test he'd be independent, and that was something to be grateful for.

A smoked salmon and scrambled eggs breakfast was the tradition for the Hedge's. After which they reconvened in the lounge to open the presents under the tree from one another.

The rest of the day was Mum in the kitchen, with Dad popping in from time to time to peel things and pass things in between removing dolls from unfeasibly secure packaging, and building toys that were always a cause of mind meltdown.

And then there was the inevitable hunt for essential and precious parts which had been removed from their package by impatient little fingers in the mess of all the wrapping paper, against parental and brotherly advice, and Neil trying to watch a film through all the kerfuffle.

The exhausted family, having consumed vast quantities of Christmas dinner ended up snoozing in their chairs wearing silly hats, and aching after the inevitable mince pies, Christmas pudding and forced-in turkey sandwiches, and maybe even a few Roses or Quality Street for good measure.

Boxing Day was different. The quiet family time gave way to a raucous open house where what was left of the mince pies and turkey would be joined by a giant ham they had cooked on Christmas Eve, and some expensive cheeses and sausage rolls.

Guests would turn up throughout the day and the last few gifts would be dragged from under the tree and exchanged with friends and relatives. Although there wasn't a set guest list, there were guests where it would be a huge surprise if they were absent—one of those being Psychic Auntie Sylvie.

Her own family, since her divorce from her ex-policeman husband, was an only daughter who had married a Canadian banker. She lived in Toronto now and rarely made it back for the holidays.

Sylvie travelled over the water on occasion, but it was expensive, and her and her offspring didn't get on particularly well. She'd been a daddy's girl and had taken his side since the divorce despite his being discovered by Sylvie in a compromising situation with his commanding officer in their front room.

Having a gay dad seemed to thrill their daughter who always said the best ones were always gay or married. The solution to her own prior fruitless search for a suitor had been to break up a young family when she'd travelled to Canada in her gap year.

Sylvie's presents were unusual, incredibly thoughtful and always treasured. Today, apart from a gift, there was something else Neil wanted from her. Hovering on the outskirts of conversations, he opened his mouth to speak a number of times before family gossip shut him down and left him with a simpering smile.

Auntie Sylvie shot him the occasional squint-eyed look, wondering why he'd become her shadow. The longer it went on, the more anxious Neil felt. On the umpteenth try and fail, he debated walking away. He didn't want to talk about number twenty-four much anyway. He'd enjoyed not thinking about it over Christmas, but he knew he needed her assistance.

"Auntie Sylvie…?" he mumbled.

"Ah, Sylvie. How's the Canadian contingent?" a regular freeloading neighbour, Mr Uzzleworth, asked enthusiastically. "I used to live in Canada too, remember?" and Sylvie's attention was taken for another ten minutes.

She'll be here for the day, Neil knew. Just calm down. She can't talk all the time. But he needn't have worried. One of her many conversations was with his mother who couldn't wait to discuss Neil's supernatural goings-on, and a plan was hatched in no time.

"Oohh. Of course I'll help," cooed Sylvie. "I love this sort of thing. I knew something was up with you, Neil. I knew it." She looked around the surrounding mob, nodding, inviting affirmation of her psychic talents. "We'll need to call all the occupants of the house together and perform a séance."

"A séance? Can't you just command it to leave or something?" His eyes wide and face white, he hadn't given enough thought about what Sylvie's methods might be, but he was determined to avoid a ghostly conflict.

"No, Neil. Not without knowing who, or what it is, sweetheart." Who or what? He struggled to hide his trembling. His half-hearted smile did nothing to disguise the terror in his eyes.

"I don't think I'll be able to get everyone there for a séance, Auntie Sylvie. I'm kind of the only one who thinks it's a poltergeist." Sylvie frowned.

"What do they think is happening?"

"Just people in the house moving stuff about."

"Neil! You saw a girl in the bath. Emma saw a girl in the lounge. It's a ghost, alright?" A rush of heat thrilled him. Put like that, he suddenly knew that far from being the house fool, he was the only one clever enough to understand the truth when it was staring them all in the face. He also knew that inviting his housemates to a séance would be embarrassing.

"Well, just ask them to get together and don't tell them why. They'll certainly be convinced by the time I've finished with them!" Sylvie smiled.

# Chapter Fourteen

Jon was back in The Railway after his recuperation. The break had been beneficial, even though it was forced upon him by Gareth (not the first time someone's older brother had shown him the error of his ways). And he'd been coerced to pay them both double time, and give Gareth a full-time job.

Hospital treatment was required for a gash above his eye where he'd fallen to the ground, and for a broken wrist from where Gareth had bent it back to the point of snapping. He would have snapped a lot more, but Efa was moved enough by his pathetic snivelling to call her brother off.

Even so, he was grateful they were here. He'd been badly shaken by the falling spirit bottles, more than by Gareth's ambush, and he wasn't looking forward to being alone again in the bar anytime soon.

Efa reported that the optics stand had just been a bit loose. Gareth tightened a couple of screws and they'd had no kamikaze bottles all the time Jon was away. He almost allowed himself a chuckle at his foolishness, but he still felt uneasy, especially next to the; he was about to think haunted but decided better of it, barstool which seemed to have prompted the tumbling bottles previously.

He decided to test his mettle and stand closer to it. A shiver ran through him. Goosebumps covered his arms, and his teeth began to chatter. Was it really colder in this part of the pub? He looked around for possible causes: an open window, or a previously unnoticed vent. There was the chimney. Maybe he was feeling a draught from that.

Breathing deeply, shaking his head and smiling, "Come on!" he commanded himself. "It's only a stool. What's the matter with you?"

Leaning towards it, fingers extended, he was trembling again. All the hairs on his head and body stood on end. Outstretched digits edged towards the stool in slow motion, his hand shaking, he couldn't find the courage to touch it.

He didn't have to. With his hand still inches away, the stool flipped over, landing with a loud thud on the floor. The supposedly fixed optics released their grip on a bottle of peach schnapps, plunging it to the ground, cracking in half. As the clear liquid puddled on the stone floor, the glasses hanging from their stems began to rattle. Shuddering more violently, they edged forwards

One glass reached the end of its hanger and toppled, exploding into a hundred pieces on the black slate. And then another, SMASH! Then more and more until the entire stock of wine glasses lay in glistening disarray upon the slate floor. The light shining through them and onto the schnapps looked like diamonds to Jon's bewildered eyes.

He wanted to get away but was paralysed to move. "Stop!" he mumbled and shouted almost at the same time in a pathetic sounding directive he knew he'd no hope of enforcing. "Please!" he whimpered, hoping to placate this demon he could not see.

The entire shelf of tumblers tipped, allowing all the contents to cascade spectacularly to the floor, crashing at once in an incredible cacophony of ear-shattering uproar.

The scream reverberated just as Gareth and Efa rushed into the bar to investigate the ruckus and were confronted by Jon, petrified to the spot, surrounded by catastrophic chaos all over the floor. Standing open mouthed, struggling to take it all in, they exchanged looks of disbelief.

The arrival of his colleagues gave Jon the impetus to finally move, which he did, fleeing the bar and the building.

# Chapter Fifteen

The holidays flew by too fast for Neil. New Year's Eve had provided promises to himself to get fit, study harder, pass his driving test, and a few other things more wishes than resolutions—like getting a girlfriend. The very notion gave him butterflies.

Something else giving him butterflies was today's return to Swansea. At least he had a plan. It would all be better soon. He'd phoned, texted, and messaged on Facebook, the rest of the group and had their agreement to be present for a special gathering with his Auntie Sylvie when he arrived later on that day.

He'd needed to tell them the nature of the get-together to gain their cooperation. No-one was up for another meeting so soon without a bloody good reason. Their positive reactions to a séance surprised him to say the least. Matthew offered the only objection but had been easy to sway through his fear of missing out.

Approaching Bronwyn made him most anxious. She was already back at the house with Aeron, missing one-another, she said. Neil frowned. Either they'd had a lovers' tiff, or something else had taken the colour from her voice. After their clash before Christmas he had expected more of the same. But when he told of Emma's vision of the girl in the lounge, she'd become mouse-quiet, then agreed to the plan immediately sounding unexpectedly grateful.

Aeron's acquiescence was a given. Bronwyn said she would tell him, and Josh was happy enough to go along with what everyone else was doing, but not without the caveat of it being a definite waste of time.

One person not included in the plan for a séance was someone who would dearly like to be. Emma, deemed too young and innocent for such things would be collected from school by one of her real Aunties and was to spend the night in the company of her cousin, Charlotte.

The family, minus Emma, and with the addition of Auntie Sylvie, made very good time back to Swansea, despite some frequent stops for tea, which Sylvie obsessed over. They arrived after lunch at Magor services (just over the big bridge.) With everyone in and awake it made perfect sense to get straight on with things.

Bronwyn opened the door. Her paleness might have been due to fear of their ghost, or it could have been from embarrassment at the untidiness with no-one to blame but her and Aeron. Venturing through the scruffy lounge to the kitchen revealed a sticky mess of boiled over pans soaking in days old dishwater emanating effluvium like a putrid pot pourri.

Closing the door without offering refreshments, Neil introduced his dad, Collin who most of the group had met before, his mum Carole and his Auntie (but not really)

Sylvie; the expert. Once familiar, she took control and directed them to where she wanted.

There seemed no rhyme or reason behind the seating plan, but they all sat where they were told around the small table in a cosy arrangement. The introductory chat made it clear there was a lot more belief in the room that number twenty-four might be haunted than Neil had expected.

The credibility of sensible adults conducting things gave them relief and comfort and a determination. Rather than feeling foolish, as he had feared, Neil felt like the hero of the hour.

All the group loved Emma, and hearing of her sighting of the blonde girl convinced them what they were doing was necessary.

"I saw her too," confessed Bronwyn to her small, rapt audience. "Just for a moment, and after alcohol admittedly. But with Emma seeing her too... I'm sure it was real. The girl was there. I feel her looking at me sometimes. I'm sure it's not my imagination." She shuddered.

Matthew and Josh's scepticism lost its voice in a dry mouthed whimper. Instead, giving full credibility to the haunting, they were happy to suggest the broken crockery and clothes thrown about were down to her.

"And the noises in the night," Neil directed at Bronwyn in an 'I told you so' tone.

"Unless you have more than one spirit here." The group convulsion was evident. Neil hadn't considered that prospect and wished he hadn't now. He was relieved when Sylvie's next statement referenced only the one.

"Neil has done a bit of research into who our visitor might be…"

He filled the others in on the results of his Googling. It was critical they put right whatever wrong poor, murdered Jacqui Lloyd needed them to.

Neil set about drawing the curtains and closing the doors to make the room dark and peaceful, but the cheap curtains were no match for the winter sun low in the sky.

"We need to put our hands on the table with our fingers touching," instructed their expert. After initial confusion, once one got it, the others followed suit. They all sat solemnly awaiting further instruction.

"We must all close our eyes. Do not break the circle," Sylvie ordered.

After a moments tense silence to compose herself, Sylvie began trying to make her special kind of connection.

"We are here to make contact with Spirit…Is there spirit with us here now?" The tension in the room was tangible, but there was nothing tangible in reply. Just an eerie silence. Sylvie persisted confidently.

"If there is spirit here, please show us a sign." A lengthy pause allowed time to react, but no retort came. Sylvie addressed the group with her eyes still closed.

"I'll try naming her with the information Neil gathered…. That's sure to get a response."

"Jacqui…? Jacqui…? Is that you? Are you there, Jacqui?" she said clearly to the room beyond the table. After a number of attempts with nothing to show for it, Sylvie broke the circle and announced the séance to be over, for now.

"It might be a bit early. Did you say you normally notice these strange things happening at night?" Nervous glances were exchanged. No-one knew exactly what the others had experienced; they hadn't talked about it. But if they were attributing all the odd things to this spirit, it was fair to say it happened any time of day.

Sylvie pursed her lips, tapping them with her fingers. "Sometimes dark is better. I don't know why. Let's get tea and try again after dusk, shall we? Agreed?" They all agreed.


Picking at their dinner in a family friendly pub nearby, they talked uneasily about what they should do.

"Do you think she might have left already? Or maybe she only haunts at Christmas. Maybe she was murdered then?" suggested a previously sceptical Matthew before adding "That's if she was there at all and wasn't just drunken dreams and a child's imagination."

No-one bothered taking offence at the added scathing remark. They recognised it for what it was. Denial.

Neil Googled results for Jacqui's murder.

"July," he announced. "But that doesn't mean that Christmas isn't significant in some other way. It might be when they were arguing most, or when they met or something."

"There isn't any link to Jacqui Lloyd or any other of the people mentioned in the press," Josh stared at his phone, further consulting the web. "The only thing in common with her at all is that she has blonde hair."

"But no-one was reported as having died in there," Neil said, "There has to be a reason a ghost would haunt the place."

"There usually is," confirmed Sylvie "But that doesn't mean it will have links on the internet."

Carole added, "She may be an ancient ghost, from before records. Since before the house was built even. If that's the case it would be difficult to find mention of her anywhere."

"We should all chill out," ordered Bronwyn. "When we go back, Sylvie might make contact and all this speculation will be unnecessary." Shrugs and murmurs proclaimed agreement the consensus. They were all tired of guesswork anyway.


They made to split the bill between them but Collin insisted on paying, knowing they were all on a tight budget. Everyone accepted with smiles and cheers.

The streetlights were on as they strolled back to the house. It was dark and getting quite late.

"If there's a ghost," Sylvie declared, "now is the perfect time to make contact."

"Put earlier out of your head. I'm sure we'll get a result now… I can feel it."

As soon as they walked through the front door, they could believe it. Something was different. Matthew raised his eyes to heaven. "It's just psycho-suggestion," he said under his breath.

"She's here," whispered Sylvie to the expectant bunch. They all made their way excitedly, and more than a little afraid, to the table and resumed their places.

Sylvie asked for candles to be lit to give the right ambience. They chose some nice red ones left over from Christmas, which Bronwyn had forgotten to take home with her, over the white ones in the cupboard in case of power-cuts. The resultant eerie red glow cast sinister shadows over the walls and people's faces.

Their fingers touched as before, and Sylvie talked to the darkness.

"We, sitting in union around this table, wish to speak to spirit, please," she began. "Is there anybody here?"

Bronwyn and Carole winced detecting a distinct drop in temperature. Opening their eyes against instruction from Auntie Sylvie, they caught sight of one another through the gloom. Bronwyn gasped as her eyes strained to focus when she saw her. Carole convinced herself it was the light from the flames playing tricks on her mind. Eyes squeezed shut tighter, they prayed Sylvie was as in control as she appeared.

"I can feel you here. Please give us a sign and show yourself." Conspicuously, nothing happened.

After a pause to make sure nothing would happen, Sylvie spoke again.

"Jacqui? Is that you Jacqui? We want to help you."

CRASH!

A spider-plant on the window sill tumbled from where it had rested forever and shattered on the floor. Collin would joke later that it had committed suicide, so pitiful did it look.

The table shook as everyone jumped in unison. They all stared towards the sound of the crash. When Neil saw the broken plant pot on the floor his hands flew to his mouth, but couldn't conceal the pitiful whimper.

"It's okay, Son, it's okay," Collin disguised his own terror to sound reassuring.

"Don't be afraid, Jacqui. We want to help you!"

CRASH!!

The plant's sorry companion raised up from the sill, and with all eyes welded to it, flew across the room, smashing against the wall near the table. Plant remains floated down, peppering any bare flesh with desert-dry soil. Screams filled the room as the unexpected touch was too much to take.

Gasping, Bronwyn blurted, "Did you hear that? Oh my God!" Sylvie had heard it too; a disembodied voice hissed, "Not Jacqui!" With a glare from Sylvie, she fought the urge to get up and run and kept the circle intact.

Josh froze. "We have to stop this. Come on. We must stop this now! I've got a really bad feeling. Really bad."

But even he knew they had to carry on. They had to appease this spirit if they were to have any peace.

Sylvie instructed Bronwyn and Neil flanking her to touch fingers to maintain the circle while she bent over to reach something. Her unruly hair returned from under the table, followed by her hands clutching a Ouija board.

"All of you, join me in putting a finger on the pointer," Sylvie instructed in the confident tones of an expert. "Together, we will find out what this spirit wants. Then we can help her find peace."

They struggled to get eight fingers onto the Ouija pointer but they did. Sylvie set about asking questions. She began by apologising for any offense caused.

"We would like to ask your name, please." It took a moment but then the pointer moved. Gasps all round as it crawled to its first resting place, 'N'.

"Did you move that? I swear to God I kept my hand still." Bronwyn's query caused appropriate head shaking and nodding. Apparently, none of them were responsible for the movement.

Relaxing from the hysteria, it was noticed the pointer still rested where it had stopped. Girl's names beginning with n were rattled off. Nicola, Natasha, Nadine, Nadia… The pointer was off again, rapidly this time.

'O'. Adding o caused a struggle... Nora, Noreen… Skidding across the board, 'T'. They could think of nothing but the pointer whizzed to its next letter, then the next and the next. Staring, they let the Ouija answer. 'J', 'A', 'C', 'Q', 'U', 'I'.

''Not Jacqui! That's what I heard her say and now she's spelling it out!" Bronwyn shot a glance toward Carol "You saw her too, didn't you?" Carol darted her eyes away.

"Okay. We know you're not Jacqui," Sylvie regained control. "We're very sorry we suggested that, but a girl called Jacqui was murdered, and we thought you might be her. If you don't want to tell us your name, can you tell us what it is you want?"

The Ouija pointer moved quickly. 'M', 'Y', 'H', 'O', 'U', 'S', 'E'.

"This is your house? What can we do to help?"

'G', 'E', 'T', 'O', 'U', 'T'. GET OUT!

The candles blew out, one by one, leaving the room in darkness.

'Get Out!!!" They all heard it. And they all heard the clattering and crashing as things unseen flew around the room. Crash! Thud! Clang!

Aeron made it to the light switch and filled the room with fear-reducing brightness. Bronwyn, Carole and Sylvie screamed as they saw her. A blonde girl, effervescent with rage, screaming at them to "get out! Get out of her house!"

She was there, but she wasn't entirely palpable. The boys seemed unable to see her at all. They all saw what she did next, though. As cupboard doors flew open and slammed shut, their contents spilled chaotically to the floor.

When the chairs fell over, they hadn't been pushed by the blonde apparition, but by the group scrambling to get out of the room. Tripping over one another, chivalry was barely observed as they fell through the front door Collin was the last to leave, slamming the door behind him.

Shivering under the street lamp at the end of the path, they stared in disbelief at the house. Bronwyn cwtched into Aeron's thick chest, her sobbing still clearly heard. Neil gulped down a lump, the pressure spilling from his eyes. Batting tears away with his palms, he shook his head. "What was that?"

"What are we going to do?" cried Bronwyn from her place wrapped around Aeron's neck. "What are we gonna do?" she hid her face again and sobbed.

Everyone, including Collin, looked to their expert for guidance. Shaking her head, she gave the only appropriate guidance she could think of. Ashen faced, she proclaimed, "I think we need a priest.

# Chapter Sixteen

The week between Christmas and New Year was one of tentative family walks. Tiny to start with but growing to a feeble, but reasonable under the circumstances, mile. Elin was thrilled, but not as much as the rest of her family.

"You're doing so well, Elin bach!" declared Emyr. "I haven't seen you looking so bright in ages!"

Elin's shapely lips curved endearingly, revealing her perfect white smile. She loved the crisp winter air, and the mountains covered in frost. The journey ventured barely beyond the boundary of Erw Lon, but the scenery was spectacular, and despite having lived here for months, all new to Elin.

The first word of concern came from Glenda, who didn't want her precious daughter overdoing things before she properly recovered. 'You don't want a relapse, do you?' Elin didn't, of course, but she had the sneaking suspicion her mum was reluctant, albeit probably subconsciously, for her to leave her alone at Erw Lon.

The plan had always been that as soon as she was well enough, she would find a job, and her own place to live.

She did her best to sensitively reassure her mum she wasn't overdoing it and that she felt fine.

Nightmares of her old house had decreased again and sleep was surprisingly refreshing. Twenty nineteen was seen in without suffering too badly from the late night. Her recovery seemed assured.

She put her peace of mind down to having told Glenda of her fears. Bottling it up must have caused distress within her she hadn't even realised. It was such a relief to sleep and not give thought to where her unconscious mind would transport her.

Her relief would be short lived; the week long reprieve, the only peace she would know for a very long time.

It began with Alis due to go back to Bristol. She had snuffled into the lounge, wrapped in a duvet.

"I don' ting I be abol to go bag toborrow," she snuffled. It was the first time her speech had been effected by the cold she had forewarned them of for a few days and was suspiciously affected.

Glenda suppressed a smile, but a look of amusement at Alis's transparency escaped. Elin reciprocated. It may have been a reluctance to go back to Uni, but more likely, jealousy at the attention Elin had received for months. Seeing her sister recovering must have seemed like the ideal opportunity to take her rightful place as the baby of the family.

They were secretly pleased to have her around for a bit longer. And Glenda's attention being shared would give Elin some much needed space. Her vivacity was a marvellous distraction from the unease the other Treharne women felt in the old Victorian house.

Whether it was recognising Alis's positive influence and the realisation she was soon to leave them again, Elin didn't know, but her nightmares of Rhondda Street, Swansea, began to take a very different and disturbing direction.

Elin was exhausted. The almost daily walks draining her recuperating body. She decided when her chin fell from its resting place propped on her up-turned palm, she should go to bed.

"Are you okay, cariad?" Glenda asked with moderate concern, pleased she was being sensible and resting.

"Yeah. Just really tired, that's all." She kissed her mum and dad goodnight. When she got to Alis she was fended off.

"Don't come near me! You don't want to catch my awful cold and make yourself worse!"

Elin obliged, suspecting it was a reminder that she was feeling poorly too.

Reaching the hallway, she was surprised to observe the oppressive atmosphere again. Too tired to heed a meaning, and doubtful there was one, she hauled herself up the long creaky wooden staircase to her room.

The night's chill made her shiver. She hadn't warmed up since the walk earlier. Selecting a thick flannel nightie from the drawer, she would soon get cosy under her duvet. Before she decided if she was warm enough, she fell sound asleep.

If anyone were to peep in on her, they would have seen the epitome of fitful sleep. Legs kicking, arms flailing the duvet entangled around her. Eyelids moved rapidly, whilst inside Elin's unconscious mind, a dream was forming that would quickly become a nightmare.

In the street so familiar. The street where she had lived for three years of student life, something was different. Scrutinising her surroundings, trying to decipher what had changed, it soon became obvious. Her vision wasn't in colour. Everything appeared in grey scale. Everything that is, except number twenty-four.

Not only was her old house in colour, it effervesced. A compulsion to go inside the glowing entrance fought with intense anxiety. She was aware of her heart beating rapidly. The hairs standing proud on top of her head allowed sweat to trickle down her face and into her eyes.

She couldn't wait out here. It wasn't safe. She had to get inside the house, even though it terrified her. Stepping toward it in trepidation, she was overcome by nausea. Laboured steps moved her ever closer when something spurred within her and she knew the house was safe.

Looking with fresh eyes, she was certain the threat was coming for her. Inside, she would find sanctuary, protection from the danger she was convinced she knew, but couldn't remember.

She made it to the streetlamp she always used as a landmark in the row of similar looking houses. Walking up the uneven concrete steps to the faded red front door, more pink than red now in its weathered disrepair.

Her eyes darted to every corner of the black and white street, expecting someone or something to pounce on her at any second. Trembling fingers fumbled in her usual pocket for her door key. The disbelief as it wasn't there turned her adrenaline to perilous levels.

With heart pounding, she rooted around in other pockets in the inside of a large coat she was sure she hadn't been wearing a moment before. Her fingers touched something cold. Grasping the key from its hiding place, she thrust the find into the lock.

At first she blamed her trembling hand, but she was forced to concede the lock wouldn't accept her key. Forcing it, finally it thrust home, but then it wouldn't turn. Her mind whirred, trying to understand. Somehow, the object she held in her hand, so familiar with her little Perestroika Doll key-ring, was the wrong key.

The threat was closer now. She still didn't know what she expected, but she knew it was coming. Banging frantically on the door. Bang, bang, bang. Over and over. She didn't know if she could be heard or if anyone was in.

Desperate to call out, her open mouth was useless. She couldn't recall any of her housemate's names. Standing with her quivering hand on the useless key, her floundering lips trying to form words that just wouldn't come. "Help! Help me, please, somebody!"

In her bewilderment, the menace gained ground. She screamed at a tugging on her nightdress (she now wore instead of the heavy coat). Kicking out in defence, terrified of the unseen foe, plummeting forward through the open front door, it slammed behind her and she was plunged into darkness.

She couldn't see where she was but the odour was familiar. Not a pleasant smell, but it made her feel safe. Feeling lino beneath her hands, she realised she was crouched on the floor of the lounge of number twenty-four. Feeling around in the dark for the leather sofa, she heaved herself to her feet.

Quietening her hard breathing, she stood in the middle of the floor and listened. Able to hold her breath no longer, the hiss as her lungs gasping for air filled her ears made it impossible to be sure she was alone, but she felt she was.

She made a conscious effort to calm herself now she was safely ensconced in the lounge and decided to make her way to the wall to find the light switch. But in addition to illuminating the room, flicking the switch had the effect of restoring Elin's terror.

Apparently in reaction to the light, or to the noise of the switch being pressed, someone or something was coming. Elin froze to the spot. Who was it? What would they do to her?

A whimper poised in her throat to be expelled whenever her instinct for safety would permit. The door to the lounge swung open. Elin timed the creaking perfectly with the sound of her own retreat to the kitchen, either through instinct or her familiarity with every squeak and groan of the old building.

Hidden in the darkness of the kitchen, she struggled to stifle her breathing. Eyes creased with the strain let out a tear. The unmistakable sound of footsteps tip-tapped across the lino floor. The lightness of step was a relief. It wasn't what she had expected.

Not willing to take her safety for granted, peering cautiously into the bright lounge from the darkness, confident she wouldn't be seen, but not so sure she wouldn't be heard.

Easing herself slowly to the doorjamb, she leaned until the angle she stood provided a glimpse into the room beyond. The room was empty. Taking a tentative step to re-enter the lounge, a hand reached in from the hallway and turned the light off.

The gasp escaped her mouth before her caution reigned it in. The light came back on instantly, leaving her exposed in the silhouette of the kitchen doorway. Frozen to the spot, Elin had no choice but to face her fear head on. She looked brazenly ahead, ready to take on whatever was about to befall her.

Across the room, and looking right at her, stood a girl.

Elin woke up screaming in her cold bed at Erw Lon. She fumbled with the switch for her bedside light. The button, some way down the electric cable, was at a distance so familiar she could turn the light on and off with her eyes closed, and frequently did. Now, in her panic she bungled the operation, knocking the lamp from its resting place to the wooden floorboards. The bulb forced a way through the lampshade and make contact with the hard surface, shattering into a million pieces.

"Shit!" she cursed herself. Swinging her legs reluctantly and carefully out of the bed, she hovered her feet above the floor.

Lowering her bare feet ever so slowly, feeling tentatively for broken glass. She found a patch she was sure was clear, but when she put her weight onto it, a sharp piece of the shattered bulb pierced her skin painfully.

"Shit, Shit, Shit!"

Hopping away from the bed in a giant leap, she hopped far enough to clear any more broken glass. Her blind estimate proved correct and she managed to stumble-hop to the door where she knew she would be able to locate the light switch.

With the room lit, and pain of her foot, she was back to reality with a sobering jolt. She sat on the floor and squeezed at where blood wept from the sharp little wound. A tiny splinter of glass came out onto her finger. She carefully wiped the shard on the chest of drawers. She knew it wasn't sensible, and there was every chance it would end up back in her foot if it blew onto the floor.

She was willing to do no more at whatever time it was. Vacuuming would risk waking the rest of the house. And the hoover was downstairs anyway. She lay a spare blanket over the remaining breakage and prepared to go back to sleep.

A knock at her door made her jump. Before she thought to answer, Emyr popped his head round the door.

"You okay? I heard a crash," he asked.

"What time is it?" Elin asked, surprised to see her dad. Emyr consulted his chunky, fashionable watch (a Christmas present from Alis in an attempt to 'drag Dad into the twenty first century').

"'Bout ten," he announced.

"Is that all?" Elin said with a frown before answering her dad's concern. "I'm fine. I had a stupid nightmare, that's all. I woke up and knocked the light over. Sorry, Dad. It smashed," she said apologetically.

Another nightmare. Why was she having these recurring dreams? She had to believe it had something to do with her recovery, and would end soon. It may well have a lot to do with staying in this unwelcoming house. The sooner she could get well and find her own place, the better.

Emyr invited her to go back to sleep while he cleared up the mess of the broken lamp. After he left with the Eubank in tow, Elin was wide awake. She elected to read for a little while which turned into a long while.

The cacophony of the dawn chorus from woodland birds residing in the many trees Erw Lon boasted roused her from precipitous slumber. But when she dropped her book for the third time, she gave in

Despite her struggle to get any decent rest, Elin forced her weary body from her bed at a reasonable hour of the morning, determined to build her strength and move on.

If she walked and worked hard at regaining her fitness, it would have the added benefit of making her extra tired. Perhaps, she might achieve some nightmare free nights of exhausted sleep.

She would exercise on her own today. Alis was feeling too unwell anyway, what with her awful cold (poor Diddums), and Glenda kept worrying she was overdoing it. Well, Elin wanted to overdo it. At least she wanted to push herself to her limit so she could find out what her limit was. She might never get better with the baby steps she had been allowed to take under her family's supervision.

Wrapped up warm, she snuck out the back door. In no time she was at the stream bordering Erw Lon's land. She impressed herself, carefully picking through the stepping stones, even leaping the final few feet where the last stone was covered by fast flowing water after some heavy rainfall.

Slipping as she landed, she giggled and regained her balance. Walking at almost a normal pace for nearly a mile meant a return journey would be a post glandular fever record. She felt pleased with herself, until halfway back, she realised her mum's concerns had been well founded.

Fatigue set in hard and she was struggling. Fire in her legs and arms caught as her muscles burned, her limbs shaking uncontrollably. She had no choice but to rest.

It took a good twenty minutes for her to recover enough to attempt moving again. Aware she might be causing concern back at the house if they'd noticed she was gone, she tried to hurry. Soon, she was once again stood on the muddy bank of the boundary stream.

The stride to the first uncovered stepping stone was too far to make safely. She stood ponderously on the side, debating if she could make a leap for it. She knew in her shattered state it was far more dangerous jumping to a wet stone than it had been jumping from the same wet stone an hour earlier.

She had no choice but to get across. Any alternative route avoiding the stream was far and uphill. She would never make that distance, so decided stepping onto the nearest stone which was underwater, and then quickly moving to the higher stone, was her safest bet.

It took a while to coach herself into action. But as soon as her weight leaned forward towards the submerged rock, she knew it had been a mistake. Through the rippling water she misjudged its position. Her ankle slipped, and she brought her other foot to join it for balance.

The current was surprisingly strong, and she immediately fell forward. Icy cold water splashed her face, then pain as she hit her head, then… nothing.

The strong arms of her retired father plucked her from the water. Cradling her like the baby she would always be to him, he lay her on the flat grass. "Come on Elin. Come on!" he bawled preparing to do CPR.

Without much of a cough, she opened her eyes and roused, cognisant again. "I think I slipped," she offered apologetically. Emyr gave her a look that told her exactly how foolish she had been before helping her get soggily to her feet. He put one arm around her wet waist and another under her elbow, supporting her back to the house.

"Thanks, Dad," she said, squeezing his arm. "I'm getting better. But I think I'll take it easy for a while longer."

"And don't go out without company until you are completely better!" Emyr berated. Elin nodded. That had been a close call.

Reaching the house, they were greeted by a frantic Glenda and Alis.

"I know you want to build your strength, but if you want to go swimming you should go to the pool!" Alis joked. Elin glared in scathing good humour. Glenda embraced her daughter, and when she was convinced she was okay, she pulled away with distaste at her cold wetness.

"Go and have a hot shower and get something dry on. I hope you haven't put your recovery back," she said, more to show her displeasure than from keenness for the day Elin went on her way. "We're having your sister's favourite, fagots, for dinner. She's decided to go back to Bristol tomorrow."

Elin called 'okay' as she walked upstairs, trying hard not to show the pain she was in and how exhausted she felt. She struggled to haul her weakened body all the way up. She turned on the shower and undressed, leaving her clothes in a heap on the floor.

The scolding water was gorgeously purging. Her aches and pains soothed under the hot flow. After a long wash and soak she exited the steamy room in a fluffy dressing gown of her mother's. It was all extremely luxurious, and for the first time since she had arrived at Erw Lon, she felt a reluctance to leave.

At dinner, Elin ate the fagots purchased from the local butchers who declared them to be 'the best in the world', with a sweet potato mash and thick tasty gravy. Very heartening after her exhausting mini adventure.

Alis, unsurprisingly, took over the conversation, with the others happy to let her because they would all miss her after she left tomorrow. They all gave Elin the benefit of their opinion that she had been an idiot, and a lucky idiot at that.

As if to appease her family, but in reality to compensate for her utter exhaustion, Elin agreed to an early night. It was a very early night in fact as she ventured upstairs after food and just after it became dark. Despite the early hour, she didn't recall her cranium colliding with the duck down pillow before falling fast and heavy once again her nightmare. Her only hope, that somewhere in the depths of her subconscious, she might have answers that would make sense of it all.

At once, she was back in the lounge of number twenty-four. The girl wasn't there, but noises of movement came from somewhere. Icy goose pimples were quick to cover her arms. The noise came closer, and this time was definitely more than a girl on her own.

Their voices, loud and animated, paid no heed to quietness. If whoever she could hear were confident and fearless, it was in exact contrast to Elin's swelling dread. Her racing heart shifted into high gear preparing her for action.

As she scouted the room for somewhere to hide, she realised the futility. It was small, and any space had been filled to brimming with furniture and junk. The couch touched two walls, and any room under the table taken up with boxes and empty beer cans. Why? Why were they there? It was usually tidy, she always made sure of it.

In the last moments before she would have to confront whoever was coming, instead of bracing herself for battle, she fumed at the mess. She scrutinised the room. So many things wrong. Whose clothes were they, hanging on the backs of her chairs? And who was in the photos in frames dotted about? She didn't recognise anyone. It didn't make any sense.

The door burst open, and they were upon her, shocking her back to her fear, forcing her to confront them. Adrenaline surged through her as she prepared to fight, and then caused her to judder as the conflict she had anticipated gave way to utter bemusement.

There were half a dozen or more. Most of them young, about her own age and a few of her parents'. What astounded her was their apparent unawareness of her. None of them even looked as they pulled out the clothes laden chairs and proceeded to sit around the table.

One of them squeezed past and lit a candle. And then… it was her! The girl from her last nightmare, standing right in front of her.

"Er… hello!" Elin barked, no longer afraid and more than a little peeved. "Hello. Am I invisible or something? Hellooow!" she cried, waving her arms from side to side. Still oblivious, the intruders began to talk in hushed tones.

The red candle-light gave the room an eerie glow which only added to Elin's bewilderment. The group laid their hands flat on the table, little fingers touching. One of the older members of the group, an scruffy, tousled haired woman spoke.

"We, sitting in union around this table, wish to speak to spirit, please." It was an authoritative, floaty voice "Is there anybody here?"

Elin moved towards the table.

"What on earth are you doing?" she demanded to no response. Just then, the girl she had seen before opened her eyes and looked straight at her. Elin would have been afraid but for the abject terror obvious in the other girl's eyes. The woman next to her looked too, but it wasn't clear if she could see her.

The untidy woman spoke again,

"I can feel you here," she said, in the same eerie voice, and then, "If there is spirit here, please give us a sign."

Elin wouldn't give them a sign. She wasn't spirit. She was a girl having a nightmare about her own house. What these people were doing, messing the place up and acting in such a peculiar way, she struggled to comprehend.

"Jacqui? Is that you Jacqui?" the odd lady persisted."

Jacqui? Who's Jacqui? Elin was annoyed now.

"We want to help you," the woman said.

Heat rose within her. Eyes bulging and fists clenched, ready to explode. This was too much. This was a liberty too far. Coming, uninvited, invading her home, her sanctuary and calling out someone else's name!

An evil, wry smile formed on Elin's taut features as a glimmer of conception shone into the dark recesses of her disgust. She reached over to the window where a pretty pathetic looking plant sat, almost begging to be put out of its misery. Elin took hold of it and slid it off the sill and onto the floor. CRASH!

She laughed as the group jumped back in unison, causing the table to rock on its unstable feet. There were murmurings of disdain, and then the odd woman riled her when she piped up yet again,

"Don't be afraid, Jacqui. We want to help you!"

'Me afraid?' Elin's mind spluttered. 'No! Not anymore,' she fumed.

She picked up the sickly companion to the already sacrificed plant, and threw it, with considerable force, at the wall behind the table.

'CRASH!'

"I am not Jacqui!" she spat at the foolish group.

Elin couldn't believe what happened next. In amongst the nervous kerfuffle she had created with her kamikaze plants, she watched open mouthed as the strange woman set up a Ouija board.

The people around the table put their hands on the glass and proceeded to ask questions of whomever Jacqui was. Elin leaned over and moved the pointer for them to spell out: *not Jacqui*. She yelled at them that this was her house.

When they still failed to listen, she spelled that out for them too. And the terse command to get out!

"Get out! Get out of my house!" she screamed. She was so incredibly angry, and wasn't even sure why. Of course, they had invaded her refuge. Broken her sanctuary. But she didn't want to hurt these people. They appeared not to know what they'd done. And it was just a dream, after all.

So, instead of hurting them, she threw things. She barely looked at what they were. When she ran out of objects within easy reach, she opened the cupboards and continued to empty their contents to the floor, screaming and yelling the while.

Gratified to witness the group hot-footing it from the room, tumbling over one another along the narrow hallway in their haste and leaving her house, she yelled after them following behind and slamming the door. Standing in the centre of the hall, she laughed with relief; a guttural purging of long trapped emotion. Her safe haven returned.

Her raucous laughter cackled through the dark silence the house had briefly sustained. She laughed and she laughed. Her sides began to strain with the hilarious relief of it all.

She was still laughing when she woke up.

# Chapter Seventeen

It was a peculiar sensation, to be woken by the noise of her own mirth. "What was all that about?" she demanded aloud of her empty bedroom.

Dawn broke, and Elin felt calm and rested. It wasn't until she attempted to move, she realised how rigid her overworked muscles were. "Damn!" Flopping back down, she prayed more rest might just do the trick.

She was still laying, staring at the ceiling, when Glenda came in with a cup of tea.

"How're you feeling, cariad?"

"Stiff," Elin had no choice but to admit. It was all too clear as she shuffled painfully around to reach the fresh cup that 'stiff' was an insufficient description.

Glenda couldn't help but further reprimand her for her foolishness yesterday.

"Sorry, Mum," she shrugged. Glenda smiled and leaned in for a cwtch which turned into helping her out of bed and steadying her down the stairs. Elin hobbled, clutching her mum's arm for support and letting out a yelp of cramp pain with each step

A few more 'tuts' and Glenda successfully assisted Elin to the couch where she'd spent so much time. Elin hunched miserably, clutching a blanket about her. Remembering her suffering was self-induced, she plastered a smile on her face.

"Alis will be off later."

"Oh. I'll miss her," Elin said, as a look passed between the two demonstrating just how much, both sure the terrible atmosphere would inflame in her absence. To lighten the mood, Elin decided to tell of last night's visions. Glenda sat with the forced smile of anyone required to listen to someone else's dreams.

As Elin recounted, her cheeks reddened, realising that apart from waking up laughing, it hadn't been uplifting at all. Just peculiar, and slightly unnerving. She neglected to mention the séance, initially due to poor recollection, but then a conscious denial. Mention of ghosts and spirits seemed unwise in her mother's current delicate state.

Her cheeks flushed and her mouth dried as telling of her nightmare became a lamentable tale. From the horror on her mum's face, she regretted it at once. The ill-prepared narrative ended in an embarrassed hush.

Glenda broke the silence, and what she said, Elin couldn't believe she was hearing. "I've done it, too. To our old house, I mean."

"You've had dreams about our old house in Bridgend?" Elin asked, not grasping the significance.

"Not dream. It's more than that. Much more," Glenda revealed. "I actually go there"

It made no sense. What was she inferring?

"What do you mean? You go on the train and visit?"

"Not on the train, no," Glenda said, trying hard not to show irritation at her daughter's denseness. "Or the car, or a bike," she added, in case Elin planned investigating other modes of transport.

"I travel in my dreams. I put myself in a quiet place in my mind and picture it. And then I'm there," she explained. "It's nice to be back in the old place." She paused to gauge if Elin understood before continuing. "But I do become resentful, I suppose—of the new people living there. And I sold them the house! They clearly have every right to be there, but I do resent them. It still feels like home. And so I punish them," she revealed guiltily.

"Punish them. How?"

"Well, you know… shake the curtains, hiss in their ears, throw stuff around, that type of thing…" she finished sheepishly. "I suppose they must get scared." She allowed a dry smile to decorate her face at the power she enjoyed.

"It's nice to go. And it's nice to feel I could scare the new owners enough to take it back if I wanted to…" Realising she might have gone too far, Glenda revised her gleeful tone. "But truly, it is good to touch base. I did love that house…" she drifted off, misty eyed.

Elin shook her head. This was unbelievable. Was she seriously suggesting she physically appeared in their old house? That she could interact with the people there?

The story was just like her own. She had done those things in her sleep. And more besides. But it wasn't real, was it? It couldn't be. It had to be a dream. It all stopped when she'd woken up. But her mum believed it was true.

Her mind struggled to make sense of it. From anyone else, at any other time, she would laugh. But from her strong, sensible mum? Still in shock, she asked simply, "How?"

"Because, like I said, I loved that house. I'm connected to it." She glanced in the direction of the hallway and gave an involuntary shudder. "I sometimes wish we still lived there. This is lovely and everything, but…" Stopping abruptly, she folded her hands neatly in her lap as she was prone to do.

And that made even less sense. Elin didn't feel connected to twenty-four Rhondda Street. She didn't even like it much. Unlike her mum's love of their perfect neat home in Bridgend, there was absolutely no question of her yearning to live back in Swansea.

"I don't think that's what's happening to me, Mum," Elin stated decisively. "I'm just having nightmares because I'm on the mend, and my mind is restless—anxious to start thinking about something. Anything. I didn't even like that house much."

Glenda looked unconvinced. A flicker of irritation, or maybe anxiety, flashed behind her emerald eyes. Sighing, she let it go. There seemed little point in arguing. Removing, and then replacing her hands in her lap, she smiled at her daughter.

"More tea?" she offered. And that was that. Subject closed.

Taking occasional sips of tea, the conversation declined to 'nice weather for the time of year' interspersed with simpering smiles and interrupted starts. Before the atmosphere became too tense to stomach, the doorway was filled with the effervescent presence of Alis announcing her goodbye.

"Don't you have a big hug for your favourite daughter and best sister?" she demanded, hands on hips.

After the exhausting departure, Erw Lon and its remaining occupants, breathed a sigh of deliverance and slumped on the comfy lounge furniture.

Elin had tentative plans for a short walk to clear her head and try to release the toxins built up in her muscles after yesterday. Instead, she realised when called for dinner that she had fallen back asleep. Probably just as well. She must be more tired than she'd appreciated. Going out again might have been insensitive to her mum's apprehension.

They managed an affable family meal of typical hearty country food. Elin helped, as best she could, with the after-dinner clear up and promptly fell asleep during one of the evening's earliest television programmes.

"Why don't you go up to bed if you're so tired?" Elin snapped awake to her mother's irritation. Doing as she bade, still guilty for the worry she'd caused, Elin hugged

Emyr and Glenda goodnight. Hurrying up the stairs before she could identify anything untoward in the hall, she was soon asleep again.

# Chapter Eighteen

"We definitely need a priest," Neil concurred vehemently with the expert of the group. "I am not going anywhere near that house again until we get one!"

Collin shrugged, looking skywards, giving the impression he considered his son might be overreacting, but he knew he wouldn't want to go back in either.

"Where will you all stay until this is sorted out?" he asked, trying to be practical.

"A park bench would be better than in there!" Neil huffed. "Or you could bring my car. I'll sleep in it until I learn to drive!"

The rest of them ignored Neil's pitiful protests but agreed they needed a practical solution. Aeron came up with the best idea when he suggested a room at The Railway. "Me and Bronnie don't live too far. We could commute for a couple of days or so." Bronwyn agreed.

Neil almost mentioned Aeron's alarmingly similar tale of weirdness at the pub. He stopped himself, keeping quiet until who would take the room was established. It was decided Josh should share it with Matthew (who insisted he wasn't scared to stay at number twenty-four, and was only doing it to keep Josh company.)

When they arrived at The Railway Tavern to book the pair of them into its spare room, and have a nerve settling stiff drink, they were greeted by an uncharacteristically meek Jon, who looked delighted at the prospect of extra company.

Their real motive for refusing to stay at number twenty-four should be omitted it had been decided; not wanting to alienate Jon if he was a sceptic. But he didn't question their reasons, and offered them the room straight away.

"Welcome aboard, shipmates," he enthused in an idiotic pirate voice. They agreed a very reasonable rate whilst Neil arranged to share a Travel Lodge with his mum, dad and Auntie Sylvie.

Sitting in the snug enjoying a few medicinal tipples, Sylvie began making calls to local chapels and churches to ask for help with the aid of smartphone searches from Neil. She had no luck finding anyone to answer their phones, so left messages instead.

"I'll make one more call, and then I'll admit defeat for today." Dialling the number, her look of frustration transformed to surprise, and she stumbled over a greeting. "Ah, Hello. Is that... Father Jenkins?"

A deep, stern voice answered. "Yes, that's right." She estimated him to be about thirty. His dour tone unsettling, she struggled to describe eloquently their situation. The priest tutted and she could almost hear him shaking his head. "You really shouldn't dabble in things you don't understand," he rebuked. "If you play around with Ouija boards and the like, what do you expect?"

After some pleading, and Sylvie's reassurance that the trouble had started well before the introduction of the Ouija board, Father Jenkins grudgingly consented to at least consider helping.

"I will have to speak to my Bishop before I can agree to assist, and I am extremely busy. But I shall endeavour to give you an answer tomorrow." The frown gave way to a grin as Sylvie ended the call. "He's in!"

Father Jenkins's gloomy timbre had been clearly heard from the phone's earpiece, so Sylvie's optimism gave scant assurance.


It made more sense for Aeron to take the room at The Railway, given his bar work there. But Matthew and Josh lived much too far away to travel. He'd regretted the suggestion as soon as it came out of his mouth. There was no way he'd consider staying there himself after recent incidents. So it was with relief he had nobly relinquished the convenience of living above his job in favour of Matty and Josh.

He justified his guilt at not warning them with convenient false cynicism. Away from the evidence, it was almost easy to doubt the supernatural explanations. Although Bronwyn's scepticism had waned since the séance, he couldn't help but be embarrassed at his own wussiness. At least with accommodation arrangements settled, he wouldn't have to admit to being scared of the pub as well as of the house.

He and Bronwyn were the first to leave as they were governed by train times. They said their goodbyes to the group and walked the steep descent to Swansea Central Station. They then set off on their respective tracks home to hole up until it was safe to return. The Hedges family and Auntie Sylvie left shortly afterwards, as though they had waited for the excuse to leave.

Matthew and Josh, once alone in the pub, had no plans to leave the comfort of the bar. Living in a pub had obvious advantages they were well prepared to make the most of. They proceeded to try every beer available until last orders were called.

A look of annoyance was shared through hazy inebriation as the cretinous Jon joined them at their table. They tolerated him, now seriously drunk. And because he brought the promise of yet more drinking with him.

"It's a shame your house is… " Jon frowned, puzzled, "What is wrong with your house?" he asked for the first time. Before giving it any thought, Josh blurted his answer.

"Poltergeist," he stated, matter-of-factly.

"No!" protested Matthew. "It's not really. The others think there's something strange going on, but well… I don't believe in that nonsense."

"You believed it well enough when you were running out of the house!"

"I was just caught up in the moment, that's all. Wait. You don't believe we've got a poltergeist, do you?"

Josh gave a scathing look which Matthew chose to ignore. Glancing back at their host, they noticed he'd gone a very quiet shade of pale. Before they thought to ask him what was wrong, he pushed himself up from the table and made an excuse about washing glasses. Matthew and Josh accepted without care and returned to their drinks.

"We'd better go up to bed soon," Matthew suggested sensibly. "We've got lectures in a few days. Gotta take it seriously." He pointed his beer bottle indiscriminately to something, failing to emphasise his point at all. Josh nodded along anyway.

"Yeah. You're right," he slurred. "One more?"

"One more," Matthew agreed, aiming his bottle in the air again. "Bar keep? Two of your finest beers from around the world, if you please."

He wasn't heard, so struggling to perch higher on his seat, he scanned the room for Jon to serve them again. An old man sat nursing an inch of warm beer two tables down, whilst a girl slouched on the end barstool hunched over the bar.

"What's that guy's name?" he whispered loudly, leaning conspiringly towards Josh. Josh shrugged and burped vociferously.

"Can you run that by me again? I don't think that was it!" The two of them found it immensely humorous and laughed raucously, spraying their mouthfuls of beer in an alcohol and saliva mist across the table.

Aeron and Matthew's talk of ghostly happenings shook Jon. Nothing had happened over Christmas and he was starting to get his confidence back and forget about it. Standing out of sight in the kitchen, he tried to regain his composure. Trembling fingers poured a generous shot of whiskey which he threw down his throat, pouring another before it hit the sides.

The fiery liquid warmed in his stomach sending a shudder up his spine which rested as a broad grin on his sallow face. Fear abating, he washed some glasses. Pressing a bar towel into the annals of a long pint glass, he planned his clearing of the pub. It was something he hadn't done for ages, leaving the duty to Gareth whose size seemed well-suited to the job.

He had given more and more duties to Efa and her horrendous thug of a brother. He would be in danger of losing his role as manager if the brewery knew just how much. The pair had lost interest after New Year's Eve and its associated double and triple pay time shifts. They still worked whenever they wanted, but Jon had been forced to retake the reigns.

He asked the patrons to leave in the order he'd like them to go. Obviously, the old man was first. Nodding, he glugged down a centimetre of very warm beer, scooped his coat and rose from his chair in one seamless movement, hailing a hearty goodbye to the others as if they were good friends.

Matthew and Josh convinced their host for 'one more.' Leaving the girl to her drink, Jon hoped the uni lads would drink up quickly so he'd be alone with her. From behind at least, she looked extremely attractive. How had he missed her all evening? Not like him at all.

He pushed himself past a moment of nerves to walk towards her. As he did, he realised she was perhaps familiar. Yes. The closer he got the more convinced he was that he knew her.

The unmistakable uproar of drunken spewing suddenly assaulted his ears, followed by the offensive effluvium which fresh beery vomit emits. Jon had no choice but to react.

"Lads! Go to bed, for fu…" he didn't finish his profanity. His beating from Gareth had made him more of a coward than ever. He tried to disguise it by demonstrating his generous spirit. "Go on. I'll clear it up."

As the two helped one another, Jon went to the cleaning cupboard and fetched the necessary tools for the job. He noted with disdain that the girl from the bar had made her departure in the commotion so he swabbed the disgusting mess with extra loathing. "I should have made you two clear this up, you ignorant plebs," he muttered under his breath, carefully inaudibly, even though there was no chance they could have heard.

Time and again, he smeared the disinfectant soaked cloth hatefully across the brimming with vomit table top and wrung it out until he was as convinced as he could be that it was clean. Walking away with the disgusting slop filled bucket, he noticed some sick trickling its way down the table leg onto the floor. Retching at the sight, he swallowed hard.

After a brief examination of his bucket's contents, he deliberated how revolting it might be to use the water one more time. "Shit," he said, realising the rancid yellow soup was too disgusting. Turning, he stomped off to the sink, bucket slopping from side to side threatening to spill the vile fluid. With every slosh, bile odour assailed his nostrils.

Finishing clearing, he made a final trip back with a clean cloth and bucket to wipe the bar. Glancing up from wringing out the new cloth, he almost fell over at the sight of the same girl sitting back on the same barstool, seemingly nursing the same drink, stooping, head down over the bar again.

Standing rigid with surprise, scrutinising the figure, he was unable to clearly see her face, her hair obscured her features. But not enough to disguise her breath-taking beauty. Or, that he was all the more certain he knew her. Didn't she used to come here a while ago, and didn't they..?  As his loins stirred at the memory, the girl swept golden curls away from huge, piercing blue eyes and looked up.

At once, upon seeing Jon, her face distorted. Eyes blazing with intense fury, a deep scowl furrowed her formerly flawless forehead. Leaping to her feet, what was left of her drink flew across the bar. The heavy bar stool thudded to the floor as an ear-splitting shriek erupted from her snarling lips, becoming an almost primal scream.

"Youuuuuw!" The cry rang from every corner of the room. Jon quaked open mouthed, desperate to move but petrified to the spot.

The girl lunged for him across the bar. When the distance proved too far to reach him, grabbing spirit bottles on the shelves and in the optic dispensers sufficed. One by one, she sent them toppling to an explosive demise on the hard pub floor.

He didn't see her leave. She didn't walk towards the door, didn't open it and exit to the street. She just vanished. Jon, alone with his thumping heart, his trembling legs struggled to support him as he stood on the shards of glass and a puddle of liquid, not all of which was from the broken bottles.

# Chapter Nineteen

"What will we do if we can't get a priest to take us seriously? Is there someone else? I mean, does it have to be a priest?" Carole was asking her friend.

"Maybe not. I'd certainly look at getting one of my friends to help, or at least recommend someone," Sylvie responded. "We can't just leave such a malevolent spirit without doing everything we can to help; for the spirit's sake as much as for Neil and his friends."

They were freshening up in their room at the Travelodge before meeting Collin and Neil at the Little Chef attached to the motel.

"Do you think Neil will be happy to go back?" Sylvie asked, rubbing a cream onto her haggard complexion in the vain hope it would offer the miracles the blurb on the jar promised. "He looked pretty scared." Her voice strained, compromised by the open mouthed gurning necessary to give the cream its best chance.

"As long as you can assure him it's safe again, Sylvie, he'll be fine. But over dinner, we should talk about anything but ghosts. It's going to be hard, considering we're staying in a hotel explicitly because of one, but hey, we can try!"

Sylvie agreed. "It will be hard, but we need to try to calm him down. There really is nothing to be afraid of anyway," she smiled, but her credibility had been somewhat dented when she'd been the first to run terrified from the house.

When they arrived downstairs at the Little Chef café, Neil and Collin were already there, and had been for a while judging by their peeved faces and number of tea and coffee cups and beer glasses littering the table.

"What kept you?" Collin demanded.

"Have you been waiting long?" Carol asked, genuinely surprised. "We just had to freshen up, that's all." Collin chuckled, seeing the lighter side and relieved he would at last be able to fill his grumbling stomach.

They ate heartily, being sure to leave room for dessert. Just as Collin settled the bill, Sylvie's phone rang. Everyone held their breath.

"Yes. Yes. Mm Hm. Okay." 'It's Father Jenkins' she mouthed, affirming things through the mouthpiece. She gave the address and handed the phone over to Neil to give directions to his house.

"I have agreed to help because you've had problems since before you chose to dabble with the occult. But I don't want to hear of any more playing with spirits. It always leads to trouble. Do you understand?"

Neil didn't have courage for anything but complete compliance. "Yes, of course. We're really grateful."

And so, it was on. The exorcism of number Twenty-four, Rhondda Street, Swansea, was to take place tomorrow at seven.

Bronwyn and Aeron were both dubious yet relieved when they received their phone calls that their student lives could resume relative normality again so soon.

Josh and Matthew weren't answering their phones, which wasn't too much of a surprise. They were most likely taking advantage of their residence in a public house. Neil left voice messages for them, but was sure the exorcism could take place with or without them.

They all tried their best to gain a worry free night's sleep and put out of their minds what they might be expected to do tomorrow. Or, perhaps more poignantly: how the spirit might react to them.

No-one ended up sleeping well at all. But it was a fact they kept to themselves for morale, instinctively acting as one, like a colony of insects, each putting their own fears aside for the group in their conquest of the perceived enemy.

It all felt a bit melodramatic now they were away from the malevolent poltergeist activities. In the cold of night, each of them confessed to themselves they felt foolish, even after the undeniable presence of something supernatural. So it was with false nonchalance they met Father Jenkins outside number twenty-four.

Matthew and Josh picked up Neil's message with relief. Staying in the pub hadn't been the relaxing home from home they'd hoped. From scant memories of their drunken night, things were not what they should be at The Railway Tavern.

Jon had been very jittery serving the cooked breakfast Matthew insisted should come with the room price.

"Yes, yes, of course," Jon had agreed with a nervous laugh and a tilt of the head.

"That went better than I thought it would," Matthew winked. "And a couple of strong coffees too," he called out, before adding as an afterthought, "please."

The sausages arrived singed and charred, but succeeded in being the best part of the breakfast as burnt was as good as it got. Fried eggs managed to be both crunchy yet runny. And the bacon was so crisp it could be constructed into a tee-pee of on-end rashers which thankfully entertained Josh sufficiently to pardon the catastrophe.

Matthew picked round the least grotesque food and glugged down the coffee. Fortunately the portions were generous, so there were enough bits of edible bacon, sausage, and baked beans to stave off the worst of their hangovers.

When they asked for the bill, Jon stammered his assent.

"You can't be leaving 'Chez Railway' so soon?" he tittered timidly, wiping a line of sweat from his brow. Matthew and Josh exchanged glances. They couldn't be sure that whatever Neil and his crazy aunt had cooked up would actually work. They might need to come back again tonight, and for perhaps many more nights. It wasn't worth upsetting Jon unduly.

They left with vague arrangements that they might return later. And, without paying their bill. A barrier Jon seemed unwilling to pose.

In spite of each of them having decided how silly it all was in their final moments of consciousness before sleep had consumed their thoughts for the night, it was outside in the cold, not sheltered within number twenty-four they awaited Father Jenkins arrival. Despite his lateness, and the bitter cold of Swansea in mid-January. Waiting inside crossed each of their minds as the cold bit into their extremities, but none of them were brave enough to suggest it.

Josh's fingernails were bitten to his elbow, whilst Bronwyn squeezed Aeron so tight, he thought she might consume him. The colony of heads jolted in unison to the direction of footsteps as they echoed down the lamp-lit street.

Due to a peculiarity of the light, his diminutive size, and his dark clothing, Father Jenkins avoided visual detection until almost upon them. A collective shudder moved the group back a step as his sudden appearance shocked them.

The priest examined the house, peering for a door number to confirm the correct address, apparently oblivious to the group gathered outside, adding to the disquieting creepiness.

"Father Jenkins?" Collin interjected the uneasiness.

"Mm Hm," came the brief confirmation. "Mr Hedges, I presume?" Collin nodded, stepped forward and held out his hand. The priest's own reluctant hand shook it weakly and immediately returned to the denseness of his habit. His other hand then appeared from within to sweep his short, blonde fringe from his forehead needlessly, before his right hand reappeared clutching a large wooden cross which he held valiantly before him.

"Come along then. No time to delay. We need to remove this spirit before it's too late and it possesses one of you."

He walked with purpose and defiance up the uneven steps to the door. Neil had to lean past him to unlock it before returning to his place behind the squat, square little priest as quickly as he could. The brief moment where part of him was the closest of the group to the house left him in a cold sweat. His heart throbbed sickeningly in his ears.

Father Jenkins shoved the door open and waited. It creaked, and slowly fell back on its hinges until the darkness inside goaded them to enter its inky blackness. They all blinked when the hall light pierced the dark. The scene appeared at once less menacing, but the priest's warning tolled in their ears.

With crucifix held aloft, Father Jenkins crossed the threshold. One by one, the others tiptoed behind.

"Where does most activity take place?" the priest demanded. Nodding to the lounge, they made their way behind him. Crowding into the tiny room, detritus littering the floor from the poltergeist's fury, the short figure of the priest intensified the disquiet.

Father Jenkins prepared to ask about the nature of what went on here when the unit of remaining drinking glasses began rattling.

"Get Out!" Not a full voice, more a distant shout, but the most sensitive members of the group heard it.

"Holy shit," Bronwyn whimpered, clutching Aeron's arm tight. She mouthed an apology for her outburst to Father Jenkins who silently pardoned her.

"MY house!" Unmistakeable this time. The shrill words reverberated, shaking the walls. Everyone shrank back further behind Father Jenkins.

"Who are you?" the priest demanded, thrusting the crucifix in the direction of the rattling glasses. Suddenly, the kitchen door slammed and the glasses stilled.

"Someone definitely wants us out," the priest declared.

"Where has she gone? The kitchen?" asked Neil.

"Yes," answered Sylvie. "I saw her. Did anyone else see her?"

"What did she look like," Carole asked, surprised when Bronwyn answered, showing that at least someone other than psychic Sylvie had seen her.

"Blonde, strikingly beautiful. Wearing a floaty nightdress." Sylvie nodded in agreement.

"Stunning. But the angry look on her face spoiled it."

"Aren't you scared?" Carole probed. Bronwyn and Sylvie answered at once, with opposing opinions.

"It must be a girl who used to live here," Sylvie clarified with a shrug. "It's an old house. And she wants us out because she doesn't know she's dead. She obviously has a connection here for some reason, so she's trapped. It doesn't make her scary though."

Wide eyes fell on Sylvie. From the abrupt silence, it was clear Bronwyn's panic was the consensus.

"This shouldn't be taken blithely," warned Father Jenkins. "In my experience, there is always a good reason why a spirit fails to pass into the light when they die. It's because they are afraid where they'll end up," he said, signposting up or down with his gaze.

"If they're afraid of God, it begs the question... why? She has shown her aggression. This is not likely to be a virtuous person. Don't be fooled by the pretty packaging... it's what's in her soul that counts. God will pardon her sins if she repents. But she shows no sign of that, does she?"

Sylvie postured herself to argue, but Collin raised a hand to stop her. "You had your chance to help, Sylvie. And the spirit became much angrier and more aggressive as a result. And now she's worse. We have no choice. We must listen to Father Jenkins."

Sylvie had no argument. It did get worse after the séance. And she was the one who'd insisted they needed a priest. Her cheeks flushed. "You're right," she admitted. "Sorry, Father. Please, carry on."

Father Jenkins sighed and resumed his stance like a teacher who had waited for a rowdy class to settle.

"Okay. Step back. We don't know how this spirit will react." They didn't need telling twice. As Father Jenkins stepped towards the slammed kitchen door, the rest huddled in the furthest corner of the room.

"Who are you?" the priest demanded again. "The spirit residing here beyond life... Listen. You are not welcome here. You need to move to the light."

From deep within the dark robes of Father Jenkins's Habit, a container of Holy water appeared. Reciting orders to the poltergeist, he sloshed the water liberally around the room as he spoke.

"Repent and go into the light. I command all operatives of Satan to go into light for eternal judgement. Go into the light now, in the Name of The Father, The Son, and the Holy Ghost."

# Chapter Twenty

Elin had never been more tired. Perhaps at the height of her glandular fever, but she'd been too ill to notice. Now, wanting to get on with her life, she found it harrowing. Getting ready for bed, she threw her clothes down with heavy hands and slammed drawers, signifying to the powers that be she had had enough.

Her noisy sister wasn't even around to cheer her up, and Emyr was always busy-busy doing his own thing, while Glenda worried too much, berating her for over-doing it (and that was really irritating because she seemed to be right).

Clean, fresh, and minty, she put on a long cotton nightie, comforted it used to be her mum's. It reminded her of a Christening gown, all comfy and crisp, and being Glenda's, cosy, like her mother's bosom.

Washing wakened her, so she flipped open her book, determined to wrest away the fatigue from her long walk. The wakefulness proved short-lived. Having read the same page three times with less and less comprehension, she finally gave in when she made herself jump by dropping the book onto her lap.

Turning on her side, she switched off her bedside light and within moments was gently snoring. Her eyes fluttered in the rapid fashion which denotes dreaming, and there she was. Back in the confines of number twenty-four, Rhondda Street, Swansea.

It was peaceful and dark. Safe. Bathed in relief, tears of gratitude welled in her eyes for this room, for this house. Asylum from her fears. Allowing the stillness to wash over her, she stood in the darkness breathing it in.

Then noise. Murmurings of hushed voices. "Shit!" A yellow glow leaked under the door and she knew she was no longer alone. 'Damn. I don't want the dream of messy students again. I want a peaceful dream. Why can't I dream of butterflies and ponies?' But there was no time for that. In her deep sleep, this dream was her reality.

The lounge door flew open allowing light to infiltrate the darkness, shattering her peace. The crowd from before huddled behind the stout figure of a priest holding aloft a crucifix. A priest! Why?

She yelled at them to get out. Why were they here? Barging into her personal space, her sanctuary. She needed time alone. Time not to be bothered by people invading her lounge. Except, it wasn't her lounge. She knew that. It used to be, but now she was the intruder. But the feeling of self-righteous tenure wouldn't shake. Nor the need. The protection this house offered was vital, and she couldn't let it go.

"This is MY house," she screamed, rage boiling up like an egg in the microwave. A fury she'd never known in her waking life. These people stole her peace. It might not be her house, but it was her bloody dream and she should be allowed to dream it undisturbed.

Desperate to scare them away, she grabbed the drinks cupboard and considered knocking it over. The glasses rattled at her hand, snapping her back to herself. Her innate calm encircled and impeded her. Instead, she flounced into the kitchen, making sure to slam the door good and hard.

Gagging at the lingering cooking smells, she reached a hand out to steady herself, then shot away from the touch of stickiness, her disgust displaying a grimace on her pretty face. The room was horrible. But at least she was alone again.

The group of exorcists listened for a response. None came. "Who are you?" the priest demanded again.

"I'm getting something," interjected Sylvie. "Hold on." An expression which might have been mistaken for an imminent sneeze formed on her face. "It's coming," she assured, before announcing clearly, "Elin. That's her name."

Despite his misgivings about dabbling with spirit, Father Jenkins seemed pleased with the new information, and used it to order her directly. "The spirit whose name is Elin. Listen to me. You are not welcome here. This is not where you are supposed to be. You must leave this place. I compel you in the name of Jesus Christ, our Lord. I compel you to leave this place!"

The kitchen door flew open. Silhouetted in the doorframe, Elin Treharne stood defiantly. Blonde hair flowed down to her white christening gown nightie; not solid, more otherworldly. The very epitome of a spectre.

Her beauty did little to disguise her fury. The exorcists trembled behind Father Jenkins who held his crucifix haughtier and higher.

"Elin," he ordered, a fresh determination to his voice. "You must leave this house. You are not of this plain. Go to the light, Elin. You must go to the light." Elin glowered at him, rage burning in her eyes sending a shiver of terror through him. He carried on resolutely. "Elin, I command you: go into the light. I compel you in the name of Jesus Christ, our Lord, go into the light. Go into the light now!"

The kitchen door closed, then flew open again. The drinks cabinet rattled, this time sending several glasses to their doom. A sound grew from deep within the spirit of Elin and echoed round the room, shuddering in the ears of the exorcists. "Nooooo!"

The light's flickered. The chairs around the kitchen table rocked in their places.

"Go into the light NOW, Elin! Elin, I compel you into the light in the name of Jesus Christ. Christ compels you. Christ compels you! Christ compels you, Elin, to leave this house and go into the light NOW!"

An icy breeze shot through the huddled crowd. The hallway lights flicked on and off, the front door rattled in its place then flew open. It banged against the junk mail chair, swung back on its hinges and slammed shut.

And then… And then nothing.
Number twenty-four Rhondda Street was silent.

# Part Two

# Chapter Twenty-one

Glenda was pleased, sitting working through her daily Sudoku puzzle, that she hadn't heard a peep from her eldest daughter today. Elin was getting the rest she needed, just as she had advised.

She sipped her coffee and wrote figures in the squares of the app on her new tablet computer (a Christmas gift, supposedly from Father Christmas, but actually from Emyr.)

He walked in with an approving look on his face that his gift was being used again.

"You like your tablet, then?" he asked quizzically.

"Yes, Emyr. For the hundredth time. I do like my tablet. Thank you. I mean, thank Father Christmas!" She flashed him a smile and looked immediately back to the screen, partly engrossed in her puzzle, but primarily because refocussing her eyes with her reading glasses was uncomfortable.

"Any sign of Elin this morning?" Emyr asked, filling the kettle with his back to his wife. When he didn't see her shaking her head, he asked again.

"No!" Glenda retorted, clenching her fist around her pen —she had nearly finished her Sudoku. "Why don't you go up and see her if you're so concerned."

"I'm not concerned." Bumbling around the kitchen he added, "Sorry. I was only asking."

He made his tea, plonked down opposite his wife and plumped up his newspaper to read. He was soon mesmerised and unaware that Glenda had used the remaining water in the kettle to make a cup of tea for the sleepyhead upstairs. She supposed it wouldn't be good for her to lie in too long. It was important her routine get back to normal.

Glancing with well-accustomed anxiety around the hallway, she trod up the stairs with her eye on the hot tea, careful not to spill any. She paused at her daughter's bedroom and knocked. As expected, there came no reply. Slowly opening the door, she could see why. Elin was dead to the world, deeply asleep.

Despite thoughts of routine and its benefits, Glenda was reluctant to wake her. She knew how exhausted she had become on her ill-adventure across the stream. She placed the hot tea on the bedside table and announced its arrival. Elin didn't stir, so she left her in peace.

As she came out, an unsettling feeling troubled her. Nothing unusual in this creepy house. Hurrying back downstairs, she decided to have another coffee and calm her nerves.

It was late in the afternoon when she decided enough was enough. Tired or not, Elin would have to get up now. Armed with a new cup of tea, she ventured out to the hallway, the earlier anxiety still fresh. She hurried up the stairs without her usual care, slopping hot tea onto her wrist. She swapped hands to wipe away the scolding liquid.

Cursing under her breath she reached the bedroom door again. She knew Elin was likely to still be asleep. Darkness greeted her, the lamp off despite the fading light, and no sound of movement reached her ear.

"I've brought you another cuppa, young lady! I presume you didn't drink the first one." Her suspicions confirmed by the mug of milky tea exactly where she'd left it.

"Come on now, cariad. You must wake up. It's nearly tea-time. Wakey-wakey, rise and shine!" This would take more effort than she'd expected.

The initial worry gnawed at Glenda's heart as she touched her daughter for the first time. No response, not even a murmur, or a mumbled 'I'm tired'. She gently shook her, then harder, and then so hard she was certain it would wake her.

When it didn't, the shock made her drop the scolding tea. She screamed in anguish as the hot fluid penetrated her thin dress, but she didn't care about the burning. She only cared that her beloved, beautiful daughter wasn't waking. Something was wrong. Something was terribly wrong.

"What is it?" Emyr asked breathlessly, having rushed two stairs at a time. "Oh you've burned yourself," he said, noticing the large steaming mess on his wife's clothes.

"No… It's not that. Elin… She won't wake up!"

Emyr side-stepped his trembling wife and gazed at his daughter. He was heartened to detect her chest rising and falling, an observation he shared with Glenda who failed to be reassured. "Why? Why can't I wake her?"

Emyr tapped his daughter, then shook her, and even slapped her gently on her cheeks. A flood of fear rushed through him and he looked back at his wife. "You're right. What should we do?"

"Call and ambulance. Oh my God, Emyr. That fall in the stream might have killed her. Call an ambulance. Now!"

Emyr scurried from the room. The last thing he saw as he turned the corner to the stairs was his wife holding Elin in her arms, rocking her back and fore. "Hurry!" she sobbed as he disappeared.

The nearest hospital was in Swansea. An estimated thirty minutes away according to ambulance control. The phone operator stayed on the line and talked to Emyr, who shouted questions to Glenda throughout.

They were reassured Elin was still breathing, but gave instruction on how to keep her airways unobscured, and keep her warm. In this January cold, Hypothermia was a real danger. Elin felt cold to the touch, Emyr confirmed. He supposed she hadn't moved since falling asleep early last night. Her blood hadn't pumped hard enough around her delicate body with the lack of movement.

Glenda rubbed her extremities and made sure the radiator was turned up. She tucked an extra blanket round her sleeping daughter and whispered, "There, now, cariad. It'll be alright. The ambulance is coming, Elin, bach."

After what seemed like several hours, but actually quicker than the estimated ETA, the ambulance crew pulled into the driveway of Erw Lon. The phone operator wished them well before leaving them in the capable hands of the paramedics.

Emyr hurried to open the front door. Flashing blue lights looked purple in the hazy twilight. The iridescent 'Ambiwlans' sign shone almost neon in the strange glow.

"Mr Treharne?" enquired a burly, bald headed driver. From behind his huge bulk, a small woman peeped out and asked "Where's the patient?"

Emyr guided them upstairs where Glenda was sitting holding her daughter's slender hand. She got up silently from her chair to allow the paramedics room to make her baby okay again.

They placed one of her fingers into a small device, attached to a handheld piece of electronics by a thin grey wire. "This just checks her pulse and oxygen saturation."

"Has she hit her head at all?" the man asked.

Glenda told them about her slip in the stream.

"She seemed fine. I don't think she lost consciousness then." Emyr shrugged, his memory blocked by his current distress.

"It may be a slow haemorrhage. She may have had a stroke," the burly paramedic warned, the wincing grimace at the thought remained on his face as he continued with his procedures.

Glenda and Emyr gasped.

"We won't know until we get her to hospital," the woman warned. After a brief check of the monitoring machine, she reported with a look of surprise, that both were normal. Her blood pressure was taken. Her eyelids were forced open, and a torch shone into her eyes.

"Just checking her neuro-responses," the hefty man said. They too were apparently normal. "Is your daughter on any medication?" he asked.

"Only some painkillers for glandular fever. She was on various anti-biotics, too. But she finished those before Christmas."

"Do you still have the packets? I'd like to see them," asked the woman.

Emyr bustled off to find them.

"Are there any other… er, substances she may have taken?"

It took a moment for the question's meaning to seep into Glenda's consciousness. "No! Of course not. She's barely left the house in weeks. And besides, she's not that sort of girl."

"I'm sure you're right. But we have to investigate all possibilities. It's not making much sense at the moment."

The woman wrote something in a notebook whilst the large man bustled with thermometers and such.

"Could anyone else have brought drugs into the house? Are there any siblings? Friends who might have visited?"

"She hasn't taken drugs. I'm telling you," objected Glenda. The paramedic nodded in sympathetic but sceptical understanding.

"I know, I know. But if you could think of anything?"

"I'll have to phone her sister. She's a student at Bristol University. She only went back yesterday," Glenda said brightly, momentarily caught up in the conversation. Reality hit hard as her focus returned to the room. Eyes brimming with tears, she croaked instruction for Emyr to call Alis.

He tottered back downstairs in a daze, having taken Elin's medicine bottles to show the ambulance crew. It was one occasion when he wished they owned walk-about phones like everybody else, or that his bloody mobile had signal in the house.

He dialled with a pseudo-calm. It was his job to take charge in a crisis. Alis's bright tone, oblivious to her sister's plight, broke Emyr's heart when he heard it.

"Hi Dad. Missing me already?" After an unnerving silence where Emyr was unable to speak, Alis's tone changed. "What is it, Dad? What's wrong?"

"It's your sister. The ambulance is here…"

"Ambulance?"

"Yes," he rasped. "We can't wake her up, you see." A pause of eternity passed as Emyr's mind fought to speak the very purpose of his call. Clenching his fist and his jaw, he forced out the words. "Have you brought any drugs here, Alis, bach?"

A brief but poignant silence followed from the other end. "Just a bit of weed. Sorry, Dad. Elin has never had any though, and I'm sure I didn't leave any there. Sorry, Dad," she said again. "You don't think that's what's caused it, do you?"

His jaw still stiff, he answered reigning in the urge to spit blame at his youngest. He knew it wasn't fair. "I don't know." Alis's distress was palpable through the phones earpiece. He didn't want both his girl's suffering. "Try not to worry, cariad. I'll keep you posted," he said, replacing the handset with numb fingers.

When he re-entered Elin's room, the paramedics were just completing an examination of her skin. After he reported Alis's admission, they considered marijuana an unlikely culprit for Elin's unconsciousness.

Happy with her vital signs, the crew stretchered her to the ambulance and set up monitors for the journey. Glenda joined the lady paramedic and Elin in the back. Emyr followed in their car.

When they arrived at Morriston Hospital, Swansea Accident and Emergency Department, Emyr couldn't follow into the ambulance-only parking area, and the visitor parking was unfeasibly busy. He eventually parked outside the denoted bays and slightly on the curb. He anticipated a ticket, or maybe even a wheel-clamp, but his priority was to get to his daughter.

He arrived in the department to a long queue at the desk. He noticed his breathing becoming faster and forced himself to calm down. He'd be no use if he fainted.

The queue moved forward slowly. A boy whose finger dripped with blood (Emyr heard when it was his turn that he'd caught it in a car door) waited behind a middle-aged woman in a onesie, who complained of a sore throat and cough.

At last he reached the desk. "My daughter was just brought in by ambulance—Elin Treharne?" Emyr blurted at last.

"Oh, yes. The doctors are with her now. If you could wait over there, please." She point towards a few tatty looking chairs next to a silent television which must have been donated around 1987.

"I need to go to my daughter," he argued. Then faced with the immobile features of the receptionist, numb to the agony of a distraught parent after decades in a job where empathy is a luxury she'd been forced to forego, he changed tack. "My wife. She came in with Elin. She'll need me."

"Your daughter's in the best hands. It's not possible to be with her yet, but a doctor will let you know soon, okay?" she managed a smile.

"But my wife…?"

"I'll try and find out where she is. If you could take a seat for now?" Pointing back to the tatty seating area, she added, "sorry," before turning to the next patient in the queue.

The mild distraction of a mindless early evening chat-show, all the more pointless with the lack of sound, took Emyr's attention. He couldn't stand to think what could be wrong with his beautiful daughter. He hoped he would have answers soon.

The talk-show gave way to some soap-opera or other when a doctor, who appeared to be about twelve years old, stood beside him. "Mr Treharne?" he asked. Emyr was surprised his voice had broken.

"Yes. How is Elin?"

There was a pause while the young man considered what to say.

"I've explained to your wife. We're not really sure of a cause for your daughter's unconsciousness at the moment. We think a head injury—from the fall she had a couple of days ago—is most likely. It could be a relapse of the glandular fever, but from her notes, I can see that we were happy it was clearing up nicely.

Tests have been done for glucose levels. They are quite low, as is her blood pressure, but it doesn't necessarily indicate diabetes, although we can't rule it out.

"She'll be on fluids, and we'll help her with her breathing, just as a precaution. She seems able to support her own at the moment, but she's showing no neurological signs and is unresponsive to all stimulate: verbal, and painful. Her eyes aren't responding normally to our tests either. We'll take bloods and test for the

185

presence of drugs or underlying infection. Meningitis is a possibility. Although she's showing no signs of a rash."

Emyr nodded, pretending he'd taken it all in, but his brain stopped receiving at the mention of 'unresponsive'. The doctor was still talking. Emyr looked searchingly when Elin being moved was mentioned.

"…to ICU." Then, in response to Emyr's quizzical expression, "Intensive Care."

It sounded so serious.

"Where is that, exactly?" he asked, frowning, already sure the instructions wouldn't reach his brain. With the junior doctor gesticulating directions, he staggered away, along corridors, peering at signs along the way. Confronted by glass doors, the other side of which seemed a world away.

Nurses busied silently, machines flashed lights and pulsed with urgent information, all unheard through the glass. Somewhere in there, his little Elin was desperately ill.

Pressing the buzzer, he waited to be allowed access. When he explained who he was, a sympathetic looking young nurse took his arm and guided him to a side room where Glenda stood staring at their daughter.

Elin already looked unrecognisable. An oxygen mask covered most of her face. Two different bags, one large and one small, hung from a drip stand beside the bed; pipes from which attached to her elegant wrist.

A regular beep coincided with a graph plotting her heart rate. Other numbers changed apparently randomly. Emyr worked out one showed her oxygen saturation level, but didn't know about the others.

A nurse in a different colour scrubs to the blue ones the others wore, came into the room.

"Hello. I'm here to take some bloods," she announced, inappropriately cheerful. Opening her mouth as though to chat, she thought better of it. Having little trouble finding a vein on Elin's slender forearm, she took bottle after bottle of blood, placing them in a receptacle designed for the job. Standing to leave, she flashed a breezy smile and disappeared in a mauve haze.

Another nurse arrived, this time in green, and proceeded to fill in what she called an admission form, requiring enough information to author Elin's biography. She updated the anxious pair that a scan of Elin's head was being arranged and that she'd been started on a course of strong antibiotics just in case.

"Don't worry. Elin's doing fine. We'll get to the bottom of this, I'm sure."

Emyr smiled wanly, but Glenda didn't react. She sat, motionless, clutching her little girl's hand willing her life into her daughter. Her eyes blinked slowly, squeezing a cascade of tears down her cheeks. She made no move to dry them, nor the drip of snot steadily forming at the end of her nose.

# Chapter Twenty-two

Shaking all over, her mind struggled to function. On pure instinct, she knew she must hide. The rasping of her breathing seemed sure to give her away. As the sound grated in her ears, her thumping chest seemed set in joining it alerting her attacker.

She had to compose herself. Forcing deep breaths in and out, she counted to ten over and over until calmness enveloped her. Whatever the danger was, she believed she had outrun it for now.

Attempts at hiding thus far appeared limited to squinting her eyes tightly shut. As she relaxed her eyelids, she realised they were closed for protection from a bright light. Go into the light, the priest had ordered. And now here she was.

She squinted her lids open a crack. It was bright, but not searing as she might expect. And yellow, which surprised her. Heaven in movies was always white. Why was her dream faint yellow? Flame. Flames are yellow. She was heading to Hell. A dream of peace and quiet, away from the awkward atmosphere of Erw Lon had mutated into a nightmare of wretchedness. Great.

Why? She was a good person. Not a church goer, but she'd never believed it necessary. It must have been important after all. Still is important, she corrected. She wasn't dead. This was just a dream. She hoped she'd remember it when she woke up and would make a belated New Year's resolution to start.

Recollecting the priest in the house, she frowned. She'd never dreamt of a priest before. Maybe the glandular fever had made her realise her own mortality. There had been times she could easily have believed she'd die from it.

Her attention fell back to the amber hue with a sudden thought. There was no heat from the flames. And the light was above her, which didn't fit in with the netherworld she was imagining. Screwing her eyes, she forced herself to stare directly at the source of the light but couldn't make it out. Something familiar sent her mind spinning.

Recalling those quizzes in magazines: photos of familiar objects taken from unusual angles, she squinted more, straining to identify it.

"Thank you, Father," a voice resonated behind her. The direction of the sound immediately reoriented her, and she knew where she was: under the streetlamp outside the house in Swansea. It had looked so peculiar because she'd never seen it from this angle. Floating inches away, circling around seven or eight feet from the pavement. What a weird dream.

She turned to look towards the sound of voices from the open front door.

"I don't think you'll have any more trouble," the priest's deep timbre filled the cold night air.

"It already feels different," the girl she knew from previous dreams declared. There were murmurs of agreement from the others. Elin watched as the stumpy little priest waved goodbye and walked down the path.

He paused as he got to the streetlamp. A frown flecked his face, his hand rubbed his stubbly chin. His face pointed toward her, she tried to meet his eye, but his gaze chilled her. Looking right through her, he didn't seem to see her at all. He shook his head and turned away.

"Bye then, Father," the older man called out, the rest joining in, well-wishing a safe journey and thanks for coming. The front door closed firmly shut, and the cleric disappeared along the street.

Elin longed to wake from this peculiar circumstance. A familiar fear of being outside the house bubbled within her. "Come on. Wake up," she ordered, slapping her own face. She couldn't stay here, it wasn't safe.

"It does feel different, Bronnie," Aeron agreed.

"So, are you happy to stay here again?" Collin addressed his son then looked at the rest in turn.

"Yeah, I think so," Neil began, and soon the others mumbled in agreement.

"Right. I'll treat us all to a takeaway, and then Carole, Sylvie and I will get on our way and leave you guys in peace. Okay?"

A moment of apprehensive silence passed, but then, with nods and nervous smiles they acquiesced.

"I'm sure we'll be fine, Dad. Thanks. What do you think, Auntie Sylvie?"

Sylvie pursed her lips and looked about the room. Fiddling with the hem of her nylon cardigan. A smile broke on her face as confidence returned.

"Yes. She's gone. You'll be fine now."

They decided on Chinese food as there was a takeaway at the end of the street. Bronwyn dug out a menu from a drawer full of miscellaneous crap and they took turns perusing the selection.

Fifteen minutes after phoning through their order, Collin left to collect it. Josh agreed to go to the off-license for beers. The rest bustled finding enough plates, cups and cutlery for everyone to eat.

With the relief of resolving the poltergeist problem, appetites were vast. Collin stood in the shop picking dead skin from around the edges of his fingernails, salivating at the delicious smells from woks, battered from beyond the takeaway's counter. When temptation got too much, he ordered some extras.

Despite the additional food there was no wastage. Josh had to fight for the last spare rib, surprisingly not with Matthew, who having piled his plate high, seemed to be struggling with eyes bigger than his belly! Even the obligatory prawn crackers were devoured to the last crumb. Everyone, except driver Collin, drank copious amounts of beer. As the last can clattered from a failed basketball-litter bin attempt, dregs of Jack Daniel's and Tia Maria were dragged from the cupboard.

Mugs were rinsed and the vestiges shared.

"To Elin. May she rest in peace," Neil tipsily toasted.

"To Elin," the group joined in.

When it was time to go, hearty goodbyes were hailed. And because of the raucous party mood and excess alcohol, Sylvie's psychic abilities deserted her. She, along with everyone else, failed to notice the presence at the end of the path. The presence noticed them.

# Chapter Twenty-three

The calm she'd strived for was lost to panic. She didn't know why, but she was desperate to be inside. Bracing herself, she rushed headlong toward the house. Moving closer was like wading through treacle. Before she even touched the door, she sprung back to the lamppost as if attached to a bungee cord.

"No!" Squealing her torment, she sprinted for the door again, propelling back harder for her trouble. She had to get away. Being here, at the end of this path was the worst place. Whatever was coming would find her here for sure.

She ran, not towards the house this time, but away. Away from here, the path, and the threat. As she reached the margins of the streetlight's beam, the bungee thrust her back again, landing her with a shock beneath the lamp post.

Go into the light, Elin. You must go into the light!

Slumped, stunned on the floor, she considered her situation, the priest's words ringing in her head. Banished to the light. Not Heaven. The light at the end of the street! That can't be what the little clergyman had meant. Frustrated, she bit down on her clenched fist to expel her rage.

The exertion of her failed escape at least left her fully alert. She still had no idea what might come for her, but now she'd be ready for it. Her heart began to race. Closing her eyes, she took a deep breath and calmed again. Ready might be an overstatement. She was trapped here to face her fears.

Yelling at the top of her voice, she vowed not to put up with it. Expelled from her own house. Her own dream! She floated as far as she could to where the light faded. Standing defiantly glowering at the house, she pictured them all. Her exorcists.

"Let me in," she wailed. Brandishing her fists, she bellowed again. "Let me in, now." But she knew she was wasting her time. No-one answered. No-one heard. Falling to the floor, she wept. Gabbling to herself, over and over, "Let me in. Please. I'm not safe out here. Please let me in."

At the hundredth inaudible whimper, the front door burst open. "Bye-bye then, guys. Bye." Elin, grasping the opportunity, jumped up grabbing at anything she could. But everyone was just beyond her reach.

"Let me IN!" Jumping up and down, flailing her arms, shouting and screaming was all lost in the cheery farewells as the older three sauntered to where they had parked. As their car disappeared from view, and the door to number twenty-four slammed shut again, Elin stood open-mouthed, torn looking one way then the other, alone again in stark disbelief. What else could she do? She gave in.

Slumping beneath the streetlight, huddling closer, trying to quieten the discord, she distracted herself gazing at the constellations. There weren't many she knew, so she tried making up names for the dot-to-dot images, but her heart wasn't in it.

A worry twinged that it was unusual to be tormented like this in a nightmare. She comforted herself with the tentative notion that she didn't know if this was normal. She never remembered her dreams in enough detail to decide. Still the fear worried at her, snapping at her intent when it could.

Hours passed until the wonderful cacophony of the dawn chorus raised a dubious smile. The beautiful, musical shrill of nature lightened the air, and Elin loved what it symbolised—it would soon be morning, and she'd wake up and forget this horrific night. Gratified, believing the sounds must be penetrating her dream from the real world, she hugged her arms, the first glimmer of hope glinting in her pan of despair.

But all that glisters is not hope. And as dawn broke above row upon row of Swansea's terraced houses, Elin's turned to the dust it had always been. The sun rose above the end of the street, and the shadow of the long terrace shrank until it disappeared and bathed her in the first light of dawn.

With it, a sudden nausea caught her unprepared, she swooned, dizzy and confused. Tingles in her arms and legs made her look down at herself. Gasping in shock, her limbs appeared translucent. The brighter became the sunlight, the dimmer appeared her body.

When morning broke fully on Rhondda Street, she could scarcely see herself at all. The nausea was too much, and she closed her eyes, a solitary tear tracking down her cheek. Limbs and torso slowly fading, the sensation grew from a visual phenomenon to an increasing numbness. She couldn't feel her body, and then she couldn't feel her mind either.

In the brightness of the morning sun, Elin disappeared.

# Chapter Twenty-four

Neil stretched and yawned. He felt like laughing after the best night's sleep he'd had in ages, certainly this year. He hadn't realised how stressed he'd been. Even over Christmas it had played on his mind.

Last night he'd stayed awake and listened intently, just to be sure it was alright. When after a long time he'd heard absolutely nothing that troubled him, he fell soundly asleep.

He hopped out of bed and skipped down the small hallway to the bathroom. Turning the taps on full, he basked in the hot steam. Immersed in the warm water, he couldn't resist singing, the moist air aiding his vocal chords.

Concerns of what his housemates might think of his performance found no foothold on his buoyant mood. Twenty nineteen was going to be a good year, he could feel it.

Mulling over his year's goals: doing better with studies, passing his driving test, and maybe, with this new confidence, even find a girlfriend. With a shiver and chatter of teeth, he ran the hot tap again to warm up the tepid water.

An optimism bubbled through him like he'd never known. Ideas flashed to his mind. He'd ask his driving instructor to put in for his test. Picturing driving around in the little Daewoo dampened his enthusiasm momentarily. But then he imagined better grades, and a good job on the back of them. He'd soon be cruising in a BMW or something.

He couldn't quite put a face to the babe who would ride shotgun, so implausible was it even to his bubble soaked thoughts. But there could be a girlfriend one day, couldn't there? Maybe he'd grow a bit. He'd heard of people growing until they were twenty-one. He could even sort out his bucky teeth.

He shuddered at the image of himself with train track braces; bits of food repulsing every girl at whom he dared smile. Putting that on the back burner for now, he refocused on passing his driving test. He was sure he could do that.

The bath temperature was cold again. Watery wrinkles gave the appearance of trench-foot so he hauled himself out. Wrapping his scratchy old towel around himself to drip dry, he decided he might buy some fluffy new ones.

Student-life reality raised its hand when he glanced at his alarm clock and remembered he'd be back in lectures in a couple of hours. He hadn't completed all his assignments yet, but with the peace in the house he'd be able to settle down to good work.

Bronwyn and Aeron made up for lost time apart in bed together. The mood in the house was so different now. They realised that for months they'd been intruders. It wasn't the smartest house in Swansea, but at least now, it felt like home.

For Josh, the fear had been intermittent. Acute and terrifying at times, and then quickly forgotten in his immersion into the absorbing world of computer code.

With headphones on and eyes focussed on one or more of five monitors set up like a virtual reality cylinder, he'd stay awake all night, falling into exhausted sleep at the break of dawn.

A series of alarms on his computer and phone with complicated maths conundrums to solve were the only way he could wake up to go to lectures. It wasn't fool proof though. Puzzles which would baffle most mathematicians, Josh could literally do in his sleep.

He was happy to assume what the others said about peace being restored now was true. When he drifted off at six thirty this morning it may have been better quality sleep, but he wouldn't know until he woke up again at tea-time.


Matthew didn't feel safer. He couldn't consider whether the poltergeist was really gone. Up until yesterday he hadn't believed in it. He thought the séance must have created auditory hallucinations due to suggestion. Sylvie's voice was hypnotic when she was doing her 'is anybody there?' nonsense.

He'd rushed from the house, unwilling in that moment of terror to go back; particularly as he'd have been alone, what with everyone else being so scared.

But yesterday he saw her. The glasses rattling, her rage filled face, the kitchen door slam, he'd seen it all. And he saw her float right through them, huddled behind Father Jenkins as he ordered her into the light.

So whether she was gone? He wasn't about to leave his room to find out.

# Chapter Twenty-five

"What's happening, Dad?" Alis asked urgently, barging in the door of the family room at ICU.

"We don't know. They've done all sorts of tests and scans. She's in a deep coma, but there's no sign of trauma as they'd suspected. They thought she'd hit her head when she fell in the stream. They still think that's the probable cause and they're missing something. They'll arrange different scans and things.

"The blood tests showed zilch. White cell count slightly raised, consistent with getting over glandular fever, but nothing to explain this. No drugs."

Alis nodded in uncharacteristic silence. "How's Mum coping?" A look passed between them. No words were needed to express that she wasn't.

"I really want to get her home. She hasn't slept for two days. Just sits by the bed, holding Elin's hand."

"Maybe I could offer to take over. Let her get some rest?"

Emyr was too choked to speak. He nodded gratefully, glassy eyes belying the agony which threatened to destroy him.

"Can I see her now, then?" Alis nobly asked. She followed her father from the room and swallowed down a gulp of grief as she watched him fail to hide his anguish.

Her dad, always in control, brought to his knees by this unknown threat to his eldest daughter, the apple of his eye, Alis accepted. He loved them both equally, but Elin had always been the good one, whereas, Alis knew she'd always been 'a bit of a handful'.

He forced a smile onto his face as he pushed open the door to Elin's room. Glenda's vacant countenance told all there was to tell about any developments—there were none.

As recognition of Alis's arrival surfaced in her awareness, Glenda stood up suddenly and threw her arms around her. Her face creased in despair, her body convulsed in hideous, silent sobs. As she let out a wail, Alis guided her from the room so as not to trouble her sister.

"What are we going to do?" she managed at last through her throat, raw with emotion.

Alis, unaccustomed to being the comforter, always feeling like the baby of the family, didn't know what to do. Squeezing her mum tight, certain that if Glenda detected her torment she'd stop crying, ready to soothe her in place of herself.

Tears stung her eyes and a lump of pure emotion strangled her, but somewhere inside her she discerned it was more important for Glenda. If she didn't express some of the grief she was feeling soon, she'd implode on her own despair.

As she held tight, her mother's body racked with grief filled shudders. With every one, Alis's heart broke a little. Seeing her mum, her best friend and her pillar broken like this was too much. She felt tiny, and so fragile in Alis's robust embrace.

She gazed through the window at her sister. Tubes stuck out of her nose and mouth and into her arm just above the wrist. Monitors told their tale of woe as they showed no reason for her sister's coma.

"Come on Elin. Wake up," she breathed, still clutching her mum.


As the light of day faded in Mount Pleasant, Swansea, Elin re-emerged with a vague awareness of herself, gulping for breath as though from drowning, circling the streetlamp in a whirlpool of hazy illumination. Glancing at her limbs and torso, she gasped seeing their translucency. Fanning outstretched fingers in front of her disbelieving face, turning her hands back and fore, she sighed.

In reverse of fading away last night, as dusk turned to dark, Elin appeared solid again. So solid, it was unthinkable she couldn't be seen. But that seemed to be the nature of this peculiar dream.

Chewing an errant shard of fingernail, she leaned against the lamppost wondering what was happening to her. Why this dream again? She didn't even remember being awake in between. Whether that struck as unusual she could only guess. But just as before, this seemed so real and not like a dream at all.

It was boring. Time stood still as she could do nothing but dwell within the confines of the light thrown from the streetlamp. She tried slapping and pinching herself to wake up, but wasn't surprised when it proved futile.

Footsteps! Someone was coming towards the house from further down the street. Elin searched her limited horizon. The view beyond the lamp was no more than a blur, but she could tell the footsteps were closing on her. She knew she couldn't run. There was no point trying. She'd end up facing her attacker in a heap on the ground. Adopting a Kung-Fu type stance, she braced herself for whoever was coming. She wouldn't go down without a fight.

Clip-clop, the clumsy steps advanced ever closer. Something of their awkwardness didn't sound threatening, but Elin wouldn't drop her guard. A figure emerged from the darkness. A young man, a couple of years younger than her, tall and scruffy looking.

Crumpled trousers sporting stains from wiped hands and spilled food hung over scuffed shoes, the heels of which had ripped holes in the hem. An unkempt beard, born more from laziness than a desire for facial hair, collected crumbs and gravy morsels from the  pasty he munched clasped in one hand, the other gripping a phone inches from his face so he was in danger of eating them both.

She recognised him from the house despite being obscured by his constant scrutiny of the small screen, chuckling to himself at its content. Elin's fear evaporated, the tension slower to disperse.

"Hello," she yelled in his face. "Can you help me, please?" The boy walked past her, completely oblivious. Reaching the front door, he fumbled in his pockets as though he couldn't remember which one held his keys. He found them and proceeded to unlock the door.

"Help. HELP!" Elin cried out louder. He gave no indication of having heard her. Reengaging with the display on his phone, he entered the house and slammed the door.

Elin shook. This was too weird. Time passed. She stood. She walked in circles. She floated around the light. Because that was all she could do, apart from think. And she didn't have a clue what direction thoughts might take.

More footsteps. Another boy. This one older, more mature looking. She called out to him too, with equal failure to gain a response. As he stepped into the house, Elin noticed him remove ear-buds from his ears, a quick burst of thrash metal emanated to the street.

Slumped against the lamp post, Elin's thoughts ricocheted round her head as she tried desperately to piece the clues together. She was stuck here. Stuck within the confines of the lamp glow. And the last time anyone had spoken to her, it had been that bloody priest ordering her into the light.

I travel in my dreams. Her mother's words scratched at her psyche like fingernails on a blackboard. Waves of memories crashed over her, too rapid to absorb: Her in the lounge throwing clothes from airers and out of the tumble-drier, angered because they weren't hers.

Piles of fetid crockery shoved to the floor with screams of "Stop messing up my house!" She'd been so angry. Keeping the place tidy seemed important and she had no idea why. Tears streaming down her cheeks now, she slapped them away with unsympathetic palms. "Why! I don't even like the shitty little house!" she sobbed.

Glenda told her how she moved things and flapped the curtains to scare the new owners of their old family home because she was jealous. She didn't like Erw Lon. It had been her dad's plan, not hers. Her attachment to the old place made her go there in her dreams… haunting it.

That's what her mum was doing wasn't it? Certainly if the new owners saw the curtains flapping and whatever else, they'd believe they had a ghost, wouldn't they?

And Elin had dreamt about this place for weeks. Not deliberately like her mum, but often. If these memories were true. If she had travelled here somehow in her subconscious, she'd caused a trail of destruction which must have terrified the poor students living there now.

As her predicament dawned, with her hand covering her gaping mouth, her shoulders shook and giant sobs thrust their way from deep within her. Her brain rushed to her defence. Logic raising its hand to be included. But she knew. The part within her that made choices. The part that knew what she liked and what she didn't; who she loved, who she was. That part knew. It was true, and she was in terrible danger.

She hadn't known it was real, she'd thought it was just a dream. If they'd seen her, they'd had no choice. This is what they would have done; hold a séance and exorcise the house. If this wasn't just a dream, she really had been commanded here, and she wasn't about to wake up.

Recalling the séance with cold clarity now, it was obvious they'd thought they had a ghost. They'd called her Jacqui, and she'd chased them out of the house like a psychotic poltergeist. Of course they'd come back with a priest. Who wouldn't? There was no Jacqui. *She* was the ghost.

Except, she wasn't a ghost. She wasn't dead. She was just dreaming.

She would love a stiff drink to calm her nerves. The notion of what was happening to her was impossible to understand. What was she to do? Constricted thoughts slogged through possibilities, reeling at each dead end.

Was she merely a dream; the real her getting on with her life? That was too weird. She felt authentic. She couldn't be just an escaped thought. Or was she stuck in an out of body experience? Her body sleeping while she lingered here?

She choked back a sob at the awful connotations. Her poor mum and dad, and Alis, would be frantic. Unable to stir her, they'd have called an ambulance. She'd be in hospital, comatose with pipes and beeping machines all around. She shuddered.

If that was true, what on earth would wake her? She didn't know if it was even possible to go against the priest's commands? But she wouldn't wait around for someone to save her. There had to be something she could do. Getting back inside, back into the house; she was convinced that was key.

Her eyes sprang wide open at a sudden realisation, a rare positive in an utter catastrophe. Having established this as a dream, what harm could come to her? Maybe to her body miles away. But here, now? Whatever had frightened her about being outside had been part of a different nightmare. No-one could even see her now, let alone hurt her. Just as well, she mustered up a minimal smile, because if she was imprisoned here until she came up with a plan, it might be a while.

A sudden recollection of the séance flagged cognition in her mind. With excitement, she concentrated on the memory and was certain. The girl had seen her. Elin knew because she'd nudged the other woman whilst looking right at her. They had both seen her.

A plan took shape. Two of the housemates had arrived home already. It stood to reason she would join them. And when she did, Elin could get her attention, being careful not to scare her, and then she'd fetch the priest.

He'd been so adept at trapping her here. His skills would surely extend to reconnecting her with her body, and all this could be over. Convincing the girl had to be her priority. How long might her coma stricken body be available to reclaim?

She waited, sure she'd come home soon. Resting wearily against the lamp post, excruciating seconds crawled on. The cold of the hard ground meant nothing to her. Interacting with objects in the house had been second nature. Out here the same physicality seemed lost. Just as well. She'd have frozen to death otherwise.

The hem of her nightdress smoothed between thumb and forefinger provided a distraction from her stake out. Eyes darted up and down the street each time her ears pricked to feminine footsteps, but upon each instance they stopped short, turning into different garden paths and houses.

Annoyance creased her forehead. Where was she? Why wasn't she back yet? There was nothing she could do. Nothing but wait and hope her plan would work. But first she needed the bloody girl to show up.

As is frequently the case in waiting situations, it was when expectation turned to resolution of failure that relief arrived. New footsteps approached closer than others, dispersing softly into the night air.

Elin hadn't paid much attention to them until their proximity demanded it. They'd resonated differently. Quieter. Not what she'd anticipated. But as she got close enough Elin recognised her.

Leaping up, she stood, staring, waiting, her heart assailed by a thousand butterflies, some of whom tried escaping from her throat. Quivering fingers smoothed over her mouth. Gulping down her nerves, she was ready to speak.

She didn't want to say anything until she was close enough. Shouting would be a bad idea. It was imperative she didn't frighten her. But the chance escaped before it even arrived. Considerably before the range of the lamp, and therefore not close enough to Elin, the girl stopped, glanced at her phone and turned around. Shit!

Walking off, she dragged Elin's hope away with every soft, trainer-clad step. Where was she going now? The corner shop? Chippy? Maybe meeting friends in the pub; all of which pastimes Elin was immensely familiar. "It doesn't matter," she persuaded herself. "She'll have to come back sometime. I'll be here! Then I'll get her to help me." She ignored the little voice nagging her determination.

"Not if it's after first light," it whined.

# Chapter Twenty-six

Neil's lectures had gone well, as he'd promised himself they would. Assignments he'd been behind with, he'd studiously sought advice from tutors, and now felt more than capable of completing them.

He'd followed up on his ambition to pass his driving test and telephoned his old instructor, Sioned. A note of ambiguity had been detected in her voice. He knew he'd not been the easiest person to teach. He'd been a little highly strung. But his calm tone today convinced her. They'd even arranged a lesson this evening to kick things off.

Neil met her outside college and took his first driving lesson in months.

"Have you been having lessons with someone else?" asked Sioned as she began to relax next to her newly skilled pupil. "You certainly have come on well." She smiled at him

"I've had a few with my dad. I got a car for Christmas."

"Ah. I see," she smiled again. "We can put in for your test if you like? For about a month's time?"

"That's fantastic. Do you really think I'll be ready?" He couldn't believe how today was turning out. Sioned nodded and wrote in her diary.

"I'll see you again on Friday then?" and with that, Neil got out of the car and made his way to one of the popular bars in Uplands above the city centre. On Wednesdays, they had student discounts on food and drink and Neil was in just the mood to celebrate.

A car pulled up outside the house.

"Thanks a lot. You're a star. See you at the weekend... Bye."

Elin couldn't hear the reply, but recognised the girl as she got out. Her heart raced, and bizarrely, beads of perspiration (a dream with sweat?) formed on her brow and chest. This was it. What should she say? When confronted with what she thought was a ghost, she'd called a priest. What would she do now?

The car pulled away leaving the girl stood in the street waving noisy goodbyes until it disappeared round the corner. The anticipation was getting too much for Elin. "Come on," she whispered, "this is important."

The girl laughed and threw her arms out like wings. Head flung back, her laughing got louder.

"I am sooo drunk!" she exclaimed.

Disappointment trickled into Elin like a filling cistern, ready to flush her hope down the toilet yet again. Even if the girl heard her or saw her, would she be able to get any sense from her anyway?

Stepping out of the road, the girl stumbled forward and cackled at the hilarity. Elin counted three attempts at least for the drunken girl to make it over the kerb and she was losing patience. Maybe she should scare her and teach her a lesson. She stopped herself. She knew the silly drunk was oblivious to the fact she'd exorcised someone in the middle of a dream and it was important she should have stayed sober.

'Calm down Elin. Keep it together.'

Stumbling along the pavement, she paused within a few feet of the lamp post. 'She can see me,' Elin gasped. Clearing her throat, she smiled in an effort to appear friendly.

"Hello," she said cheerily. "Don't be afraid. I won't hurt you, but I need your help."

The girl looked thoughtful for a moment. Elin raised on tiptoe in nervous anticipation of her response. Stumbling again, the girl rushed, lurching towards her and grabbing the lamppost for support.

"Hi," Elin tried again, but gave up when the reason for the girl's headlong pitch forwards became disgustingly apparent. Still holding the post, she bent over double and spewed all over the pavement.

Rage coursed through Elin at the revolting sight of vomit trickling down the post. She shocked herself at her anger. This dream Elin was so unlike who she thought she was in real life. With the admission, the fury dissipated as quickly as it had arrived. The poor girl didn't realise what she'd done. She couldn't be accountable. And Elin needed her help when she sobered up.

Once the girl hauled herself up the steps to the front door, fumbled surprisingly efficiently with the key and disappeared inside, Elin was left to her thoughts again. Her thoughts, and a revolting puddle of alcoholic puke. Relief her state of consciousness excluded her sense of smell was marred by worry over her belligerence.

Everything life had thrown at her she had dealt with calmly with compassion. 'There, but for the grace of God, go I,' was a faithful mantra. Yet here she was, quick to judge and even quicker to a violent rage. She had controlled herself, but that had never been necessary before. It was a difficult situation of course, but something about being here at this house brought the worst out in her.

Her plan to acquire help wasn't going at all well. She had no choice but to wait for the students to come and go, and try to get their attention. When she could expect the next arrival she had no idea, but light would break the darkness soon and she'd no doubt fade into the air as she had before, like a puddle after summer rain.

Her natural optimism held steadfast to the fact she would reappear at dusk. But festering within was an ulcer of fear that knew it wasn't a fact at all.

# Chapter Twenty-seven

Neil's day was the best he'd had this year. It was amazing what a positive mental attitude could achieve. He'd felt good about his lectures and assignments, and better yet about his driving—not least because he'd found the courage to call Sioned in the first place. Using the phone always made him awkward. Knowing she'd not been keen to teach him anymore worsened it. And yet he'd turned it around and even had a brilliant lesson.

He could really see himself passing his test and driving his car wherever the mood took him. The beaches of Swansea Bay and Gower beckoned. Maybe he could take up surfing! He precluded himself picturing his pasty body in trunks and instead imagined a flattering wet-suit.

After his day of achievements, he deserved the curry with half chips/ half rice and sparkling wine on special offer. Sated and slightly merry, he almost found the courage to approach a pretty girl he spotted sitting at another table. One of his classmates also enjoying the curry with half chips/ half rice and lager instead of wine egged him on. But his positive outlook didn't quite stretch to being adroit with the opposite sex. And he didn't want his high to plummet dismally when he was inevitably shot down in flames.

But in just a few weeks he could be driving, offering lifts and trips to Gower to bikini-clad babes and… he rested his musings before they overwhelmed him.

He raised his glass of bubbly.

"Here's to a great year!" he proclaimed.

"You're a bit late, Neil, but yeah, here's to a happy 2019!" his friend added.

When the effects from the wine wore off, he chose not to top up his tipsiness in accordance with his new attitude as a star student. He wanted tomorrow to be as satisfactory as today, which meant not waking up late with a hangover.

Instead, he topped up his good mood with a game of darts which he lost. Lack of height gave him a disadvantage, he excused. And when he was defeated playing pool, his shortness took the blame again, or rather his corresponding lack of arm-span for holding the cue.

He'd lived with these trials for a long time and they didn't bother him much. It dented his confidence, but he believed his mum when she told him what was on the inside counted more, and that the right girl would be out there somewhere. She should know. She'd married his dad, a much older, bespectacled and more follically challenged version of himself.

Granted, he exuded an assurance Neil didn't yet possess. But that was probably because he'd found the love of his life in Carole and was respected in his work. Both accomplishments Neil was happy to wait for. A girlfriend would be great, but could distract him from his studies and so ruin his job prospects. So for now, he'd be content as he was.

When the pub closed its doors at midnight, a momentary pang of anxiety knotted in Neil's stomach, before he remembered it was all okay back at the house now. He laughed and walked up the hill with a spring in his step, knowing nothing could spoil this wonderful mood.

He could see the lamppost outside number twenty-four, one of a few that still worked on Rhondda Street; his beacon in the dark night. Nearly there, he thought, stepping from the glow of one streetlight into the next. And then he reached within a few feet of the last lamp that signified home.

As soon as the ambient light greeted his slight build from the shadow cast by the faulty lamp flanking it, he stopped, a shudder of dread shaking him from his reverie. There was that feeling again! That weird feeling that had bothered him in the house for months.

A revolting smell assaulted his nostrils. Noticing the pool of vomit on the pavement and staining the lamppost, he cursed whoever had sullied his path. But it offered a fortunate effect. Where he'd been reluctant to go back into the house, reminded of the horror he'd felt; his priority now was to get inside quickly, away from the awful stench.

As soon as he reached the top step he felt better. By the time he'd stepped indoors and closed the door, the feeling was already becoming a distant memory. Just a moment of fear because he couldn't believe his luck, he rationalised.

"Come on Neil. Just enjoy the new positive you. Don't spoil it!" And with that, he got into his comfy penguin onesie and hopped into bed.


Elin saw him coming up the street. She didn't expect much, but when he got closer, it seemed he sensed her. Calling out 'hello,' as before, he appeared to react, but then he smelled the vomit and the moment was lost. Damn!

Optimistic cogs cranked out positivity as they were pre-programmed to do. He was another hope, just not for tonight. Anyone who came close enough was fair game. She had nothing else to do. But these two, the girl and the small lad had to be her best bet.

Boredom was an alien concept to Elin. Even from her crib she had entertained herself. Whilst 'I'm bored' was a cry never far from Alis's lips, Elin was sure she had never uttered the words. There was always so much to do. A mountain to climb, a woodland camp to be made, a good book to read on a quiet beach.

But she had to concede that rather than being a quality she possessed, her ability to entertain herself had been largely attributed to her blessed surroundings. Imprisoned in this twenty foot diameter circle, she was struggling not to go mad.

"I'll be out of here soon. My body will be well looked after. Everyone's mission back home will be to wake me. And I'm sure I'll get these guys to help me soon. Tomorrow. I bet I can be free from here then." Doubts surfaced and were batted away by insatiable positivity.

Now she had time to herself. A rare commodity in this busy world. And, she could fly. Hindered by her ring of light, it could still be fun. When else would she get to do this?

Swooping round the light like a giant moth. Soaring in the light, nightie flowing out behind her, springing back whenever she reached the extremities of the dispersing light like a recoiling magnet. Convinced it was temporary, Elin enjoyed herself, laughing maniacally in the still night.

There was a lesson here. Enjoying the moment, not dwelling on her plight. She remembered a Buddhist story she'd read somewhere of a hunted monk, who trapped on a sheer cliff, paused to eat a delicious strawberry. As he ate, he noticed a concealed cave where he hid from his pursuers. Elin's strawberry was the fun she'd found. But she didn't find a hiding place. She found something else.

If she travelled from one extremity to the other, she was able to gather enough speed to move slightly further with the momentum. The glow almost reached the house. If she reached out as far as she could, stretching her arms, it might be possible to touch it.

They wouldn't be able to ignore her tapping on the window, would they? Not if she did so constantly! Her heart fluttered with excitement. This could be her ticket back to normality; back to her body.

She flew back and fore, gaining speed with every turn. Reaching outstretched fingers, she couldn't quite touch, but the next time she was closer.

Her heart skipped as she was so close she was sure she'd make it on the next pass. Whoosh. At improbable speed, she achieved the merest brush against the glass before catapulting back on the elastic light. And then, the faintest tap. She had touched the house. It felt so good. A giant leap back to reality.

She had refused her apprehension that her physical communion with the house might have been lost to the exorcism, and she'd been rewarded. It felt as real and as tangible as anything she had ever touched.

Suddenly, in response to the glancing stroke, the curtains at the bedroom window flew open. "Yes!" It had worked already. A proud grin parted Elin's granite face, her eyes glowing with the force of her being.

A face appeared at the glass shielded from the light with framing hands. Elin tore towards it. "Hello! Please help me!" she cried. Eyes widened and the face shot back. The curtains ripped closed faster than they'd opened, the tops fiddled with to obscure any chance of the outside penetrating the room.

That could have gone better, Elin supposed. But, she was still buoyed by the interaction. "It might take a night or two, but I know I'll make contact."

# Chapter Twenty-eight

Matthew hadn't left the house today. Seeing the girl during the exorcism had spooked him badly. He'd been awake all night but that was nothing new. A frequent night-owl, he would stay up playing 'X-box Live' with people in different time-zones and often lost track of when he should go to bed.

Last night was not one of fun with cyber-friends. He couldn't relax and had lain awake, chewing at his already non-existent fingernails. From his Doctor Who Tardis Fridge he'd pulled out a cold lager. After seven cans, he finally attained some relief from his anxiety and drifted into uneasy inertia.

Jumping awake throughout the night, he'd numbed his brain with yet more lager. When he woke again near lunchtime, it was with the inevitable throbbing head and dry mouth. He had to get a drink of water, but he couldn't face going downstairs. He knew it was because he was afraid, but he excused himself as being too fragile to tackle the stairs. Instead, he ventured next door to the front shower room and glugged his fill from the tap.

He hoped he wouldn't get sick from the bathroom water. A notice declared it unsafe to drink, but today wasn't the first time Matthew had succumbed to laziness.

He staggered to his room and got back into bed. Sometime in the afternoon he realised he felt better. Something about the daylight calmed his spirit. He didn't venture downstairs. Instead he switched on his X-box and got comfy.

He whiled away hours, getting his nutrition from half a dozen bags of Red-Hot Doritos and a giant bar of hazelnut chocolate. Snacking and gaming proved a great distraction. When fatigue forced him to remove his ear-crushing headphones, it was pitch black in his room.

He leaned back in his office chair and yawned. A gust of wind blew branches against the house, the tap-tap on the glass making him jump. With racing heart, he took a few deep breaths but a flickering from the window began to irritate him. Is the bulb going in the street light, he wondered? He staggered across the dark of his room guided only by the disturbing flicker of light coming through a gap in his curtains.

He was breathless by the time he reached the window, having trodden on a couple of empty cans and tripped over a damp towel. When he drew back the curtains to investigate the dodgy bulb, his heart stopped.

Tears dried in his panic filled eyes as he couldn't blink or wrench them away. His feet stumbled over themselves in his desperation to escape. Tugging at the curtains, they refused to close without a fight.

"Come on. Come on!" he hissed.

Running across the room, almost breaking his ankle in the process, he leaned against the wall, staring at the covered window, his hands impulsively searching the wall for an escape route.

How he wished he had expensive, lined curtains instead of the worn out dishcloths that presumed to do the job in his tatty digs. If only he'd invested in black-out blinds as he'd considered many times, he wouldn't be faced with the horror of the ghostly silhouette overwhelming him now.

"No, no, no," he repeated over and over, hitting his head with his palms. Still he stared at the window, the apparition whizzed past every few seconds, tormenting him to the edge of insanity.

He longed for the days when he had believed it all to be ridiculous, just the others' foolish imaginations. But since seeing her, he couldn't stop thinking about her. And now he knew she hadn't gone like the priest had assured. She was here to torment him. Why else would she fly outside his window?

Another tap-tapping on the glass made him shriek in anguish. He sank down to the floor, his eyes refusing to be prized from the window. With his arms wrapped around his knees, he cowered, rocking back and forth. "Please go away. Please leave me alone. Please. Please. Please."

As soon as the first light of morning breached the curtains and the blankets Matthew had pulled over his head, he phoned his dad to collect him. He couldn't stay another night in this house.

Outside, Elin had given up. She really thought she was onto something for a while. It was obvious the boy had seen her. Why had he been so afraid? Looking down at her appearance convinced her she looked like her normal self—apart from floating outside his window, of course. That must look scary.

But if he'd just look again, she'd make sure she smiled and looked her most appealing. She practiced fluttering her long lashes and smiling, showing her perfect teeth, hoping the anguish she felt didn't make the whole performance appear grotesque.

Tapping the window again, attempting, if it was possible, for it to sound friendly. She waited expectantly but he didn't come back. "Come on. Look out of the window again, please," she begged.

Having tapped the glass a dozen times or more, the light of dawn finally forced her away from the house and nearer to the street lamp. Daylight would claim her soon—taking her to the oblivion she'd disappeared to when the sun peeped over the row of terraced houses. Tomorrow, she'd try again. Sooner or later he'd peer out and she'd charm him into helping her. They owed her that much for exiling her out here.

As the sun rose higher and brighter, reaching the familiar point of no return, paradoxically, it consigned Elin to darkness for another day.

# Chapter Twenty-nine

"It's the freakin' weekend baby!" Aeron fist-pumped, placing a tray of drinks on the table for his housemates, minus one. As it was early, and he wasn't needed behind the bar, he joined them, keen to discuss the gossip of Matthew's departure.

"So, is he coming back?" he asked Josh, arguably the closest to the absentee. Josh shrugged.

"He wouldn't say. But he didn't go to lectures yesterday. He was getting stressed before Christmas. It just got too much for him, I guess." The group nodded.

"What about you, Neil? Did he say anything to you?" Neil shook his head too. Memories of the ghostly mood he'd sensed returning to the house last night rattled in his mind.

"What is it?" Bronwyn asked, noticing his expression.

"Nothing…" Neil muttered.

"It's obviously not nothing. Go on, Neil. Tell us."

He paused, then decided feedback from the others might be reassuring.

"He went weird after the exorcism." A simultaneous frown descended on the faces staring at him.

"He didn't eat much when Neil's dad bought us that Chinese," Josh recalled to a gasp from everyone else.

"That is weird," Bronwyn sneered.

"So, what do you think made him behave oddly then, Neil?" Aeron asked, impatient to find out before Jon summoned him back to the bar. Neil fidgeted with his beer mat and ran his fingers round the rim of his glass.

Without looking up, he said, "The ghost. Elin. I'm not sure she's gone."

Bronwyn groaned. Aeron shifted uncomfortably in his seat. "Why?" he asked.

"Last night. When I came home from the pub, I felt strange. Just outside the house."

"Outside? Well that's not the same then is it? Were you drunk?" Aeron demanded.

"No! I wasn't."

"Oh, Neil. You felt strange? You are strange!" Bronwyn teased. "Listen. Father Jenkins said the ghost had gone, and I can tell you, I actually saw her leave." Pausing, she took a deep breath and looked around the group for dramatic effect. "And we could all tell how different it was afterwards, couldn't we?" Everyone nodded in unison.

"It was pretty late when you came back, Neil. You had a fleeting bout of nerves. Nothing real. As for Matthew. He was stressed before Christmas without the poltergeist to blame. He probably realised how much he was struggling with his course after spending time at home. Loads of people drop out. Let's not make it something it's not and start blaming ghosts again, yeah?"

Bronwyn's scathing reproach left him regretting airing his concerns. But with arched eyebrows and pursed lips, he decided to take heart in the other's vehement rebuff. Of course she'd gone. A priest, not to mention his psychic Auntie Sylvie, had confirmed it. Why was he so set on self-destructing just when he was doing so well? He didn't know, but he wouldn't let himself succumb to doubts.

Aeron re-joined his boss, who was surprisingly upbeat; noticeably different to his demeanour before Christmas.

"What was all that about?" Jon nosied.

"Nothing much. Matthew left today. Neil reckoned it might have been because we've got a ghost. We haven't," Aeron asserted in reply to Jon's perplexed expression.

"How have things been here?" he inquired, not wanting to upset his boss with bad memories, but seeking reassurance things truly were back to normal.

"You mean the ghost we had?"

Aeron nodded.

"Never better, fingers crossed, touch wood," he placed his hand flat on the bar. "It seems to have settled down. I was just under a lot of stress, I think. Had a couple of er… issues with the staff. "It must have affected me more than I was ready to admit. But everything's A-Okay now." Making the okay sign, circling his thumb and index finger, he turned toward a waiting customer. "What can I get you?" he beamed.

Aeron nodded, squinting at confirmed instincts. Just as he'd thought. Everything was back to normal, even here at the pub. Neil was just being a wimp as usual.

A lengthy night of serious relaxing in the form of indulgent inebriation followed. Jon kept the bar open for extra time and let them stay behind while Aeron cleared glasses and wiped tables. When the doors finally closed, they staggered home clinging to one another for mutual support. Aeron was the only one sober.

Elin saw them coming. She made her usual pleas for their help, but seeing the state of them, wasn't surprised she couldn't get their attention. Where was the other one, she wondered? The one who'd seen her last night?

She cursed herself when she realised he must have been in his room all along. How many hours had she squandered not tapping on the window? She wasted no more time and hurled herself backward and forward until she attained the necessary momentum to reach.

The room was in darkness. He must be asleep. Tapping as hard as she dare without breaking the glass, she muttered to herself. "He'll soon be awake! I can't spare any more time for him to have a rest!"

It was quickly apparent he wasn't going to answer. Maybe he wasn't there, she fumed. Gulping to the pit of her stomach, she was terrified she might have scared him away. What if he never returned?

Her plan to get help was going from bad to worse. A giant sob erupted from deep within as despair began its consumption of her every thought. Her resident optimism prepared to wave the white flag. The hopelessness of her situation was crushing. She didn't want to give up. The consequences were unthinkable. But what else could she do?

The sensitive ones amongst the students residing at number twenty-four Rhondda Street would admit, if pushed, that it did feel spooky outside the house. It passed when they walked away or went inside. A conscious effort combined with natural distractions meant it was becoming easier to ignore.

Neil was too excited to notice anything peculiar today. He had a date for his driving test. In three weeks' time, with the right preparation, he could be driving around freely. On top of that, he was due to hand in the assignments he'd been behind with today. Catching up and being back on track felt fantastic.

A horn made him jump as the 'Learn 2 Drive' car pulled up behind him. Sioned smiled approvingly at news he'd booked his test.

"You're ready now, I think. We'll polish the skills you have already, do a couple of mock tests, and you'll breeze it."

As Neil drove away, he couldn't help grinning like a lunatic.

# Chapter Thirty

"You must have some clue why my daughter is still in a coma," demanded Emyr. "It's been weeks now."

The consultant looked at his shoes, embarrassed he had no answers. He knew it was unjustified. There were so many possible causes. "We can't be certain, Mr Treharne. I do understand your concerns."

"Concerns! My daughter's lying in a coma and no-one knows why, and you call it 'concerns'?"

"We're doing everything we can. As you've been advised, we suspect the fall combined with the glandular fever has caused the problem. There's no sign of infection, and scans have revealed nothing. That should be viewed positively. It's good news we've not found anything dire. But it's just a waiting game at this stage."

"And how long are we expected to wait?" Emyr wasn't sure what he was even asking. He just wanted answers, and the man in front of him was where the buck stopped.

"That is something we can consider at another time. We haven't yet given up hope that she will wake up. Try not to worry for now... I know that's easier said than done."

"Yes. Thank you, Doctor." Emyr, puzzled but managed a smile as he walked away. As he reached the door, his true emotion crumpled his face. He sucked it back. He had to be strong for her mum and Alis… and for Elin too.

"Well. What did he say?" Glenda demanded, having sent her husband to find answers, she expected him to deliver. This was no good. There must be a test. There must be something they could do; that they should have done to find out what's wrong with her daughter. She couldn't just be left to not wake up. It was ridiculous.

"They still don't know. But they haven't given up hope. He said try not to worry."

"Don't worry?" she spat. "I'm so glad they haven't given up hope," she added caustically. "Did you tell him we'll sue them for negligence if anything happens to my little girl? Did you tell them?" Clutching her daughter's hand even tighter, she broke down into silent sobs.

Later on that day, Alis arrived at the hospital to relieve her from sitting with Elin. She'd willingly stay there all the time, but Alis and Emyr persuaded her that rest was crucial for her own health.

Alis brought some of Elin's favourite music on her phone, and a little speaker to play it on. She'd read on the internet it sometimes helped.

"Oh, you are a good girl, Alis bach," Glenda said, hobbling, exhausted from the room.

Shuffling down the long corridors of the hospital, one phrase played round and round her mind, chipping away at her with every pass: *We haven't given up hope*. It was a phrase loaded with threat. It meant at some point in the indeterminate future, they would give up. And then what?

# Chapter Thirty-one

Driving Test day had arrived and Neil couldn't feel more ready. Sioned was due to collect him at eleven to take him to the test centre. A glance at his watch revealed it was only ten now. What could he do with himself in the meantime to stay calm? A cup of tea or coffee? What if that made him need a wee mid-test?

A knock at the door startled him from his dilemma. Sioned was early he thought, walking down the hallway. Some pre-test practice her likely plan. He opened his mouth to greet his instructor but was left gawping, surprised at who stood on the doorstep. A less familiar face smiled sheepishly up at him. It took a moment for Neil to recognise Matthew's dad.

"I just wanted to get a few things from Matthew's old room. Is that okay?" he asked.

"Sure," Neil answered. "Old room? He's not planning on coming back, then?"

"No." He shook his head disparagingly. "The rent's paid to the end of term, but basically, you guys might as well look for another housemate."

"I'm sorry. I didn't realise he was so stressed."

"No. Neither did we. Christmas was great. But then, when he came back… I don't know… It must have all got on top of him."

Neil nodded slowly, trying not to think about Matthew leaving and what he'd worried about then. He went with Matthew's dad upstairs to his room. Pushing open the door they were greeted by the putrid smell of old food wrappers and drinks cans giving a strangely unique rotting yet floral aroma.

"I've got my driving test in a little while. I'll have to leave you with it, if that's okay?" Neil was grateful for the excuse.

"Yeah. That's fine," said Matthew's dad, pulling a roll of black bin bags from his back pocket. "I'll lock the door when I leave," he said. And as Neil turned to go, he added, "Good luck with your test," giving a thumbs up which Neil returned.

Neil felt slightly guilty leaving the work to someone else, but it wasn't his mess, and he did have to prepare for his test. He waited outside the house, a little way down the street so Matthew's dad wouldn't see him from the window and wonder if it wasn't just an excuse.

Sioned turned up three quarters of an hour early with pre-test practice on her agenda, just as Neil had predicted. He smiled and took his place at the wheel.

"Let's do this thing!" he said with a confidence he wasn't even faking. "Bring it on."

He walked, dour faced, into the snug at The Railway.

Already waiting at what was becoming their usual table, Bronwyn, Aeron and Josh sat expectantly.

Their eyebrows raised in response to his entrance. He looked miserable but with a tell-tale twinkle in his eyes. They went along with the façade, knowing it wouldn't be for long and not wanting to spoil the moment.

"Aww. Never mind, bach," Bronwyn colluded. Neil could contain himself no longer and burst into laughter. "Totally nailed it! First time!" he accepted his high-fives and deliberated what to drink.

"You mustn't drink and drive. You don't want to lose it on your first day," Josh advised without looking up from his smart phone.

"I don't want to lose it any day, obviously. But I haven't got my car here yet. My dad's gonna bring it down for me in a couple of days."

"Why don't you get the train? Get your car sooner, save your dad the journey. I'll come with you if you like?"

Neil quickly worked out whether it would work with his lectures. And remembering one of his tutors was off sick and he had an extra day to himself, he agreed.

"I don't need to be back 'til after the weekend. We can make a trip of it. I can show you where I live. There's actually a couple of pretty good clubs we can go to. You can be my wing-man," Neil suggested, without the foggiest idea what that entailed.

"Cool," agreed Josh, still engrossed in his phone.

They popped back to the house to grab a few things for the weekend and walked down to the Victorian grandeur of Swansea Central Railway Station. Waiting for the train, Neil made one-way conversation with his friend. Josh said 'yeah' and 'mm hmm' in the right places, but Neil knew he wasn't listening.

Halfway through the journey, Neil decided to say.

"You're great company, you are."

"Yeah. Mm hmm," Josh replied nodding, laughing inappropriately in response to his phone.

"What's so funny?" Finally, Josh looked up and engaged with his friend. "Just some coding issues a friend from another uni is having trouble with." He went on to explain, but despite them both being on the same software engineering course, it went completely over Neil's head.

He panicked, wondering how Josh could be so much better at it. In lessons, he never spoke up. He wasn't top of the class, but he sure knew his stuff. Neil took a deep breath. He was doing fine. His grades were fine, improving even. They were just different that was all.

He left Josh to his coding hilarity and fired up the kindle app on his phone. Scrolling down his library, he selected an intriguing romance novel he was halfway through. It was great no-one could tell what he was reading. He'd die of embarrassment if anyone could, but he was a true romantic at heart.

They arrived in Bishop's Stortford at just after midnight. It took so much longer by train than Neil was used to that his surprise arrival had to be warned of half way through the journey. Collin and Carole were delighted and even offered to pick them up from the station.

Collin was waiting in the car for them when they walked out.

"Hello, Son. Hi Josh." Josh looked up briefly to acknowledge Collin, trying not to be rude.

"What brings you home, then?" Collin asked.

"I've come to pick up my car," Neil tried to sound nonchalant. It took longer than it might have done at a more reasonable hour for Collin to catch on.

"You've passed your test?" He hugged Neil and pumped his hand vigorously. "Congratulations. I didn't even know you'd put in for it!"

Neil gave a coy shrug. "It's no biggie." Collin punched him jovially on the arm. "Really, well done, Son."

They were still dissecting the finer points of Neil's test when they pulled into the Hedges' driveway.

"Quiet now boys. Your mum and sister are in bed."


The next day, Neil took everybody for a ride in his car. They even ventured to Auntie Sylvie's. Emma rabbited to her confined audience about how clever her brother was driving his own car, and how he would be able to take her places—like the zoo and Toy-R-Us.

When they arrived at Sylvie's, Emma ran down the large, untidy garden where she was in the long process of constructing a den that she'd begun in the summer holidays.

When she was out of earshot, Sylvie inquired after the situation in Wales. "Tell me how it's going in Swansea, then, Neil?"

"Good. It feels totally different. Everything stays where it's supposed to." He debated mentioning the creepy feeling he sometimes had outside, but he supposed he was being foolish so kept it to himself.

Neil loved being the 'designated driver' for a night out in town with Josh and a couple of his hometown friends. The thrill of driving was far more rewarding than a few beers. They offered lifts to some girls who declined. Which was fortunate, because there weren't enough seats anyway, although Neil would happily have left the others to walk.

When Monday morning came round again, Collin treated him to a full tank of fuel to show how pleased he was. Then after lots of hugs and promises to drive home again soon, they set off back to Swansea.

After Neil and Josh had left to go to Neil's parents', and in the spirit of travel, Bronwyn and Aeron bought themselves a pop-up tent in the January sales at a third of the retail price.

Chucking it, and various warm supplies, in the boot of Aeron's Ford Focus they headed into The Brecon Beacons National Park. They spent their time enjoying one another's company trekking beside the Afon Mellte (River Mellte) and its famous waterfalls.

The absence of students left the house in darkness, much like Elin's mood. She knew they'd come back, but the lack of life within symbolised too acutely her terrible plight. She was going insane. Periods of manic tapping on the window interspersed with hours and hours of catatonic trance with no-one to interact with, nothing to read, and nothing to do. Nothing.

Her imagination failed her. She flirted with the notion that if she was stuck here in a dream—her subconscious—then if she could dream somewhere else, she could be somewhere else. But nowhere seemed real and simply faded away—street art washed away in a deluge of despair.

With images of her family fleetingly in mind, she tried talking to them. Entering their dreams, telling them her plight and begging for help. It might work, but it didn't seem hopeful. The struggle she faced evoking her beautiful family for more than a transient moment devastated her. She was losing them.

Picturing the house residents was easier given the frequency she saw them, but infiltrating their dreams was less convincing. She felt no connection. It was worth persevering perhaps. It would be foolish to dismiss any possibility of help with so much time on her hands, but it felt pointless.

Introversion tested her to her limits. The strain driving her crazy. Her own company had always been her favourite, but with her thoughts deserting her she felt more trapped than ever. This circle of light was all she had, with no reprieve.

The novelty of flying around the light had become an irritation weeks ago when her resemblance to a disorientated moth became disturbingly authentic. Now depression showed its evolutionary purpose and kept her just below the surface of her unbearable reality: prudently apathetic.

There would soon be longer periods of time when they'd be gone. Easter and Summer Holidays; and, of course some of them might be about to complete their courses and leave for good. If her body was still viable by then, she thought, choking down bitter bile that surfaced, she'd have to muster the strength to try something. But what was the point? If she couldn't get people who knew about her to help, there'd be no chance with strangers.

Sat leaning against the lamp post, she couldn't even muster a tear. Her eyes numbed to the pain. She couldn't do this forever, she knew. The time to give up and let herself go drew closer, and gripped her very essence somewhere indefinably within.

Her brain worked in the background to her thoughts, throwing up suggestions over and over; rarely new, and even more rarely positive. A hideous notion fought to the front to be acknowledged. What if things were already worse than she'd supposed. Even a coma was an optimistic theory.

She could have been found dead after the exorcism. Maybe this is what ghosts were. Fragments of consciousness trapped in their last dream for all eternity. A lump grew in her throat and she threw her hand to her mouth. Her poor mother. Her poor family.

Maybe she was missing something. If she could just think outside the box, read between the lines, or any other clichéd terms for alternative thinking, there might be something else she could do. She had to hope. If she let go of that, it would be the end.

# Chapter Thirty-two

Glenda struggled most with the predicament of her eldest daughter. It was a mother's prerogative. To make matters worse, plans had been made to switch off the life-support late next week to see if Elin could sustain her own breathing. A cloud hung over the procedure. The risks were played down, but the doctors had to admit that if Elin didn't respond favourably, it could be the end.

Glenda stifled a sob recalling the worry behind the eyes of Elin's consultant. She clung to the hope it might be positive. It could be the moment Elin woke up and came back to her. But her red eyes showed her true misery.

It wasn't good to be retired from work now. With nothing pressing to distract her, she'd become unwilling to leave her bed. For the first month she'd barely left Elin's side. But every time Emyr and Alis forced her to come home to shower and rest, it had been harder to go back.

Something inside her knew Elin wasn't really there, and part of her—a selfish part—wanted to remember her full of life and not see her passing moments. She was going back today.

Initially, she'd stayed for herself as much as for Elin. Today, and any future days she had left, she would go for Elin's sake. Much as it pained her to watch her beautiful daughter's deterioration, she knew that if she passed, she'd need her family, and definitely her mum, close by.

Alis had needed to go back to Uni. She came home every opportunity she got, but Emyr persuaded her that her sister wouldn't want her to jeopardise her future. It was too late for that. Alis's concentration was non-existent and her course-work had suffered badly. She plodded on, resigning herself to repeat the year when Elin pulled through. She, unlike her mother had not yet given up faith her sister would make a full recovery. Not that she would admit at any rate.

Her lecturers', aware of her situation, were being appropriately lenient. The distraction of lectures proved useful, but left two unscheduled days each week with nothing to do. Of course, that was when she was supposed to be using what she'd learned on her coursework, but that didn't happen. Instead, she slept her way through the days, waking only to go to pubs and clubs and get incredibly drunk.

A few guys propositioned her and she'd succumbed to temptation once or twice. But thoughts of her poor, beloved sister, lying helpless in her hospital bed crushed her desires.

Dancing was freedom. A few minutes lost in music and she could almost forget. Her guilt threatened to spoil it, but alcohol proved a worthy ally, not least in blocking memories of waking up with strangers in her bed.

Every weekend back home, she managed to appear supportive and helpful. But she knew she was spiralling out of control. If Elin didn't come round soon, she dreaded where it would all end.

Emyr remained strong for his girls. He felt confident that's the impression he gave, but really, he was fooling no-one. His haunted eyes sat distraught in his gaunt face. His appetite, beyond poor since Elin was rushed to hospital, had made him shed several stone.

The pallid smile forever applied to his features whenever Alis or Glenda were near did nothing to disguise his torment. They both appreciated the effort though. Someone had to take the strong role. Someone needed to organise practical things such as meals and travel. And someone had to speak to the doctors about Elin's prognosis. Emyr's feeble smile flagged his willingness, if not his ability, to take on this responsibility.

Staff at Morriston Hospital remained at a loss what to do. Elin was unresponsive to all of the usual tests, yet there continued to be no detectable cause for her condition. Whilst that made them optimistic if she did come round, that she may be lucky and survive with no loss of neuro-function, they were becoming increasingly pessimistic of her ever waking up at all.

They knew all too well how distressing it was for the family to keep loved ones in a vegetative state for a prolonged period. It was often kinder, and obviously less costly, to let them go. Only then could the healing process of grieving begin.

They had scheduled, with the family's consent, a time next week to try Elin without life support. They'd see if she could breathe on her own. Often the urge to breathe pre-empted other neuro-responses. If it did, it would likely still be a long recovery, but it might be something they understood, something they could work with.

They'd warned the family of the risk that Elin may prove unable to breathe independently. The moments of forcing her to try could begin the natural shutting down of her vital organs. They might have to seriously consider not resuscitating and letting her go. There was plenty to consider for medical professional and close family alike. Next week was a big deal. A very big deal.

Elin somehow sensed the urgency of her situation. There hadn't been a night when she'd not banged on the window even though she realised her suspicions were correct and she must have scared away the boy from the front bedroom. She'd seen no sign of him since that first occasion.

Now with the increasing daylight she kept missing the comings and goings. The students were coming back from their lectures while it was still light, she presumed, because she rarely witnessed their return. So when noise of raucous revellers reached her consciousness she sprang to action.

Shouting and yelling got her nowhere. Even touching them, they'd not felt. Tapping them with something? That might work. If she could break a branch from the hedge, she might get their attention with it.

As the sound of them edged closer, Elin frantically tugged at a brittle looking twig, bending it to and fro. They were almost upon her when it finally snapped just as they took their first steps onto the path. Desperate not to miss the opportunity, she lunged forward and jabbed each of them sharply with her little stick.

"Geddoff!" one of them cried, flapping at his shoulder.

"Hey, stop shoving!" another complained.

"Thank goodness," Elin gasped. "You felt it. Please, I need your help. I've been trapped out here since your exorcism! You must get the priest back and reconnect me with my body. You see, I'm in a coma, or worse. But I wasn't dead when you exorcised me, just dreaming. And I hope I'm not dead now…" Elin rambled on but no-one paid her any heed. She poked out again with her stick and it ensnared in the thread of the larger boy's jumper.

Flapping his arm round, flailing in his attempt to free himself, he slurred, "Wait up, guys. I'm caught up in the bloody hedge." The other three turned and laughed to see him comically fighting off a phantom twig just beyond his grasp. Extended fingers finally gripped it and threw it to the floor beyond Elin's reach. Soon they were all guffawing, holding one-another as they stumbled the rest of the way up the path.

"Wait! Please help me. Please. I need you to help me." As she went unseen, Elin got louder. "Hey! Don't ignore me. I need you to help me. You put me here. If you don't help, that's murder, or manslaughter," she babbled, "because if you leave me out here, I'll die and it'll all be your fault. Don't go. Come back. You have to help me!" But they didn't come back. They carried on, ignorantly slamming the door with extra gusto to underline her hopelessness.

"Come back and help me, you…" she couldn't think of a word to express her contempt and her despair. She couldn't think of anything. She gritted her teeth and prepared for her next disappearance, aching for tomorrow to bring a fresh chance.

# Chapter Thirty-three

Neil's successful driving test meant there were two drivers in the household now. Combined with the mild early spring weather, it gave plenty of opportunities to get away. They'd become frequent day trippers; sometimes to Cardiff or Newport and even Bristol, and other times into the mountains for picnics. They'd even taken a weekend at Center Parcs.

The house dynamic had changed and they'd definitely become friends. Matthew's departure was a factor, too. Everyone had found him bombastic and irritating and his absence a relief, but they tactfully avoided mentioning it.

His room remained vacant. It was difficult to fill because all the students found accommodation well before starting their courses in September. With only a term and a half before the end of the year, takers were unlikely. It thankfully wasn't their responsibility. With separate contracts with their landlord, Matthew's family would have to sort it out.

Neil had meant to check the state of the room since his glimpse at the chaos within when Matthew's dad came to get his stuff. It was no good presuming his cleaning would be sufficient. If it wasn't, they'd be in danger of attracting rats.

He must remember to look. He wasn't promising to clear up if anything needing doing, but he would tell the landlord. A pang of guilt gave him a queasy knot in his stomach. He should have done it weeks ago, and although the same could be said for any of his housemates, it was him who'd seen the disgusting state.

Promising himself he'd check it out soon appeased his guilt for now, so he got on with his coursework. Well on top of things, giving more priority to his leisure time had relaxed him and paid off. And Neil wasn't the only one. Everyone's work had improved. They were all relaxed and happy, completely oblivious to the turmoil they'd created in the Treharne family mere minutes away in the local ICU.


"Of course, you're right," Elin's consultant advised. "There is a chance attempting to incite your daughter to breathe on her own could back-fire. But even so, honestly? We're running out of things to try. We don't know how much of her cognitive capacity might already be lost.

"If she takes over her breathing. That will be an essential positive step towards her recovery. But equally, if it isn't successful; if she's unable to breathe un-aided, it would probably be the right time to let her go, I'm afraid."

He nodded in agreement with his own monologue. "Certainly, keeping her alive in a vegetative state would only serve to increase the likelihood that, if we were ever to successfully wake her; and that would be unlikely verging on miraculous, then she'd probably be a mere shadow of her former self.

"She would likely struggle to do any of the things she could do before. And that may not be fair to Elin. Certainly not fair to you." He removed his glasses in a sweeping motion to illustrate he was rounding up. "In these situations, it is usually kinder, and more practical, to recognise the limitations of what is achievable. It is the healthiest option for you to attempt to move on."

The atmosphere in the room was as black as forever. Moist eyes of her stricken parents stared intently at the middle distance, somewhere between the floor and Hell below. They would shatter if they looked away. Then Dr Lewis threw them a bone.

"Of course, there's every reason to be optimistic for Monday's outcome. The fact we've been unable to find anything wrong with Elin should be seen as a positive. There's no cause we can decipher why she is unconscious. There is, therefore, nothing stopping her from waking up. We hope breathing for herself will fire her brain into activity and begin the process of recovery.

"While we ask you to be prepared for the worst, we also urge you to try and remain positive. If Elin does wake up, she's going to need you."

Alis, a hundred miles west on a train from Bristol, glanced anxiously at her phone, awaiting a call or text to tell her the outcome of the meeting. She'd already excused her absence from lectures so she could be with her parents on Monday morning, and a lot more besides if it didn't go well. She gulped down emotion as a wave of nausea forced her hand to her mouth at the thought of what might come to pass.

How would they possibly cope? Her sister was her world. She admired her so much. Her kind, calm, optimistic cool-headedness. She'd pretended her encounters with boys might make her jealous. But she knew Elin was just waiting for the right person.

In reality, it was Alis who was envious of Elin's assuredness that Mr Right was out there somewhere whilst she had clung onto Mr Right Now. Although she billed it as her wild lifestyle, she knew it was born from desperation; a strategy to make sure she was with someone hoping that when they were ready to settle down it would be with her because she was there. Elin always told her how beautiful and attractive she was. She'd fall apart without her.

As the carriage clattered on, the rat-a-tat-tat over and over drove her crazy. Her ear buds had been cast aside some time ago when she couldn't stand any of the music. The inane drivel from the DJ's was too much today.

She'd known it had been foolish attempting to read her latest young adult novel, about a girl discovering her absent father was an elf, and gave up after reading the same page for the fifth time.

Candy Crush Saga and Subway Surfer had offered brief respite, but now she sufficed with staring steely-eyed out of the window. Flutters of adrenaline wafted through her the more mountainous the scenery became as she realised news of her sister's prospects grew ever-closer.

Eventually a text arrived. It didn't say anything bad directly, but the instruction to get off the train at Swansea instead of continuing to Llandovery told its own story.

She almost walked past Emyr waiting on the platform. His bullet-hole eyes framed with purple bags sunken into his sullen grey face made him unrecognisable.

"Cariad," he said quietly. Alis did a double take before walking back to her dad and throwing her arms around him. He felt so frail. He'd aged years in the last few weeks. Alis feared she would lose them all.

Emyr stiffened in the swell of his younger daughter's sobs. He was committed to being the strong one for all three of his girls. He knew he was failing.

"They're going to switch her off..." he managed to croak before breaking down. Alis galvanised her own courage, attempting to be a bolster, but with every quiver of her once robust dad's tortured body, her heart broke a little more.

They got in the car and made their way in silence to the hospital ready to join Glenda in staring at their beloved daughter and sister for as long as they could suffer. She looked so lovely. Her graceful elegance hadn't faded any in the weeks since she'd slipped into unconsciousness.

Beneath the covers, her muscle tone had suffered. The nurses manoeuvred her limbs regularly to maintain some of her strength. Something about her face, perhaps that it never moved, belied the fact she was not simply asleep. But none of that detracted from her exquisite beauty. A sleeping beauty. Oh, for a handsome prince to wake her with a kiss.

A few miles west, a not so handsome, vertically challenged, definitely non-royal nerd was restless.

The group of housemates returned late having cancelled a planned long weekend camping trip to the lakes of the Elan Valley. Eager for peaceful long walks and campfire singing, they'd abandoned the idea after forecasts of storms, and instead set up camp in the snug at The Railway Tavern.

When they stumbled back after midnight much the worse for wear, they staggered noisily to bed. Loud snores reverberating through the house attested to their slumber.

Neil had fallen asleep before his head touched the pillow but something bothered him. Shaking from side to side he mumbled under his breath, "no, no, no."

A loud crack he wasn't sure hadn't been part of a dream, woke him with a start. He sat up in what should have been the darkness of his bedroom, but in his insobriety, he'd forgotten to switch off the light.

Sitting blinking in the harsh glow emitting from the ceiling, breathless and a touch confused, he debated his options. Now he was aware the light was on, he knew he'd struggle to get back to sleep. At the same time, the idea of getting out of bed and walking the chasm-like few feet to the switch somehow terrified him.

Apart from the thumping in his chest, another noise, equally subtle and equally compelling dented at his wellbeing. His heart attempted to drown out the noise with its hammering response.

Neil shifted reluctantly from the bed. With quivering fingers on the handle, he prepared himself for what he might see when he opened the door. With a sudden rush of movement, he flung it open as though revealing his presence to whomever was there would scare them away.

No-one was there on the landing to scare away. Neil stood, breathing hard. His ears had deceived him in identifying the sound as coming from outside his room. Now he was here, he could tell the source was further up the landing, he suspected from Matthew's room. A scraping, tapping sound he couldn't identify.

"Shit," he exclaimed, clenching his fist into a tight ball. If it was coming from Matthew's room, why wasn't Josh on the landing with him? His room was much closer to the noise.

He knocked on Josh's door a couple of times before remembering that Josh, another all-night gamer would often fall asleep with his surround sound headphones cushioned against his ears. Music, and Halo gun fire, likely blocked out the strange disturbance.

Positive now that the sound was coming from under Matthew's door, rats was his first thought. There had been a lot of food waste. But surely they would leave other signs throughout the house?

He hoped the door wasn't locked. Matthew's dad would've had no reason to lock it unless there was still stuff worth keeping. Neil grabbed the handle. He wasn't frightened of rats. Spiders and moths were his phobias, but the lateness and the uncertainty of exactly what he'd encounter made him nervous.

Turning the handle revealed it was unlocked. Before pushing it open, he stepped back in case a large population were keen to bolt from the room as soon as the door opened. He pushed it lightly with his foot. It swung on its hinges and came to rest almost fully ajar. Neil could see inside. No scurrying little bodies rushed him. The room looked empty.

The scratching, tapping noise continued. It was interspersed with moments of silence and then tap-tapping again. With the door open, he could hear the sound more clearly. It sounded like wood tapping on glass. When he stepped carefully into the room, he realised it wasn't coming from the room, but outside, tapping on the window.

Neil pictured the front of the house. He puzzled at there being no trees close by, yet it sounded like the branch of a tree was drumming the window. He walked across the empty room, his slippered feet echoing eerily.

When he reached the window and took hold of the curtains, he felt sure he knew what he was about to see: he would be reminded of a forgotten branch and could decide what needed doing about it. But drawing back the curtains, what he did see froze him to the spot in terror.

# Chapter Thirty-four

He was there fleetingly, and she was positive he'd seen her. She couldn't afford to let another one go so she tapped again on the glass, trying to be gentle, trying to sound friendly; difficult, given she had to hurtle at the house just to reach it.

It was most unfortunate that it was whilst moving at speed towards the window, brandishing a stick, the curtains opened once more. Elin tried to slow down. Forcing a smile, determined to appear angelic and not-at-all scary. He'd be more inclined to help her then.

His goofy face, drained of any colour, gawped at her through the glass, bulging eyes fit to pop, drinking in the spectacle of her. She did her best to smile sweetly, the stick hidden at her side, but it was too late. His terror was undeniable.

Neil wished he could go back in time so he hadn't seen the faint yet unmistakable form of the girl inexplicably hovering metres above the street outside the window. His mouth opened, jaw on his chest, but no sound came out.

Stumbling backwards, he had to get away, and then she was gone, hurtling away from him fast as lightning.

The curtains still in his hands, strength sapped from his grip, he struggled to draw them closed. Clinging to the fabric in clammy, trembling palms, he tugged, desperately holding them shut, praying it would all go away, that he'd somehow mistaken what he'd seen.

His mind clumped through his thoughts searching for sense. Shaking his head in disbelief and mumbling over and over. "Why? Why is she back?" He had to look again. He had to be sure.

Struggling to tighten his grip on the curtains, with a gulp, he tentatively jerked them aside. Peering out, already flinching at the prospect, a bubble of relief escaped as a nervous peal of laughter when he was greeted by nothing but darkness penetrated only by the yellowish glow of the streetlamp.

But then from a distance, the faint figure of the girl tore towards him. He heard himself cry out as he lurched backwards, but he couldn't wrench his gaze from the window. Closer and closer she moved until she was mere feet away.

Appearing not wholly there, more as though through the crystal water at the bottom of a clear pool, her long blonde hair floating out in an unearthly mane. She gazed directly at him.

The blood that rushed to his brain to help him form a plan for survival now diverted to his icy limbs to run away. Heat in his head drained rapidly like a plunged cafetiere, tiny morsels of courage swimming in the murky waters of his mind. The sudden change left him dizzy, and then he fainted.

He fell to the floor, slowed by his grasp of the curtains which eventually gave way, snapping the plastic hooks and showering them over the floorboards like bouncing plastic hail stones. As his head thumped on the ground, he couldn't be certain, but he thought she smiled at him.

"Neil? What are you doing? Are you all right?"

Josh stood over him. It was morning and he was still lying on the floor of Matthew's old room, covered by a blanket of curtains. The memory of last night hit him like a fist in the face. He blinked away the shock and jumped up, surprising himself with his energy as adrenaline surged through his veins.

"Josh, did you hear anything last night?" Neil demanded. But he hadn't, and having established Neil was okay, was already walking from the room tapping away at his smart phone. There was no point forcing him. Josh talked lucidly about computer coding, but little else.

Arriving downstairs, Bronwyn was sitting down to a breakfast that wouldn't look out of place in a hamster's cage. Neil sat beside her, not knowing how to broach the subject of last night's apparition.

"You want something, Neil?" she asked, chewing the robust mouthful.

"I saw the ghost last night."

Bronwyn put her spoon down and looked straight at him. "Where?"

"I was woken up by a scratching, tapping noise. Tracing it to Matthew's room, I expected to see rats. But when I went in, it was empty. The sound was coming from outside."

Bronwyn gazed at her granola, wondering if Neil was about to say anything that would justify letting it go soggy. She paused briefly, but when he described the floating figure tapping the window, and then how Josh had discovered him this morning, it all struck her as ridiculous. So different to what happened before it didn't make any sense.

"Oh, stop it, Neil!" she said. "We've been having such a good time these past weeks." When she saw his dejected face, she tried to be more tactful. "You did have a lot to drink last night. You most probably sleepwalked, is it?" Neil smiled. He knew he hadn't but there was no getting through to Bronnie if she wouldn't listen.

"Maybe," he agreed noncommittally. Bronwyn pushed her chair back with a flourish, stuffing the last of her cereal in her mouth as she did. She rinsed her bowl and put it away before returning to the living room, giving Neil an affectionate pat on the shoulder on her way to her room.

Neil had little appetite. Recognising the futility of involving Aeron now Bronwyn had spoken, he knew he had to face up to whatever he was to do about their ghost alone

# Chapter Thirty-five

Alis hugged a plastic cup of hot chocolate to her as she sat with her mother beside Elin's bed. She hadn't been back to Erw Lon and there were no plans to either. They hadn't said, but they'd each accepted that if this was the last weekend they'd be able to look upon Elin alive, albeit asleep, they wanted to be here for every minute of it.

When she'd seen her mum she'd tried to encourage her to go home and get some rest. She knew she wouldn't, but the sight of her was shocking. Emyr still looked terrible, not just his waif-like, dishevelled demeanour, but everything he did was laboured and painful to witness.

Collecting plastic cups containing cold, discarded coffee from the wheeled table near Elin's bed, even appearing busy, his troubles were obvious. He moved in slow-motion and struggled to understand the mechanism of the pedal bin, even though he'd used it dozens of times.

He pressed and fumbled around the top of the bin, peering down each side for a clue as to its operation.

"Step on the bar, Dad," Alis was forced to instruct him. He offered a weak smile in gratitude, the corners of his mouth barely turning up in his chalky features.

Slate eyes suggested he'd prefer to remain lost deciphering the bin lid. Free of his litter load, he had no distraction from the gaping gulch of despair upon which he was teetering.

Glenda hadn't the presence of mind for anything as mundane as the removal of her rubbish. Her hand never left Elin's. She stroked it continually, slowly back and fore, up and down and sometimes in circles as if she were about to sing 'round and round the garden.' Emyr fiddled with a pen, spiralling it in his fingers and flicking the button 'on' and 'off' with every turn.

Even Alis had aged five years since stepping from the train. Elin looked unchanged, peaceful and unaware. The only small mercy. All the suffering was theirs and not hers.

Their consciousness caught up with their mindless actions and they paused briefly, each determined not to show their distress in front of Elin, until mindfulness became more than they could cope with and they returned to their fidgeting once again.

A tacit signal between them shook them from their silence. Micro glances of unbearable emotion prompted them to talk, for Elin's sake. Speaking in mock, cheerful tones, they implored her to recognise the importance of what was planned for Monday; how she must wake up and breathe for herself when the doctors switched off her life support system.

Talking hurt. They persevered, like holding a hand over a flame. When they could endure no more, they committed to force themselves later. No response came from Elin. Not a smile, not a twitch, nothing. She lay serenely, silently.

She was never going to wake up, was she? They would lose her forever in just three days, they were certain of it. Emotions were swallowed down with the taste and weight of lead. They had to hope. Until it became too late, they must. So they clenched their fists and hunkered down behind the hero which hope might yet prove to be. Their only faint glimmer; that she could hear them, and she would listen.

Neil could think of nothing else but the girl at the window. The good times they'd had for weeks couldn't continue with her outside. Not just because it was terrifying, but because, there had to be a reason. He'd seen this sort of thing in films. They haunted because there was something they needed doing, or something they needed to be known. The ghost couldn't leave until whatever it was had been done.

Neil knew he'd not rest until he'd helped her. He blushed, hoping he wasn't being influenced by her astonishing beauty. He'd have to be careful not to gush. People might suspect he fancied her! Which of course, he didn't. That would be ridiculous.

He'd been disappointed at Josh and Bronwyn's response but he'd thought of someone else who might react differently. His phone in his hand, he dialled the number. It wasn't long before someone answered.

"Is Matthew there, please?"

"Hold on. I'll get him." The person Neil assumed to be Matthew's mum could be heard clattering. A distant call to come to the phone was followed by a further off response of 'who is it?' echoing in the background. Then footsteps and the clump of the handset being picked up.

Neil could almost feel the warmth of heavy breathing in his ear, the effort of walking to get the phone taking its toll on Matthew's bulk.

"Yeah?" his miserable voice inquired.

"Matthew? It's Neil. I know why you left in such a hurry." The tension could be heard in the sharp intake of air. Neil came clean straight away, not wanting to risk his only ally hanging up. "Matthew? I've seen her too!"

# Chapter Thirty-six

Silence was Matthew's response, but something in the hush, even over the distance of a phone call, told Neil he'd struck a nerve.

"Matthew, I know you saw her. Tapping on the window, the ghost girl, Elin." Still quiet. "Listen, the others don't believe me, but I think she needs help."

"Count me out. I can't help, I can't!"

"So you admit you saw her, then. Good. How about I come over to you. I can drive now. We could grab something to eat somewhere," he said, hoping to tempt his former housemate's appetite, and then added, "my treat," in an effort to clinch the deal.

It worked. They were to meet for a late lunch this afternoon. Luckily, Neil had no lectures today, but he would have been tempted to skip them anyway. Helping Elin had become his priority. There'd be no way he'd settle into his uni work knowing she was there. Who could?

Perhaps speaking to Auntie Sylvie or even Father Jenkins might be a better idea. But apart from his own credibility being questionable, they'd probably take it as an unwelcome criticism of their skills and faith

They would surely emulate Bronwyn and be reluctant to believe him, keen to find other explanations, like he was drunk and had sleepwalked. Matthew's backing was credibility to get help.

It was going to be quite a long drive to the Cotswold Hills, but his camping trips with the others had been good training. After only a few weeks of driving he felt like a pro.

Whilst his dad's car (and pretty much every car he travelled in other than his little Daewoo) benefitted from Bluetooth to connect to his phone and MP3 player (even Aeron's jalopy had a multi-change CD player), Neil's dad had bought as his Christmas present a car so old it boasted a cassette player.

Neil had enjoyed cassettes when he was a kid, his embarrassing parents reminded when he'd shown dismay at the prehistoric technology taking centre stage on his dashboard. His favourite had been 'The wheels on the bus' which he'd apparently insisted on playing everywhere they went.

He had purchased from e-bay, a device which linked a cassette to his phone's headphone socket so he could play his music. It was a relief to be alone in the car. The pop music which was his preference seemed to bother his thrash metal-loving housemates in Swansea, so he took advantage of the solitude and cranked the volume up as high as the buzz-prone speakers would allow.

Fate took a hand in Neil's journey when the musical delight was interrupted by the phone ringing.

"How're you getting on? Where are you?" Neil's instinctive reaction was moderate annoyance at Matthew nagging, but soon was immensely grateful when he realised he was heading the wrong way.

"But, I thought you said you lived in Gloucester?" Neil inquired, confused.

"Gloucestershire," Matthew corrected. "I live in number twelve, Trinder Place, Cirencester, Gloucestershire, you Muppet!" Neil would ask for a sat-nav for his birthday. Fortunately, it was a good half an hour closer than his planned journey. Their late lunch wouldn't be so late after all.

The Cotswold Hills looked stunning in the bright sunshine. He was surprised to see a sight he'd come to associate more with the Brecon Beacons and other hills in Wales—several red kites wheeling in acrobatic circles in the sky.

He followed the signs from the motorway and found Matthew's directions were spot on. As soon as he turned into Trinder Place and began scrutinising doors for a number twelve, the familiar figure of his old housemate came out to greet him. Neil pulled over and he hopped in.

"So, lunch on you, my friend. Don't worry. I know some nice places, not too expensive!"

He was right. The place was lovely. Very quaint, made more so by being overlooked by an enormous gothic church, so large Neil had been amazed wasn't a Cathedral. The setting amongst the mediaeval architecture looked appropriate to their planned discussion of ghosts.

Neil began. "I'm sure she needs our help," he suggested. "I felt her presence even before everyone else knew about her. Before Auntie Sylvie's séance." Matthew nodded, but was distracted by the huge Nacho cheese mountain he was halfway through devouring. Neil hadn't started his sandwich yet. He was keen to get down to business.

"I tried to research girls who might have died in the house and came up with Jacqui, remember?" Matthew managed a grunt to accompany the nod this time. Neil finally took a bite of his lunch and carried on talking, happily letting his manners go in the face of sudden hunger.

"That was incorrect. Auntie Sylvie said her name was Elin, not Jacqui. We'll need her help. But I need you to convince her with me it's worth doing. Will you corroborate my story? Confirm to Auntie Sylvie and the others you saw her too?"

Matthew's chewing slowed for the first time since the waitress plonked their food in front of them.

"I don't know." Sitting back and dabbing his mouth with a paper napkin. "I can't see there's anything we can do. If she doesn't want to leave?"

"I've been thinking about that. I don't think she can go. She needs our help first. It makes sense, doesn't it? There must be something tying her to the house. She didn't die there, it would have come up in obituaries on Google."

"I suppose," Matthew grudgingly agreed, resuming the destruction of his food. "We could do some research. We have a name. You're the I.T. geek. Why don't you start now?"

"Software engineering. Not I.T.," Neil corrected.

"Whatever."

Neil fetched his laptop from his bag and began utilising the free Wi-Fi offered in the café. They justified their stay by ordering coffees. Matthew further pleased the establishment and requested a large slice of cake as well.

"We know where she lived. We know what she looks like and so her approximate age when she died. She might have been a student. We should check the uni database.

Surprisingly, only one Elin popped up on file, and it seemed to be her. Both boys recognised her photo and blushed at how pretty she looked. Elin Treharne had been at Swansea University only recently. Last year, which fact made her passing even more poignant.

"We should have heard about her death, shouldn't we?" Matthew sighed. "If it's that recent, wouldn't it be the talk of the town?"

But Elin Treharne brought no results for obituaries or any other searches for Swansea away from the University database.

"Do you think she was killed somewhere else but loved Swansea, and that's why she stayed?" Neil offered excitedly.

"Why would she love it in student digs?"

"Maybe her home life was bad and Swansea felt like home!"

"Perhaps. But it doesn't sound likely to me." Neil frowned, disappointed at Matthew's lack of enthusiasm before another idea struck him.

"When I researched the other girl, Jacqui, she hadn't lived in the house either, but her boyfriend had or something. Elin could have had a love interest who lived there?"

Matthew nodded, wiping crumbs from his lips "That makes more sense. What do you think she wants us to do, then?" Neil opened and closed his mouth, but he had no answer. "Do more investigation on your laptop. We must be missing something," Matthew griped.

Neil beavered away, trying every search he could think of for Elin Treharne and going through dozens of pages for each one. Surely there must be some clue somewhere why her ghost was haunting 24 Rhondda Street Swansea. There just had to be.

Whether it was the espressos or just spending more time on the problem, Neil didn't know, but one search provided a most unexpected result.

"Shit! Oh my G..." is all Neil managed to say whilst turning the laptop towards Matthew for him to read for himself. Matthew was tucking into some chips and ketchup he'd ordered when the time had dragged on. He peered at the screen through squinting eyes as though it might be hieroglyphics, but he soon cottoned on.

*Local girl in coma. Doctors mystified.*

The headline was eye catching, but Matthew didn't know why his friend had reacted to it until he read further.

*Former Swansea University student, Elin Treharne slipped into a coma on Tuesday night after suffering from a bout of glandular fever…*

*Doctors are unsure of her prognosis, but are encouraged by scans and tests… Our thoughts and prayers are with her family…*

"Shit," Matthew echoed. "But, what does it mean? Our ghost isn't the same Elin? She just looks like her?"

Neil shook his head vigorously. "No. It means we performed an exorcism on Elin and put her in a coma!"

"How can that be possible?"

"I don't know, Matthew. But what if I'm right? She was really ill with glandular fever." Matthew's eyebrows raised in incredulity. "Stay with me," Neil encouraged.

"What if she was close to death and left her body? She came to our house because of some connection to it, and then when we exorcised her, that's when she went into a coma? Look at the date in the newspaper story… it all fits. I'm right! I know it."

A second, more thorough read led Matthew to reconsider his initial scepticism. "The dates do fit. And I can't deny there is a ghost who looks remarkably like this girl, Elin, who tapped on my window. So, I may as well go the whole hog. It's no more preposterous than any other explanation, I suppose."

"More than that. It makes perfect sense."

"You're just hoping you're right and we can be the heroes to revive her from her coma. You think you're a fairy-tale prince about to give the kiss of true love to the beautiful sleeping beauty!"

"Kiss of true love? Don't be stupid." Neil laughed a little too hard.

"Don't think I haven't noticed you mention 'Elin this' and 'Elin the other' a hundred times since lunch. If you're wrong, then you're in love with a ghost!"

Neil reddened even more. "I'm not in love with her," he said unpersuasively. "She is pretty though," his cheeks beetroot as he exposed his true feelings.

Matthew's eyebrows curved into another position, perfectly expressing 'I knew it'. Neil decided he would practice his own eyebrow techniques in the mirror. Matthew's were so effective. The benefits of being a drama student, he supposed.

"What on earth do we do about it, though?"

"Well, I think time is of the essence. She's been in a coma for weeks. How long do they keep you on life support?"

Matthew spat out his hot chocolate and marshmallows in a swell of alarm. "Shit. I don't know. We might have killed her! "

Neil turned the laptop towards his friend again, displaying from the University database Elin's address.

"We should go there. There might be something they can do."

"What if she has died? They wouldn't want to hear how we might have been involved. And we don't know really if our hypothesis has any truth to it. Shouldn't we call your aunt? Or the priest?"

"Maybe. But what would they do? They probably won't even believe us, and if she is still alive in a coma, a psychic and a priest might not be who we need. Don't be a coward. Come on lets go. We can be there in a couple of hours."

Neil made sure he entered the address into Google before they left, not drive in the general direction and then look, as he'd foolishly done on the way to Matthew's.

"Are you sure you're okay to drive? You've already driven a long way today."

"Come on. I'll be fine, but we have to get there ASAP!" Matthew desperately rushed his hot chocolate and Neil paid as he'd promised he would. He hadn't planned on staying for quite so long and buying quite so much, though. He'd make sure Matthew paid for something else. It was only fair.

"It's closer than Swansea. We shouldn't make bad time if the M4 isn't too busy. Here, you can be the navigator," Neil said, passing over his phone with the map on the screen.

The motorway, when they joined it, appeared quiet as they had hoped. They crossed the Second Severn Crossing back into Wales a little after six o'clock. They were making good time when the traffic approaching Cardiff slowed dramatically.

An accident involving a jack-knifed car transporter spread over both carriageways, according to Google.

"It doesn't matter. We'll get there when we get there," Neil resigned.

"We should've come over the Severn Bridge on the M48."

"You're the navigator. It's no good saying that now. Chill out and find something on the radio."

"I'm hungry."

"We'll get food after our mission. It's important."

"But I'm really starving. I can't wait 'til then!"

Matthew agreed stopping at services en route would have to do.

They'd been stationary for at least half an hour before the traffic moved an inch. A bing-bong warning sound coincided with an amber symbol of a petrol pump flashing on the dash. Neil glanced nervously at it.

"Shit."

"At least I know you'll definitely stop at the nearest garage now," Matthew chortled.

"If we make it to one in time." Shaking his head, Neil decided on a more positive outlook. "I'm sure there'll be plenty as soon as we get moving," he declared.

Another half an hour went by before they managed to pull off the motorway and limped into the nearest filling station.

"I'll need some fuel money. I spent most of mine on your lunch!"

"I'll go inside and get some snacks while you fill up. I'll pay for it all if you like."

Neil wasn't sure if Matthew had meant 'fill up,' so he played it safe with twenty quid's worth. Matthew came out before Neil made it inside the shop, carrying a bulging carrier bag.

"Don't worry. I bought enough for you, too," he announced.


"No thank you!" Neil exclaimed to the umpteenth offer of food from his passenger as he opened a family pack of pasties.

"You sure? They're really yummy." Neil tried not to be annoyed. He was sure Matthew hadn't been this much of a pig at Uni. When all this was over, maybe he'd come back to his studies. He probably needed the distraction.

The house was difficult to find. After a few cross words and stopping to ask several strangers for directions, they were both surprised when they were suddenly very close.

"Here it is," they declared in unison as Neil pulled into the driveway. "Do you think anyone's home?"

"There's a car in the drive so I guess so. But there's only one way to find out." Matthew brushed crumbs from his clothes, easing himself from the little car. Neil's keys rattled against the door as his shaking hand struggled to find the keyhole and lock the car. "No-one will steal it," Matthew teased. "You okay, mate?"

Neil nodded, attempting a reassuring smile which displayed as a grimace on his pale green features. "Mm hmm," he managed, unconvincingly.

"Come on, dude," Matthew encouraged. "You have a damsel in distress to save."

Suddenly, the gravitas of confronting Elin's distraught parents and admitting culpability in their daughter's dismal plight was too much.

"Will you do the talking? I don't think I can."

"Sure, buddy. No problem."

With a pang of regret at his previous antipathy towards his bombastic companion, he decided Matthew was now his favourite person. His super-confidence was a real asset.

With the pressure off, Neil was happy to walk behind his friend. The few steps to the door took forever. Neil felt like his namesake, Neil Armstrong, taking a giant leap for mankind. He couldn't have felt more out of his depth if he was on the moon. Gripping onto Matthew's sleeve for balance, he felt an overwhelming giddiness of expectation when the door was knocked.

Several hours, or seconds, passed before they detected movement and someone was heard shuffling towards the door. It opened a crack and was halted abruptly by a chain. Eyes peered out at them from the four inch gap between door and frame. Encased within pale, lined skin, they shone with acuity and vigour.

"Oh, good evening. Mrs Treharne?" Matthew began with his inimitable charm. "My name is Matthew, and this is Neil," he indicated behind him with a nod in Neil's direction.

"We are students from the same university as your daughter. There are some things we'd like to discuss with you; something we need to tell you."

Through the crack, her eyes expressed concern and disbelief. The door closed abruptly.

The pair stood on the doorstep, not sure what to do next. Matthew considered knocking again, wondering how he could without seeming pushy, when it opened again. This time, it wasn't prohibited by the chain and opened fully to reveal the owner of the twinkly eyes.

She was older than either of them had expected. Older than their own mums, certainly. She looked them up and down a couple of times, deciding if they were telling the truth, but why wouldn't they be?

"You'd better come in, then," she said, finally.

# Chapter Thirty-seven

They followed her into a large reception hall. She walked along the hallway and disappeared. Neil expected he should close the door, then headed after her. In the room she'd ducked into, she sat behind a table, staring into the distance.

She didn't look up when they entered. Neither did she invite them to sit. After a minute nervously fiddling with the ends of his shirt, Matthew asked if it was okay to take a seat. Neil, who's own fiddling with his shirt, pockets, and hair had reached psychotic proportions, followed his lead and pulled out a chair.

The lady turned towards them, startling them with the suddenness of movement. Slapping her hands, palm down on the table, with a friendly, but 'don't suffer fools gladly' look on her face, she spoke.

"Now, what is it you two boys have to tell me?"

Using the word 'boys' seemed deliberate; so they'd understand that was how she saw them. The put-down was hardly necessary. They felt far less than men themselves. Even Matthew's confidence struggled with the tension. How would she react to hearing what they had to say? They had a duty to Elin regardless.

"I'll start at the beginning if that's okay?"

"That's usually the best place to start, I always find," the lady replied, as though Matthew was already testing her patience. He stuttered slightly when he resumed speaking, his edginess shattering what was left of Neil's poise.

"I… It all began before Christmas. There'd been some strange goings on in our student house: Weird noises in the middle of the night, things being moved from where we'd left them. Not being able to find Uni-work and stuff.

"Then it got worse—cups and plates smashed on the floor, washing thrown everywhere." The lady sat, taking it all in with an unblinking stare.

"I blamed the other students being careless with other people's things. Neil, here, wondered if we might have a poltergeist. A house meeting was called and we decided we probably had a rat problem instead.

"We cleaned meticulously so we could stop attracting them. I should say at this point, there were no other signs. No droppings, no chewing or anything. Anyway," Matthew was getting into his stride now. The woman's expression had softened, and he'd felt assured to carry on with more of his drama-student verve.

"When I went home for Christmas, something obviously happened because Neil phoned me early in the New Year saying we were to have a séance. What happened, Neil?" Neil's eyes widened. Gulping, he couldn't believe he was required to speak, but with the expectant eyes of Matthew and the lady of the house baring down upon him, he felt himself succumb to the pressure. He cleared his throat before telling his part.

"I was going home for Christmas too, a couple of days after Matthew. My dad and my little sister, Emma, came to collect me. After the long trip, they stopped for coffee, well Dad did. Emma had a milkshake or something. But anyway, when we left, Emma asked me who the girl was in our lounge… not Bronwyn, she's our housemate, but someone else.

"We know now, she was describing your daughter. We saw pictures of her in uni records, and in the story relating to her being in a coma…" Neil flinched at his tactlessness. The lady's eyes moistened, but she said nothing. "Sorry," Neil offered, feebly.

Matthew, concerned at his friend's ineptness, took over the telling again.

"Neil called all the housemates together for this séance where his Auntie Sylvie—who's psychic—confirmed we did have a poltergeist. It was pretty compelling," he said with a glint in his eye as though admitting it for the first time.

"Plates rattled, plants flew across the room. When we heard a disembodied voice scream at us to get out, we did. Rapidly. That's when Neil's auntie said we needed a priest." He stopped, breathless. The memory of it disturbing him.

"We have a poltergeist," the lady announced, surprising them both. "She moves the curtains. It's the lady who used to live here. I don't know why. I didn't know she'd died, but I suppose she must have." Matthew and Neil gasped. Maybe their incredible story wouldn't be so difficult to accept.

"She doesn't want me here. I'm sure of it. You can feel her. Not all the time. My husband thinks I'm mad."

"Well we don't, obviously. To be honest, it's a relief to hear you talk like this. I was worried you wouldn't believe us." The lady returned to her staring silence. Matthew took it as permission to continue.

"A priest came and performed an exorcism. It was quiet after that. For weeks, anyway. But then one night I saw her. Tapping on my window with a stick. A very faint apparition, but that made it more chilling.

"I regret to say, it was too much for me and I went back home to my parents." Guilt at Elin's predicament tweaked his conscience. "I didn't know it was your daughter then, of course." It was his turn to offer a feeble, "Sorry."

"I saw her too. Tapping on Matthew's window. Last night. I knew then why Matthew had left in such a hurry. I couldn't blame him," Neil piped up, suddenly full of confidence. They were about to get to the important bit: how Elin might wake up thanks to his brilliant deductions. Feeling like the hero of the hour, he filled her in on how he'd gone straight to Matthew's house and, together, they'd pieced it all together.

"So now we're sure it was the exorcism that put your daughter in her coma. She must have, somehow, become disconnected from her body. She had glandular fever, didn't she?" he looked for conformation. It froze his heart seeing the distress in her eyes, staring into the distance with needle precision.

A man walked into the kitchen. When he saw his wife's face he stopped abruptly.

"Everything okay, dear?" he asked.

The lady shook her head. "These boys have put our Karen in a coma. They said she was haunting their student house, so they exorcised her, and now she's in a coma!" she let out a wail of despair, turning away, trembling fingers moulding her colourless lips.

The man glared at the two boys. "What have you said to her?" He looked angry. "Come on, Stella. Karen isn't in a coma, now is she? She was here only this afternoon. Admittedly you didn't know who she was for most of the visit," he muttered under his breath.

Confusion overwhelmed them. "Mr Treharne?" Matthew enquired, but he couldn't think who else he could be.

"Mr Treharne used to live here. About eighteen months ago. My wife thinks Mrs Treharne is haunting us, but I don't even think she's dead! Not that I believe in ghosts anyway, of course. So, what have you two lads been saying to upset my wife?"

"Sorry. Er, nothing. It's all been a mis-understanding."

"She gets terribly confused, you see?" the man said. Neil and Matthew nodded quickly in unison, pushing their chairs back to leave. "Yes, we're so, so sorry for the upset. Very sorry."

"Do you know where the Treharne's live now?"

Neil glared at Matthew. He wanted to know but it seemed callous in the circumstances.

"In Wales. Llan something or other. Llandudno? No that's not right. Oh, I don't know. Please leave us in peace. I'll have to calm down my wife now."

With further apologies they left the old couple in the kitchen and bid a hasty farewell. Neil reversed the car from the driveway and roared down the road. At the first layby, he pulled in abruptly. Turning off the engine, he sat back hard, breathing heavily and staring at the ceiling.

After a moment to compose himself, he tore his gaze away and looked at his friend who was staring back, eyebrows raised so high they mingled with his fringe.

"Now what?"

# Chapter Thirty-eight

They hadn't left Elin's bedside once. Always one, usually two and frequently all three of them were at her side. They had different ideas for permeating her subconscious. Alis played her favourite music whilst Glenda concentrated on her sense of smell, knowing how that can often be the most evocative of the five senses. She ordered her favourite foods, as well as suntan lotion, different perfumes, and anything else they could think of to alert her.

Emyr read. He didn't share his daughter's passion, but he did his best to read out loud one of the novels he found crammed into the drawers of her bedside table. He wasn't sure if she'd already read it but didn't suppose it mattered. He found the plot confusing, made worse by his lack of orating skill, but he hoped hearing the words would please Elin somewhere in her core.

At the end of an exhausting day, Emyr and Alis would take turns sleeping in the dayroom. Glenda only left her daughter's side to use the toilet, and that she managed to limit to only once a day.

Tonight, rest was impossible despite their immense fatigue. Tomorrow would be harder, and Sunday? That might be the last chance of sleep any of them would ever get.

"We could go straight to the hospital. I don't know why we didn't do that in the first place."

"Because we had an address we thought was right. It might be impossible to get anywhere near her in Intensive Care or wherever coma patients are treated. That's if we knew which hospital she was even in."

"I hadn't considered that," Neil admitted. "There're three hospitals just in Swansea, and she might live closer to Aberystwyth, or Bangor, or Cardiff, or God knows…"

The blip-blip of Neil's phone declaring it would soon shut down due to low battery echoed alarmingly. Without it, he couldn't make any calls to find Elin, and charging it meant returning to the house. The idea of walking past her spirit outside terrified him, and he didn't need to ask to know how Matthew felt.

"I'm not going there! My parents will fret if I stay in Swansea with you," Matthew vehemently protested. "I haven't been too well." Staring at the floor, embarrassed, he brightened and made his own suggestion. "Why don't you stay at mine? You can use my charger. We can use the house phone. Then tomorrow, we can drive to wherever she is from mine." Neil nodded, happy an excuse had arrived, even though Cirencester was a lot further.

"Great idea. We don't want your parents to worry."

Matthew's mum and dad were more than happy to have him stay, and included him in the family tradition of Friday fish and chips. "You'll love 'em, Neil. Better than any you can find in Swansea," Matthew enthused. Neil wondered what was so special. He soon learned it was the enormous portion sizes.

The unmistakable waft of vinegar reached their noses as Neil's dad bustled into the kitchen with steaming paper parcels. "They didn't have a jumbo cod, love. I got you two normal ones instead. Alright?" Matthew looked disappointed, appeased with an extra saveloy.

Neil attracted concerned looks from his hosts at his tiny appetite. "Are you not keen on fish, Neil? It's good for you; brain food." Not deep fried in batter it's not, Neil kept to himself. "Do you want something else? I could rustle up a sandwich if you like?" Matthew's mum offered.

"Thank you. I'm just not hungry. Sorry."

After dinner they tried a few numbers and learned Hospital switchboards were closed until morning. The porters who answered didn't have access to patient information. They'd have to phone tomorrow.

They didn't remember falling asleep but must have done, because they awoke to the wonderful aroma of a full English breakfast. And when Matthew's mum said full, she meant full. Apart from the pile of fried food on their plates was a bigger pile in hot trays in the centre of the table for seconds, thirds and even fourths.

"I hope you slept okay, Neil," Matthew's dad inquired through mouthfuls of sausage and bacon. A trickle of liquid (a combination of baked bean sauce, tomato ketchup, brown sauce, and egg yolk) dribbled down his chin and onto his shirt, pooling into a nauseating stain.

Neil uttered a polite "yes, thank you" and returned the sentiment, trying not to be mesmerised by the ever-growing blemish.

"What are you two up to today, then? Will you give me a hand clearing the garden? I need to get things ready for spring."

"Sorry, Dad," Matthew answered, unimpeded by his astonishingly full mouth. "Me and Neil have some important work to do." His dad nodded in understanding, not bothering to inquire its nature.

They washed the hearty breakfast down with enough coffee to keep them awake and alert for the foreseeable future. Retiring to Matthew's room, they both flipped open their laptops.

Having phoned the most obvious hospital choices last night and been fobbed off until today, research into possibilities had also been postponed. Tapping away at laptop keys for answers, it didn't take either of them long to complete a comprehensive list.

Then the inevitable task of telephoning them. Matthew sighed, resigned to making the calls. Neil wouldn't conquer his shyness under such pressure. "Which one shall we start with?" he pondered.

Neil shrugged. It wasn't fair to offer an opinion as he wouldn't be the one phoning. "Whichever you think," he said with another shrug.

Matthew dialled at Neil's first shrug and was listening intently to some robotic instructions.

"Oh, good afternoon. I'm inquiring after a friend of mine, Elin Treharne? I believe she may be in your care. Came in about six weeks ago. She's in a coma."

Neil waited, breathless for any confirmation.

"Okay. Thank you very much," he said, and pressed the 'end call' button. He looked dourly at the floor. It was an exaggeratedly despondent display for only the first phone call, so Neil wasn't altogether surprised when his face suddenly brightened and he yelled, "Bingo!"

"Wow. That was lucky. First call. Where is she then?"

Matthew gave a scornful look. "Swansea. Morriston. It was the most likely, wasn't it?"

Neil nodded.

"Great. We can go today then. Sort this mess out."

Matthew almost laughed at his friend's grey pallor. "Don't worry. It'll be fine. I'm sure."

They pulled into the confusing hospital car park a little before four o'clock.

"Where the f'ing hell are we meant to park. Where are we heading, again?"

"The receptionist said to head for Intensive Care, but added she thought she'd been moved."

"We'll head there and ask. It can't be far."

290

Parking in what a large sign declared to be 'car park four,' they entered the building at the nearest entrance and consulted the map on a noticeboard which greeted them.

"I don't believe it!" Neil exclaimed when he spotted the 'you are here' arrow. "We've parked about as far away as it's possible to park. We may as well have walked from Gloucestershire!"

They set off, re-consulting maps whenever they came across them. A juxtaposition of old and new greeted them in a cold and spooky corridor which must have dated from Victorian times and probably hadn't seen a coat of paint since.

"You okay? Do you need any help?" a friendly uniformed man asked them.

"Er… Intensive Care. Our friend's in a coma."

"That'll be The High Dependency Unit, HDU, you'll want. It's up on Pembroke Ward. You're a long way away. Follow me. I'm going that way."

When they arrived, breathless, outside the ward, they thanked their Sherpa profusely.

"We wouldn't have made it without you!"

He grinned at them and carried on to wherever he was headed.

They looked at one another, the magnitude of what was required of them clear in the pin-hole pupils of their steely eyes. Neil's pitiful expression prompted Matthew. "Don't worry. I'll do the talking. But back me up. I may need to lie."

They walked to the door of the ward, surprised to find it unlocked, but it was explained when it didn't lead anywhere directly. The corridor forked, one way required intercom clearance to enter.

"That must be it," Neil declared. Matthew nodded and pressed the buzzer. A lengthy thirty seconds passed before a curt voice answered.

"Yes? May I help you?"

"Good afternoon," and then he added in stilted Welsh, "Prynhawn Dda. We're here to see Miss Elin Treharne."

"Are you a relative?"

"Cousins." His mouth dried at the lie and he hoped he wouldn't be asked to repeat himself. The tell-tale buzz/click of the door entry system promptly allowed them access. Matthew pushed it quickly before it re-locked, and then they were inside.

They paused and shared a look of trepidation. The next room might hold the comatose body of the spirit who had haunted them for months. It was impossible not to be terrified, not least of how they'd explain their presence face to face with her family.

"What should we say?" Neil hissed.

"The sooner we get to the truth, the better. Come on."

A nurse smiled and approached them. She didn't speak, but her raised eyebrows alluded to her inquiry.

"Elin Treharne. Where might we find her?" Neil forced himself to speak this time. He needed to step up if he was to claim the hero's welcome headed his way.

"Of course," the nurse relaxed into her reply. "The last door on the right, past that pillar and through the double doors." She waited to check they had understood before bustling off.

The corridor stretched infinitely ahead. The double doors growing terrifyingly until they were inches away from what lay beyond. Neil, dreading how he'd feel on the other side, pushed it hard anyway, reminding himself of some tough private eye in a film.

A few feet from them, a man stood, gazing through a window. Behind him, on one of a row of waiting room chairs sat a girl, about their own age. A familiarity made them think she must be Elin's sister. As they approached, she and the man stared at them, or rather through them. They didn't know they were there for Elin.

Neil and Matthew stopped, ready to speak, but the sight that dominated the man's gaze now occupied theirs.

She was there. The other side of the glass and a few feet away, but unmistakeably her. The girl they'd both seen floating outside their house. So surreal. Neil suppressed the urge to tap on the glass and say "Hi, do I know you?"

"Who are you?" the man challenged, too haggard to be aggressive. Neil looked away from the window with a start.

"We're friends... of Elin's. From University."

The man's face softened, pleased the need to challenge had passed, and glad there was someone else to share his burden. Tears streaming down his face, Emyr pulled away from the impromptu hug he had besieged upon Neil.

"Sorry. Sorry."

Neil's arms remained outstretched and stiff. "No worries," he said, relieved that their presence had been so gladly received.

"How is she?" Matthew asked indelicately.

Emyr simply waved his hand in Elin's direction.

"You can see for yourself. We're going to lose her." Darting his eyes away, he almost let out another sob, but sucked it back in.

"We don't know that, Dad. There's still hope." Elin's sister squeezed his arm. An awkwardness befell Matthew and Neil. Matthew overcame it by stating their purpose.

"There is hope. We think we know why Elin is how she is. Can we go somewhere comfortable and talk?"

Alis and Emyr stared blankly at the boys who were supposedly Elin's friends. They didn't think she'd ever mentioned them, but what harm could it do to listen? With a glance towards Glenda, and seeing her transfixed, staring into Elin's sleeping face, Emyr shrugged.

"We can go in the family room, I suppose."


The four of them sat in an uncomfortable bubble. Matthew's attempts at relieving the strain by offering a reason why Elin had slipped into a coma served only to inflate the bubble until it strained to bursting.

"How dare you waltz in here suggesting such irrelevant nonsense? We have to come to terms with my daughter, and Alis's wonderful sister, never waking up again, and you two buffoons arrive and suggest she's already a ghost! She's not dead yet for heaven's sake!" Emyr stormed from the room, leaving them with Alis.

"My sister has never mentioned either of you. And we're close. Very close. I don't know why you've come. Bloody trolls. Getting some sought of thrill out of this, are you? You make me sick."

And then they were alone.

"That went well," Matthew pronounced.

Neil's moist eyes couldn't focus on his friend and he was too upset to speak. Forcing down the lump in his throat, "What now?" he sighed for the second time today, but this time, neither of them knew.

# Chapter Thirty-nine

"**D**ad! Are you all right?" Alis rushed after Emyr as she spotted him down the corridor. She placed a comforting hand on his shoulder. When he turned round, his face was ashen and the strain of emotion palpable in his severe countenance.

"What are we going to do, cariad? What are we going to do if she doesn't wake up?"

"Auntie Sylvie, listen! I know it sounds ridiculous. And I know you and the priest both saw the ghost leave. But we've both seen her, Matthew and me, and we have to do something to save her. Her dad and sister won't listen to us, but they might listen to you."

"You want me to come all the way to Swansea on a preposterous whim?"

"Er… Yes. It might not be a whim, Auntie Sylvie. And a girl's life could be at stake. I may be able to get them to listen to you on the phone… save you coming…"

"No. She needs to come," Matthew insisted. He had just returned to the family room from a brief foray into the corridor in search of a vending machine. "I heard them talking. They're convinced she'll never wake up. They're going to switch off her life support on Monday morning!"

"You heard who talking?"

"Her sister and her dad."

"Please, you need to come. I can drive and get you if you need. Or my dad can bring you. But we need you. Elin needs you." There was a brief pause whilst Sylvie weighed her options.

"I'll come. But if we're about to make utter fools of ourselves offending the girl's grieving family, then I don't want your mum or dad involved. It'll be our little secret. Okay?"

"Okay."

"I don't know what time I'll arrive in Swansea, but I'm sure it'll be late, after ten  You may want me to speak to them tomorrow."

"Maybe. But it is extremely urgent."

Neil put his phone back in his pocket.

"We might as well get ourselves down to the canteen," Matthew declared. "I'm starving."


"Who were you talking to?"

Emyr's eyes darted towards Alis. He was sure Glenda must have seen the boys, and he hadn't thought of a cover story. But he was determined his wife shouldn't be bothered by their obscene nonsense. He dismissed them as another patient's temporarily lost visitors, and Alis backed him up.

Glenda accepted it, and continued her vigil, staring at her daughter, mindlessly counting down the hours until she may never be able to ever again.

"Come on, cariad. You need a break. Why don't you…"

"No!" The force of the objection made them both jump.

"Come on, Mam. You'll make yourself ill."

"No," she insisted again. "I'm not leaving her. You two rest if you want, but I'm staying here." She caressed Elin's hair tenderly. "She needs me." Her voice broke as she spoke, and she hid her face in the crook of her arm.

Emyr couldn't bear seeing the love of his life so distraught. And his wonderful daughter. He'd loved her as soon as Glenda presented the stick with 'pregnant' written in its little window nearly twenty-four years ago. Even before, when she was still just a twinkle in his eye.

They'd talked about having her. Planned it meticulously. Picked names, even some boy ones, in case their instincts were wrong. But they knew she was a girl. A beautiful angel child. They had always known. There had been scares early in the pregnancy, but she was born strong, even though a month premature.

She wasn't some accident. She was a hoped and prayed for miracle. And now she lay motionless, within his touch, but beyond reach. He looked away and walked back out of the room. It was more than he could endure.

"I'm in Swansea, and in a taxi on my way to the hospital. Where will I find you?" Neil told her the layout of the hospital was more confusing than Sudoku, and that he and Matthew would meet her at the main entrance.

They were soon all together. Neil let out a sigh of relief.

"What exactly do you want me to say? Bearing in mind I am a bit sceptical."

"You should believe us," Neil said in mild indignation, knowing there was no chance she'd turn round and make the long journey home. "We both saw exactly the same thing, independently, and weeks apart."

Sylvie's eyebrows folded and her mouth curved in acknowledgement that her nephew might not have imagined it. "What precisely did you two see?"

Their independent testimonies convinced her. Disappointment in her psychic powers had to be deferred. There were grieving parents and a fierce sister to convince—to let them save Elin's life.

They arrived back on Pembroke ward unchallenged. The scant staff who saw them must have assumed only family would be here at this late hour. The corridor outside Elin's room was empty. As they approached, they could see the family standing beside Elin's bed in a group hug, looking like they were saying goodbye.

Sylvie gasped. "It's her!" Neil and Matthew gave an 'I told you so' smile. "I know you're telling the truth now. I'm sorry I doubted you. You did absolutely the right thing bringing me here. That's definitely the girl I saw as a spirit leaving your house all those weeks ago. That is definitely the same Elin. We have to help her."

Sylvie hoped the three in the room would notice the three of them standing self-consciously outside the room and come and speak to them. When they didn't, she was forced to tap gently on the window.

Emyr was furious to see the two intruders again. A hand from his wife stopped him.

"They've come back. They weren't lost, were they?" Emyr opened his mouth to say but words failed him.

"What do they want?" she asked coldly, in full acknowledgement of the lie she'd been told. Not anticipating an answer from her husband or her daughter, she got up from her place beside Elin and walked to the door.

Whatever they wanted must be important to still be here. She did her very best to place a smile on her face. Less than convincing, but the effort was welcome. She stepped out into the corridor and stood before them.

"You've been here all afternoon. You must have a reason. Would you like to tell me what it is?"

Sylvie offered her warmest smile. "Shall we sit in the family room? Or perhaps we could buy you a coffee?"

"The canteen's closed, but there are vending machines," Matthew offered considerately.

For the first time in what seemed an eternity, Glenda accepted the offer to leave the tiny prison and relieve her body with sustenance. Something in the group's demeanour comforted her.

They walked in silence along the corridor. Emyr and Alis stayed behind in disgrace. If whatever these people had to say was significant, there'd be hell to pay.

Glenda ate hungrily a cheese and ham sub roll, several cups of milky coffee, and a hot chocolate. As an explorer returning from a food-short expedition, her taste was heightened. This was the best roll and coffee she'd ever tasted.

Away from the stifling horror of her daughter's sick bed; and with nourishment coursing its way through her exhausted body, Glenda felt much more herself. She leaned back in her plastic chair and declared she was ready to listen. The two boys sat back also, leaving the explanation to the greater credibility of Auntie Sylvie.

"What we're about to tell you will seem unbelievable, but please hear us out. It could be of great consequence."

Glenda nodded she would.

"I'm Sylvie, and I'm psychic. Not professional or anything, but my gift is well established and respected in my circle." Glenda tensed and tried not to be put off. Whilst she was happy to concede ghosts may be real— she was still struggling with the horrible atmosphere in her own hallway—she had always mistrusted psychics as charlatans.

She wouldn't be content leaving without knowing what this woman wanted to tell her, so decided she may as well just hear her out. Her face softened as she unclenched her jaw and attempted to replace her smile. Sylvie took her cue and told her everything, "...so after the priest performed the exorcism, the disturbances stopped."

She turned to Matthew and Neil. "You two should say what happened next." Matthew sat forward and cleared his throat. He described the tapping on the window, then seeing the beautiful, ethereal girl, floating outside. Neil took over the telling, and they were soon onto how they realised what must have transpired.

"We thought she might have been a student. Twenty-four Rhondda Street has been a student property for years. It seemed a reasonable assumption. We thought research might show us what she wanted, why she hadn't really gone after the exorcism.

"We soon recognised Elin's picture from University records. She's quite unmistakeable." Glenda smiled genuinely at the compliment to her daughter. "We searched obituaries, hoping to find a clue to her angst, maybe in the manner of her death..." Neil's throat constricted, recognising how difficult this must be for Elin's mother to hear.

"It took a while, but then we found out she wasn't dead at all, but was lying in a coma. And the date matched when we'd called the priest! He ordered her out of the house and into the light. I think she only went as far as the light at the end of our path! And she's been stranded there ever since."

Glenda's initial response was anger. Elin being a ghost was intrinsic in her having passed away; a possibility she was unwilling to face.

"But Elin isn't dead. The doctors are hopeful she'll wake up when they turn off her life support, so how could she be haunting your house?" Her assured tone was unpersuasive. Her curiosity piqued. Might it be true?

"We've considered that," Neil declared. "I read that Elin had suffered from glandular fever, and I thought she might have left her body prematurely. I mean, no-one knows exactly when the soul leaves the body, do they? And loads of people have reported out-of-body experiences when doctors are working to resuscitate them.

"I think whilst Elin was having such an experience, when she was really ill with the fever, we exorcised her and put her in limbo. We need to reconnect her with her body somehow so she can wake up."

Glenda so wanted to believe them. If it were true and they could just call the priest and she'd have her baby back... But it didn't make sense.

"Elin's been in a coma for seven weeks. Prior to that, she'd been making a steady recovery. Not close to death and in need of resuscitation. You say the haunting was going on before Christmas when Elin was better than she'd been in ages. So, as romantic as it seems, it's not possible, is it?"

Whilst Neil and Sylvie looked dejected, Matthew fidgeted with excitement.

"Before we came here, we went to see you at your house. We got it from the uni computer, and of course it was your old address. We had a confusing conversation with the lady who lives there. She appears to be suffering from dementia, but something she said suddenly makes perfect sense to me."

The other's stared, rapt. "She said she hadn't realised you had died—you!" he pointed at Glenda. "She said the lady who used to live there must have died because she was haunting the place! She'd seen you moving the curtains!"

It galvanised into a rapidly forming idea within Glenda. She almost yelped in delight.

"I dream of that house. I loved it. Didn't want to leave. I see the new owner in my dreams, and I know she can see me. That's why I tug the curtains and open and close doors… to scare her. I imagined it was real, but it couldn't be, could it?"

Further recollection hammered at her brain. "Elin dreamt of your house. She couldn't understand why. I'd told her about my dreams, how it felt so real travelling to our old house in Bridgend, and I did believe it was real. Why didn't I realise? I should have realised. We even fell out over it." Her fervour faded briefly at the memory of being cross with her lovely girl and what had happened since.

"She said she had no connection to her old house. Didn't even like it. Much messier in her dreams than how she remembered it, she said" Matthew let out an untimely guffaw.

"The situation improved a lot after we had a good tidy-up. We thought we had rats!"

"So," Glenda continued. "Elin was having dreams about your house, and somehow, just as with me, part of her actually travelled and did the things she dreamt she was doing."

"And now she's trapped outside in the streetlight," Neil reiterated, keen to remind everyone that this now accepted theory was his first.

"When you assumed she was a ghost and she was stuck at the house because she needed you to do something," Sylvie said. "You may have been onto something." They all frowned. "Glenda said she deliberately dreams about her old house, wishing it was still hers." The perplexed expressions remained.

"Elin couldn't understand why she kept dreaming of her old student house, she didn't wish she was still there, but maybe there's something she needs to do. Something she hadn't done when she lived there and feels guilty for. How was she with her studies? Up to date?" Glenda nodded.

"She did very well until her illness."

"Maybe that's it," Matthew ventured. "She felt healthy when she was a student and was trying to reconnect with feeling that way again."

"Yeah, she might associate living there with being well and independent. Not ill and living at home with mum and dad," Neil added.

With wide appreciative eyes, Sylvie agreed. "It makes as much sense as anything else, doesn't it? The important thing now is to reconnect Elin's spirit with her body. Any ideas?"

"If the priest sent her out," Neil recapped, "he can send her back in again. Yes?" Sylvie wasn't so sure.

"He didn't want to get involved in the first place, saying he needed clearance from the Bishop. I was sceptical when you told me. Father Jenkins will probably be completely unconvinced, so we're on our own." Neil and Matthew looked close to tears. Glenda's jaw clenched in acceptance.

"It might be a good thing. We don't have to wait for anyone. We can get on with things right away," Sylvie said with confident assurance.

"Why did you need the priest before, then?" Glenda asked, one cynical eyebrow arched.

Sylvie considered a moment, eyes squinting skywards as though for Divine inspiration. "We didn't. We only thought we did. We thought we had a demonic presence who wanted to harm us. Now we know exactly who we're dealing with. There's nothing we need Father Jenkins for."

"What should we do?"

"I'm not sure, but going to Elin's bedside and trying to connect with her spirit couldn't be a bad idea." Glenda had another moment of internal conflict, wrestling with letting a psychic interfere with her beloved child. But she was immensely grateful really. She knew she had no choice but to trust Sylvie, so she led the way back to the High Dependency Unit.

A pensive Emyr and Alis looked up from Elin as they returned, unoptimistic for Glenda's mood after enduring the nonsense from these strangers. When they saw her, flush faced and bright eyed, they couldn't quite believe it.

Glenda, impatient with their plan, didn't have the energy to be angry with them. She'd save that for when she had time to focus properly. That they sent the only hope for Elin's recovery away without consulting her was unforgiveable.

Sylvie and the two boys crowded in behind her. A nurse would almost certainly object if they'd seen. But there was little for nurses to do this late at night. They seemed to assume Glenda, Emyr or Alis would alert them if anything changed, which of course, they would.

While they had the chance in the relative silence: the HDU was full of beeps and bustling care at any time of day or night, they were instructed by Sylvie to join hands in a circle around Elin. Emyr and Alis didn't dare object. They were just thrilled they might be about to do something positive. If it was good enough for Glenda, it was good enough for them.

When they'd formed a circle, Sylvie took charge, instructing everyone to close their eyes and focus their thoughts on Elin. Then she began.

"We are gathered here, in this circle of Divinity, to reconnect Elin with her body. To bring her together and make her whole and happy again. Elin. Please hear our call. We are here, now, with your body. You need to come back. You need to re-join with your body and wake up. Wake up, Elin. Wake up."

She repeated similar affirmations and instructions for a while before stopping abruptly. They all opened their eyes again and looked at her for further instruction. When they observed her expression they knew none were forthcoming.

"She's not here," she despaired. "Elin's spirit isn't here."

# Chapter Forty

"She's at the house. Outside in the streetlight of course," Neil reminded them. "We'll have to go there to connect." He had surprised himself with his outburst. Was he really volunteering to go back to where he'd been so terrified and try to make contact?

He'd done it before, and that was when he thought she was a ghost. Now he knew she was just a beautiful girl who'd become trapped in a dream, that didn't sound scary.

"We can't all go. Someone must wait here and make sure the doctors are au fait with our plan. We can't have them... interfering," Sylvie advised as tactfully as possible.

Glenda decided Alis should stay. Emyr's stability creaked under the strain. Alis's level headedness was what was needed.

"Nothing will happen if we're not here. They can't switch off Elin's life support without our written consent. But just be here to make sure, okay?" Glenda checked with her youngest daughter before glancing once more at her eldest, and leaving the room and the hospital for the first time in weeks.

Squeezing together, filling all the seats in Emyr's car, the group tension was palpable. But as the engine started and they drove away, it was their driver on the precipice of insanity. Although only a couple of miles to Rhondda Street, and this late, virtually no traffic, his eyes darted from side to side at every junction and roundabout, not trusting his senses that the way was clear.

Nights without sleep allowed themselves to take their toll in the face of the possible hope they drove towards. Emyr scrutinised the route ahead as though the surface might plummet to a fiery abyss. The magnitude of what lay at the end of their short journey ever more stifling to his seized-up brain.

With a vigorous shake of his head, his mind ground into gear, beads of sweat forming a crown of tenacity. His position as the man of the household had faltered under the strain, but he knew he had to forge ahead.

She'd seen no-one the last few times she'd re-manifested under the streetlight. No comings and goings. No-one to help her. She worried she'd frightened them all away after the boy opened the curtains and fainted. What would she do then? It wasn't unprecedented, she reasoned. They'd left for weekends before and returned, but the uncertainty made her jittery.

Light from one of the back rooms filtered through to her position. Springing into action, she grabbed another stick from the hedge and flew at the window, hitting it frantically. She couldn't waste the chance. Opportunities to get the housemates attention were becoming scarcer.

It would soon be Easter. Some of them might graduate, never to return. Getting help from a whole new batch of students might prove impossible. She increased her ferocity, attacking the window with her branch.

"Come on! How can you not hear me?" she gave one more mighty bang and rested awhile at the post; the effort of racing to and fro exhausting to her ghostly form. There had to be something more she could do, but her ideas reservoir was in severe drought.

Time dragged as she stared with wavering determination at the house. Tapping the window was proving fruitless, but she forced herself to it like a fresh gym membership in January. She wouldn't have long. The hours of darkness had shortened noticeably over the weeks.

Car headlights shining at the top of the road suddenly grabbed her attention. Her heart knew before her mind that they were familiar. Was her actual heart in her actual body reacting? Were nurses and doctors monitoring her wondering what was going on?

Squinting in disbelief, she didn't imagine it was them. Just the same make of car. BMW's weren't entirely unheard of in this less affluent district of Swansea. But then it stopped right next to her, and she saw them: the fat boy, the small boy, the weird middle-aged hippy… and her mum and dad. She wept.

They were here. They were really here. They hadn't run away scared, the two boys. They'd gone to get help. Oh, how she'd thank them when she woke from this awful, terrible nightmare. The doors of her dad's car opened and they stepped out, her parents last.

She could tell they were nervous. Floating from where she hovered above the street, she reached ground level, inches from her mum.

"Hello, Mum," she choked. "Long time, no see."

It was evident she couldn't be heard and her heart broke a little more. "Mum? Dad?" Nothing. The group milled at the bottom of the path, each gazing in different directions, alluding to their failure to observe her. But the hippie woman looked right at her.

"She's here," she declared. "I can definitely feel her presence."

Relief and excitement intertwined like strands of molecules interacting in a chemical reaction, ready to burst forth in a spectacular kinetic display. She reigned herself. Scaring them away when it seemed she'd finally been discovered wasn't an option.

Apparently following the hippie woman's instructions, the five of them encircled the lamp post, which meant encircling her too. This looked good. Very promising. Eyes wide as saucers, she let out a laugh of joy. Would she soon be in her body and awake again?

Holding hands in a circle increased the potency of Sylvie's psychic abilities. She confirmed Elin's presence was strong and getting even stronger.

"Elin? Elin Treharne? I'm here with your mum and dad, and witnesses who say they've seen you here in the street light."

"I know. I can see you all," Elin's voice went unheard.

"Elin? Are you here now?"

"Yes!"

"I'm sensing strongly that she's here,"

"You've already said that twice," Glenda frowned "Find out how we can save her. How we can wake her up."

Typical of her mum, Elin thought. Straight to the point. Not suffering fools. She'd definitely find out how to help her.

"Elin. You've become detached from your body. We're here to help you get reconnected." It was difficult not to share her mum's annoyance at this strange woman's insistence at walking her through the task like a baby. But she felt so happy she was being addressed directly for the first time in forever that she couldn't help but just listen.

"We give you permission to leave the light. You can leave and go back to your body, NOW."

The group sensed nothing.

"It seemed different with Father Jenkins here," Neil said bluntly. "We all felt something happen then. Are you sure we shouldn't try and persuade him to help?"

"We don't need him!" Sylvie hissed at the suggestion.

"Are you sure she's even here?" Glenda sneered. The question sent shockwaves through her daughter, petrified they would give up before they'd even started.

"I'm here, Mum! I'm here. Please don't go. You have to help me." Glenda gave no sign of hearing her daughter. Elin put out a tentative hand to touch her. As it passed straight through, a spring of despair babbled from deep within, a despair which threatened to break her.

Then, with a sudden jolt of energy she could feel her lovely mum: all her love and all her suffering. Glenda's head shot round.

"Elin?" she said, looking right at her. "Is that really you? I felt her! She touched me. On my shoulder. Oh, is it you? Please say it is. Please."

"It is me, Mum. It really is. I love you so much. I'm so happy you're here." Glenda heard nothing. Turning to Sylvie she snapped.

"Ask her to tell you something only she and I know. I want to believe it's her. I want to believe it's my little girl."

"Who else would it be?" Emyr frowned, puzzled. Glenda scowled back.

"I want to know it's her. Okay?"

"Didn't you say you felt her?" Emyr persisted, reluctant to broach this potential stumbling block.

Before further discussion took place, lines of concentration grew on Sylvie's face.

"I'm getting something." She screwed her eyes tight. "She bought you a book for Christmas. One day, she's telling me, she moved the bookmark back several pages and giggled at the confusion it caused you."

The simple memory no-one else could know or guess, dropped Glenda to her knees. She nearly broke the circle, but she needed the support of Emyr and Matthew's strong arms to stop from falling completely to the floor.

Glenda's huge sob echoed from the row of terraced houses lining both sides of the street. Elin's own cry of anguish went unnoticed.

"We must save her. We have to save my precious little girl."

"Okay. We ordered her into the light. That's why she's stuck out here," piped up Neil. "We should order her back to her body, not just give her permission."

Sylvie looked at Glenda for guidance, her fierceness giving her the natural alpha role.

"Just do it," she barked. "We've wasted enough time with my daughter being stuck in a coma." Her stern voice apportioned blame to the foolish exorcists in the circle. The hope it would soon be over freed some of her pent up ill-feeling.

It was unwise and unfair to make Sylvie more nervous than she already appeared, so she modified her tone and tried to be encouraging. "We really need you," she managed with a weak smile.

It was all the reassurance Sylvie needed.

"Join me when I speak," she directed, receiving nervous nods of confirmation.

"Elin. Listen to our instruction. Go from the light. Go from the light now and return to your body." The chant grew louder the second, third and fourth times as the group joined in and found their stride.

"Elin. Go from the light. Go from the light now and return to your body."

*"ELIN. GO FROM THE LIGHT. GO FROM THE LIGHT NOW AND RETURN TO YOUR BODY."*

The window of the house next door flew open and an angry outburst filled the air, "Shut up! What the fuck are you doing you bunch of freaks. I'm trying to sleep." But they weren't about to stop for neighbourly etiquette. The woman shouting gave up. With a murmur of "for f' sake…" she slammed the window closed.

"Elin, go from the light and return to your body. We order you out of the light." Over and over again. Over and over the group chanted, until suddenly, "Stop!" Sylvie opened her eyes, breathless. "She's gone!"

# Chapter Forty-one

"Phone Alis. Ask her if there's any change. See if Elin's waking up," Glenda instructed her husband, a new colour to her cheeks. Rushing to get in the car, she badgered the others to hurry and get in, too.

"Her phone will be switched off. It's not allowed in that part of the hospital." Glenda's eyes widened in comprehension. She'd been so cocooned, sitting beside Elin, that against her usual nature she struggled with the practicalities

Neil and Matthew were pleased if not a little confused why they were included. Elin waking up was really a family affair. Harbouring a desire to meet the angelic beauty they'd only seen sleeping, they kept quiet and hoped they weren't just being given a lift to collect Neil's car. When they pulled into the hospital car-park with no mention of goodbyes, they happily presumed tagging along was expected.

Sylvie knew she was wanted; to revel in her success, or offer explanation and consolation if Elin still didn't wake up.

Their footsteps echoed eerily as they walked the empty hospital corridor, giving a surrealism to an already peculiar scene. Imagining the commotion that might greet them on arrival at HDU: nurses bustling, paging on-call doctors to witness the miracle; Alis trying desperately to find signal to call them to Elin's side as she woke up, they couldn't help but feel disappointed at the stillness.

It took a while to be buzzed in by a nurse so late in the night shift. Dawn would break soon and exhaustion was hitting hard. Rushing as sensibly as they could endure, they were confronted with the disheartening view of Alis sitting quietly beside her sister who appeared exactly as she had before.

"It didn't work," Glenda pronounced in a monotone. The seething resentment towards the three intruders upon her family's distress resumed forthwith. It seemed like the best and most sensitive idea to leave her to it, but Sylvie didn't want to.

"We must go back, maybe after a rest, and try again. Sometimes, with spirit, there are unresolved issues that have to be dealt with before they can leave. Whatever drew Elin to dream repeatedly about that house will be the key."

"But you said she had gone. You made us stop," Glenda protested. Sylvie managed to look both apologetic and self-righteous.

"I must have been mistaken. It is an unusual situation, after all." Her pious tone wilted in the heat of Glenda's hateful stare. "We'll get some rest tonight and reconvene tomorrow. Okay?"

Glenda seethed at the focus of her rage.

"Thank you for all you've done," stepped in Emyr. "Tomorrow's a new day. We might feel differently then. But we just want to be left alone, now."

Sylvie and the boys mouthed silent goodbyes whilst backing carefully from the room. They walked back to the canteen, and the vending machine for nourishment before discussing where they should stay tonight.

"Why does she have to be so shitty?" Matthew said indignantly. A rueful smile played on Neil's lips.

"Well, we did an exorcism on her daughter and put her in a coma. And the one hope we came up with didn't work. It's understandable."

Matthew shrugged. "Well, she did haunt us, didn't she. We had no choice."

"Yeah, maybe. But what are we going to do, now? I'm frustrated, but them," Neil nodded in the vague direction of HDU. "They must be going through hell."

"You just fancy her," Matthew scoffed.

"Like you don't," Neil defended. Sylvie coughed.

"Ahem. Do you two think it's right to be leering over a girl in a coma?" The boys reddened. "As for what we're going to do… It'll come to me after a good night's sleep. It always does."

"Whenever you put a girl in a coma, how to bring her round always comes to you after sleep," Neil facetiously deflected his embarrassment.

"Don't be flippant, Neil. It comes across as quite unkind."

"Sorry." He fiddled with his shirt hem. "We're gonna have to stay at the house tonight." He flinched at his own suggestion. Being with family and knowing what was happening helped him stay resolute. Matthew winced.

"I'm not sleeping in my old room."

"We can't all fit in mine," Neil objected. But that was what they did. Neil and Matthew top and tailing and Sylvie on an air bed.

Daylight was taking hold when they arrived. The streetlamp felt different. Switched off, it had lost its menace. They rushed past anyway, feeling irrational at their anxiety. Before the impractical arrangements received too much criticism, they all fell into deep exhausted sleep.

The scream pervaded the house, followed by a crash of breaking crockery as the tray which moments before contained several cold cups of coffee and toast crusts, clattered deafeningly to the floor.

"Oh my God!" exclaimed Bronwyn. "Oh my God. Oh my God! Aeron, come here. Now!"

A sleepy Aeron ambled into the lounge, yawning and tying Bronwyn's pink dressing gown around his bulk, almost tripping over the mess.

"Ach a fi! What happened? You alright?" he asked, taking in the extent of the disgusting disarray. "Don't worry. I'll help you clear it up."

"It's not that, babes. Look." She pointed at the wall. When Aeron looked up, he was stunned he could have missed it. Scrawled in large red letters were two words which sent his mind into a whirl.

*I'm here*

"Shit! What does it mean?"

Bronwyn gave him a scathing look. "It means that little pleb, Neil, was right. Our ghost hasn't gone anywhere."

Neil heard the cacophony but it took his brain a while to rouse from sleep enough to recognise it wasn't a dream. He disentangled himself from Matthew's tree-trunk legs, which had threatened to make him sterile on several perilous occasions throughout the night, and eased his stiff body from the bed.

How the other two managed to continue sleeping through the noise he was making he couldn't believe. As he left the room, he decided he didn't. He suspected they were pretending to be asleep until he established if they had to get up.

He trudged heavily down each step, pausing to rub sleep from his eyes. The atmosphere was tense. He soon saw the mess in the doorway, and beyond, Aeron and Bronwyn.

"What happened, Bronnie? You, alright?" she stepped over the mess, arms folded, nodding her head slowly.

"You were right, Neil bach."

"What do you mean?"

"Go and look. Go on," she gesticulated toward the lounge. Neil saw the scrawled red writing immediately. The grin which grew on his face was evidently not what Bronwyn expected.

"Are you demented, Neil, mun? You look really pleased."

"I am," he said. He ran upstairs, stumbling on the middle steps in his rush.

"She's here!" he yelled, barging through his bedroom door. The wide eyes of last night's roommates confirmed they had been awake as he'd suspected.

"How do you know?" Matthew asked.

"Come and see for yourself." He turned for them to follow.

They stood in the lounge, staring at Elin's message.

"We'll have to go back to the hospital and get her parents. We need to find out why she's stuck in this house."

"I'll do us some bacon butties, shall I?" Bronwyn suggested.

"That's the best idea I've heard all day. But I thought you only ate healthy stuff, Bron," Neil asked in surprise.

"Needs must, Neil. Needs must."

# Chapter Forty-two

They used the three bathrooms the house boasted and showered whilst the bacon cooked. After half an hour, they were clean, presentable, fed and watered (coffee'd), and back in Neil's car.

The car park was full to burst. Sunday was a popular day to visit. A fact confirmed when they passed the hospital shop in the foyer, crammed with queues of people buying flowers, cards and grapes.

They had trouble convincing the nurse on duty they were relatives. A change of shift bringing a new proficiency in visitor discrimination. She eventually said she would have to ask the family. Neil, Matthew and Sylvie weren't convinced that would gain them entry, unsure if they were still welcome.

The nurse returned briskly. Unsmiling, she buzzed them in. They said thank you to her disappearing back as she walked off to her duties. As they approached Elin's room, they came face to face with a rigid Emyr, standing tall, arms folded, sent out to intercept the intruders and ascertain if they had anything useful to say.

His demeanour melted at their revelation. "She actually wrote on the wall?" he repeated misty eyed. He went back into the room to consult his wife and daughter. Glenda pushed her chair back and walked with Emyr to the door.

"Here we go again," she said.

Sat tightly around the table, they dispensed with the need for candles, it being bright morning light, and because they knew who to expect. As the resident psychic, Sylvie led what she still called a séance.

"Elin. We have seen your message. We're so pleased you're here. Can you give us a sign? If it's you Elin, move the curtains for us?"

Instantly, the curtains flapped back and fore to a gasp. Glenda stifled a sob of joy and relief and an array of emotions she had no hope of getting a handle on. Emyr determined as always to be strong for his girls, did a good job of keeping it together, and him coping helped Glenda cope too.

"Thank you, Elin. We need to ask you why you are still here and not back in your body. I'm going to use the Ouija board again. Is that okay?" The curtains flapped again. Sylvie took it to be Elin's agreement. With the Ouija board on the table, she began asking questions. It soon became apparent that Elin had less idea than they why she was stuck here.

"What do you feel when you're here?" Neil asked timidly, the first time he'd ever attempted to speak to the beautiful creature who had terrified him for months. After a few moments while Elin considered her response, the glass moved. 'S, a, f, e.'

"Why? Why does she feel especially safe here?" Sylvie frowned at the group

"It's her glandular fever. We talked about it yesterday—well, I suggested it," Neil recalled. "She was fit and healthy here. When she left she got really ill. It makes sense she feels safe here."

The murmurs round the table showed concordance. The Ouija glass remained still. Elin wasn't objecting. Sylvie led them in an impromptu prayer.

"Elin. We thank this house for providing you with a feeling of safety; a refuge from your terrible illness. But you don't need it anymore. Your illness is gone and you are needed in your body.

"You are safe to leave this house. You don't need it anymore. Go back to your body, now, Elin. Go back to your body. You are safe. You no longer need this house." She went on and encouraged the others to join in.

A compelling chorus swelled in the lounge of number twenty-four Rhondda Street, Swansea. It had to work. It was real, and they were helping. Everything would be all right. She would listen. She had to.

After repeating themselves until any more seemed ridiculous, they stopped. Bronwyn and Aeron first, then Neil and Matthew and Emyr and even Glenda. Only Sylvie carried on a few more times because nothing had changed. She didn't feel as though Elin had gone back to her body.

When even she fell silent and opened her eyes, the curtains flapped furiously, confirming their failure.

"Why hasn't it worked? My daughter's here. She responds to us, yet her body is two miles away and close to death. "Elin! Get back to your body. Now!" she ordered, her voice cracking.

The glass on the Ouija board vibrated and moved swiftly from letter to letter.

"I c a n 't," quickly spelled out. With it, their hope stagnated and they were once again at a loss.

"We'll find a way, Elin. Don't you worry. We'll get you back, cariad. I promise." Emyr never made promises he couldn't keep. He prayed this wouldn't be the exception.

"We'll go to the hospital and make sure everything remains fine there," he said, anticipating the doctors not approving of their reasons for postponing the planned switch off.

"You three can find that priest. Make him see sense. Do you think you can do that?" Sylvie, Neil and Matthew nodded assuredly, displaying a confidence they didn't trust.

"Is there any way we can help?" Bronwyn's sing-song Carmarthenshire accent asked.

"I don't know. But stick around. More people connecting round the table may prove to be the crucial key."

Aeron and Bronwyn were left in the house, alone. A normal, cuddly Sunday was impossible. Whilst they felt silly to be afraid of Elin, it was just too weird to cope with.

Was she there only during a séance? Or, was she there all the time, watching them, judging them? Why could sometimes they see her and most times she was invisible to them? Was it their strength of feeling or hers which brought her to the surface?

Recalling the treatment of the dirty dishes before Christmas suggested she was there whether they could see her or not. A flush of embarrassment at personal and intimate times they'd shared reddened both their faces. Did she see everything?

"Let's go out, shall we?" Bronwyn agreed with Aeron's suggestion before the idea of where was even considered. They threw on jumpers and coats and hurried from the house.

When she'd been ordered from the light and back to her body, Elin had felt something change. Like she was dissolving into the ether, ready to be divided and cleverly fused with her body again in spiritual osmosis or something equally incomprehensible.

She found herself lying in darkness. "This is it," she'd said to herself, "I'll open my eyes and be back to normal." She peered out at the room beyond.

Breaking dawn offered just enough illumination to recognise her surroundings. It was with more than dismay she saw where she'd ended up.

"Shit. Why?" The light pierced the room and polarised Elin into action. "I've got to do something before I disappear again," she muttered. Seeing the lipstick, she knew what she would do.

Her mum and dad and the others would get to the hospital and wonder what had happened and where she was. A simple 'I'm here' should do the trick. Then the weirdy woman could do her stuff and sort it out.

Once she'd written in giant red letters on the wall, she felt a pang of guilt at the job she'd created for someone to scrub off. But not for long. This was life and death. The thought hit her like a body blow.

Seeing her mum and dad, devastated, gave it all a realism that giddied her, like viewing video footage of a lucky escape, or revisiting the site of a car crash and seeing how bad it could have been.

She felt especially mortal again, and extremely endangered. The relief she may have got from disappearing to wherever she usually went during daylight, didn't come. The morning, bright now, and she was still present and aware.

The lounge of number twenty-four was the most excitement Elin had enjoyed for weeks. The change of scene more than welcome. It was about to get a lot more interesting when she gained some company.

The girl student walked in carrying a tray laden with remains from student snacks. She saw Elin's message scrawled on the wall, screamed, and dropped the tray. The largest boy followed sleepily to see what the commotion was wearing a ludicrous pink dressing gown, and then the small one and finally the chubby one and the hippie woman. Quite a crowd.

The message was having the desired effect. The three newest arrivals appeared to be relieved to see it, just as she'd hoped they would. They talked about what it meant, and what their next move should be.

It was wonderful to have company, to see life happening. As a child she'd often imagined what it would be like to be invisible. Now she was, her mind giddied at the fun of it. She eavesdropped, effortlessly, reassuring conversations about her. Everything would be good soon, and she was excited.

Before long, she was alone again, but she didn't mind, confident her saviours were striving for the answer. She wished someone would put the telly on. So resigned to being stuck with nothing to do, it took a while before she attempted to do it herself. She didn't feel part of this world. Trying only confirmed the feeling. The small buttons needed more dexterity than her ethereal self could provide.

She entertained herself instead reading the piles of mail stacked on the dresser. Nothing she read interested her, but she was grateful for anything to break the monotony.

The group returned, and this time her mum and dad were there too. It was wonderful to see them again. The table was yanked out, and they arranged themselves in a circle around it as the séance before. Elin did her best to give encouragement, flapping curtains and pushing the glass on the Ouija board, considering each answer carefully.

When the hippie woman prayed and everyone joined in, the power was undeniable. She desperately tried to obey. Picturing herself moving towards her other, sleeping self; every time she got close something drew her back. The idea of being away from the house seemed treacherous.

Failure tipped over her like an ice-bucket challenge but without the exhilaration. Just desperate emptiness. What was it going to take to rescue her? Realising for the first time; she despaired she would ever know.

Alis was exhausted sitting beside her sister. She had regaled tales from childhood, played music, offered food and drinks, including wafting items under her nose, and nothing had made any effect to her expression, nor to the machines monitoring her vital signs.

Her parents' strange comfort at the three strangers and their unbelievable twaddle was a mystery to her. They were clinging onto any little thread of hope. It was ridiculous. She had been happy to step up and give her mum some time to rest. As that wasn't going to happen, this at least was a distraction she supposed, but it was wearing a bit thin now.

They shouldn't leave her as the only one doing anything practical to help her sister. It was foolish and unfair. Relief quickly turned to irritation when the two of them returned, talking animatedly and loudly. She tried to not let her annoyance show. It wasn't her intention to make things worse. But they wouldn't have noticed anyway. So preoccupied were they with their psychic claptrap they barely paid her any attention.

The Ward Sister hustled into the room

"Dr Overton is doing his rounds. He'll be in shortly, so hang around if you want to speak to him." She left without waiting for a response. Striding away, straightening her skirt with one hand and adjusting her short hair with the other, she addressed more patients and their families in other rooms.

On her return, she took her place backing up the entourage of fawning junior doctors, including the Dr Lewis they'd seen before; bobbing and weaving in their efforts to impress the great man. Minions to a super villain. Dr Overton would look like Darth Vader but for being far too short. An expression of smugness only that amount of obsequiousness on a daily basis can invoke, carved his face.

The Treharne family waited anxiously, but with a united determination, knowing they were about to go against the great doctor's plans and insist Elin remain on life support for a while longer. If he didn't like it—which he wouldn't—he was going to have to lump it.

The anticipated reaction proved accurate. Dr Overton thundered they were being foolish. Putting off the inevitable. It really was best for them to let go so they could begin the grieving process. But they shouldn't forget that there was every chance forcing her to breathe on her own might be the very thing to wake Elin up.

A monotone Glenda addressed the doctor.

"With the greatest respect, Dr Overton. I don't care if you understand our reasons. We won't be granting our permission to switch off our daughter's life support as we had planned tomorrow. Why don't we discuss it again in another week?" The consultant flashed a bright smile.

"Of course. As you wish." With that, he turned and walked from the room. His unique skill, to show immense rudeness, cloaked under a guise of good manners.

When he was confident he wouldn't be overheard, he leaned toward the Sister.

"Schedule Miss Treharne's life support removal as originally planned. I'm sure they'll come round." And with no further words, he walked from the ward in arrogant, self-righteous certainty.

"How are we going to find Father Jenkins?" Neil inquired without thought, his brain too fatigued to consider the simplicity of the problem.

"We'll go to his church of course," Matthew said. "Which one was it, Sylvie?" She looked sheepishly at him, stiffening before admitting she couldn't remember.

Performing an internet search of local Catholic churches, it didn't take long to match one with his name and the phone number they'd used previously. They pulled up outside St. Benedict's church half an hour later.

"Are you sure this is the right place, Neil?" Matthew asked in disbelief. "It doesn't look much like a church to me. More like a school or something."

The grey building sat miserably in a shabby car-park, looking like offices of an unsuccessful group of solicitors or accountants. Multiple windows stared out wistfully, knowing they were a disappointment. Its appearance, entirely incongruent with its purpose.

"You were navigating," Neil snapped, stressed from negotiating Sunday drivers.

"It's definitely the place. There's the name above the door," Sylvie said, pointing.

"Where will Father Jenkins be?" Neil wondered out loud. They'd taken note of mass times from the web, so knew they wouldn't interrupt. Wiping their feet outside the door of the unattractive carbuncle, they pushed it open and stepped inside.

The interior was far more inviting and church-like, and happily, the square, squat figure of Father Jenkins entered from another door when they walked in. He stopped, staring open mouthed for a moment before exclaiming, "What do you want?"

He was forced to listen. Not doing so would have appeared extremely rude.

"I suppose I could come to the house again, but it really is nonsense. I've never heard of anything like it before." A smile found its way onto Neil's tense face, heartened by the promise of the Priest's help.

"I will have to get the permission of my Bishop, and to be honest, he was reluctant for me to get involved before. I can only guess what he will say about this," he said with a dismissive shrug. "It will be Tuesday or Wednesday before I will have a chance to speak to him. I'll get back to you after that."

"You can't!" Neil exclaimed. "She needs you. She'll die."

"It's true, Father. We can't wait," Sylvie confirmed.

He held aloft a dismissive hand. "I cannot act without the support of the bishop. It's just not possible. I have a lot more experience in these matters, and can assure you, if this girl is trapped in a dream-state—and I really don't believe she is—then I'm sure she'll be fine for a few more days."

Holding both hands up, he interrupted the objections. "I fully expect to come to the house just to put your minds at rest. But it will be as I say. You are mistaken. You'll see."

"No! You must come sooner. They'll switch her off. Please," Neil begged.

"Listen to me." The priest was angry now. "I've agreed to humour your nonsense, but I'm not going to jeopardise my position. For my own satisfaction, as well as for the spiritual well-being of my parish, I must do things properly. I've told you my opinion, but graciously agreed to speak to my bishop and risk ridicule anyway.

"Question me again, and I will have no compunction in leaving you to your ridiculous plight by yourselves. I've done more than enough for you already." And with that, he flounced back through the door he had entered moments before. They weren't sure where it led and couldn't help picturing Father Jenkins hiding in the broom cupboard until they left.

Matthew took a step after him. Neil put out an arm to stop him. "Leave him, Matthew. We can't risk provoking him further. We need him."

They walked dejectedly back to the car. "It wasn't a complete disaster," Sylvie suggested. "He did agree to help."

"If the bishop lets him," Matthew sniped. Sylvie ignored him.

"We just have to make sure the doctors don't switch her off before he does."

They didn't want to go back to the house so decided to go to the hospital and check on Elin and the rest of the Treharne's. Informing Glenda of their less than successful mission with Father Jenkins wasn't a prospect they relished.

They were buzzed into HDU, familiar faces, now, to the nursing staff. Glenda's countenance welcomed them as naughty children to a particularly stern headmistress's office. And that was before reporting their relative failure.

The fury in her eyes was tempered with fear. She couldn't afford for things to go wrong. "Well, I'm not prepared to leave it there. He's the imbecile who exorcised a spirit who wasn't a spirit at all. Let's see if mention of 'murder' and telling the police doesn't motivate him to help us immediately. I'm sure he wouldn't want his bishop to hear of that!"

Sylvie and the boys wished they'd been more assertive. It hadn't occurred to them to remind him he was to blame. Glenda doing the reminding would be more effective. She appeared to be a very persuasive woman.

For the second time that day, Neil, Matthew and Sylvie arrived at the drab grey building on the outskirts of the city. This time, as the passengers of Glenda and Emyr.

"Right, Father Jenkins. You are about to be persuaded. Because I'm not going to take no for an answer!"

# Chapter Forty-three

Going out in Swansea without a plan inevitably led Aeron and Bronwyn to the pub. They had begun with the good intentions of going for a walk and had ended up high on the hill over-looking the city. Struck with awe, they were also struck by bitterly cold wind and were now warming their cockles beside the roaring fire of The Railway Tavern.

They were on their third or fourth pint when Bronwyn pulled a bitchy smile whilst looking across at the bar.

"Wos a matter, babe?" Aeron asked, missing the problem.

"Jon. He keeps looking over and smiling at me."

"He's just being friendly."

"You know what a smarmy little perv he is. He seems to 'ave got worse."

Jon smiled again and walked over to their table.

"How's my favourite couple?" he said, placing two more bottles of beer on the table. Aeron usually drank pints of bitter, but there was a special offer from a local brewery they were taking advantage of.

"Not too bad thanks, Jon." Aeron answered, all too aware he was addressing his boss.

"And how about the lovely Bronwyn?" he inquired, moving in to kiss her on the cheek. She repealed his advances more curtly than she might have without the copious beer. Concern for Aeron's employment usually forced a modicum of politeness.

"Fuck off, creep," she spat, shoving him enough to knock over one of the bottles.

It splashed onto Jon's trousers. He seethed with rage, but in fear of what Aeron, or Bronwyn for that matter, might do to him if he let it show, he kept it hidden. "No worries," he forced a smile. "I'll bring you another bottle... on the house." He shuffled away, dabbing at his crotch with a bar towel.

"Fucking perv," Bronwyn said, slumping back into her seat. "I don't know what's got into him. He's not normally so cocky."

"Do you want me to have a word?" Aeron asked, reluctant to upset his boss who'd been especially generous with overtime recently, but overruled by greater loyalty to Bronnie.

She gave him a sideways glance over the lip of the beer bottle she was still draining the dregs from. "No. It's alright, babes. I think I can handle 'im." She winked, holding her beer in the air.

Aeron was in no doubt.


They arrived to a car park full to over-flowing. They were forced to join a dozen other cars parked half on the pavement further down the street.

"I presume it wasn't this busy when you were here before?" Emyr commented. The others shook their heads. "It must be time for mass. Great."

They tried to sneak in through the back door. Most of the congregation didn't look. Those who did offered beaming smiles to the newcomers. Emyr touched the signs of the cross. Neil and Matthew nervously followed suit, but the two women didn't.

Father Jenkins paused briefly and sighed when he saw them. He glared, certain they were not there because they'd had a sudden conversion to the One True Faith. They flinched from the fury streaming their way, except Glenda, whose conviction gave strength to the others to ignore the imposing presence of the stocky priest.

There was obviously nothing to do but sit and join the mass. Whilst it could have been frustrating, there was an indubitable comfort from the atmosphere of holy worship. The onslaught of love from the congregation, from the priests words, or perhaps even from God himself washed over Glenda, eroding the control she'd fought to maintain over her emotion.

Sitting in stunned silence, tears streamed down her haggard face. She prayed, and felt truly she would be heard.


"I think you've scared him, Bron. This is the third round 'on the house' he's bought us!"

"I know. Do you want mine? I'm getting a bit pissed."

Aeron happily glugged Bronwyn's as well. Watching Jon's timid figure behind the bar, he turned and whispered.

"He's definitely gone jittery. Look at him. He'll be dropping bottles again soon!"

"What do you mean?"

"I told you. Bottles and glasses smashed regularly for a while. He thought he had a ghost too. But I reckon he was just having a break-down or something. He went weird for a while… weirder. You must remember. It happened about the same time we had our strange goings on."

Bronwyn sat up, a sudden alertness to her features.

"About the same time, or the same time?"

Aeron frowned in puzzlement and took another sip of his beer.

"Why would you even think he was 'avin' a break down? Our Elin could be his ghost too! When did he start behaving his cocky, arsehole self again?" Aeron looked up and to the left as he pursed his lips in cogitation.

"It's hard to say. It could have been the same time as Father Jenkins did the cleansing. More like a week or two after."

"It took him a while to notice she wasn't haunting him anymore! He didn't know about our situation, did he? And I'm sure you didn't tell him about the séance or the exorcism?"

"Why would I?"

"Exactly. So when he did notice she'd gone, he put the whole thing down to stress or whatever and got all cocky and leery again."

"Do you really think she was here as well?"

"Why not? She travels in her dreams. We don't know how. No-one does. Why not here?"

"I suppose. But why?"

Bronwyn drummed her fingers on the table while she considered.

"Elin dreams of our house because she has an association... right?" Aeron nodded. "But she doesn't understand what the link is. She doesn't know why she dreams of it, but she feels safe there. If she dreams of here too, and whilst she's here, she's angry and she frightens Jon... You have to see the connection?" Aeron's acutely angled knitted brow, exhibited that he didn't.

Emyr placed a comforting hand on his wife's knee. His own moist eyes met hers and she broke further.

"It's going to be okay. I can sense it. We were meant to come here," she managed through her sobs.

Seeing the evident distress in his newest members of the congregation, Father Jenkins was duty bound to at least hear them out. He nodded his submission, so the group sat in silent contemplation while the rest of the worshipers made their way from the church in a steady flow, pausing to congratulate the Father for his insightful sermon.

When they'd all gone, the priest walked decisively to them. He did his best at a warm smile and invited them to join him in his office.

"She feels safe in the house, and furious in The Railway Tavern… with our pervert of a landlord. Don't you see?" He thought he was getting the gist, but still wanted clarification. He nodded slowly to give Bronwyn encouragement to carry on.

"If he behaved with her the way he behaves with most of the other girls, no wonder she's angry. Perhaps he really tried it on with her. More than with me. She's supposed to be a real looker."

"You're perfect."

"Thanks, babes. But I wasn't fishing for a compliment, just making a point. Maybe he took it too far, frightened her or something." Aeron snorted a contemptuous laugh.

"I can't see him scaring anyone. Scrawny git."

"I know. Not scared, then. Maybe, deeply offended."

Aeron nodded earnestly. "That, I can believe."

"Give me your phone a minute. I wanna try summin."

# Chapter Forty-four

"You must help us. You have to help my little girl," Glenda demanded from in front of a vast desk in Father Jenkins's well-appointed, plush-looking office. His large throne of a chair gave him an unusual height advantage which seemed to delight him. Uninhibited by the confrontation from the larger group, he gave his dispassionate response.

"My hands are tied. I've already explained to your friends."

"Well you haven't explained to me."

Father Jenkins began his self-vindication once again

"I must seek the advice of my bishop. I am the representative for the Bishop of the Diocese for this Parish. It is paramount I represent faithfully his wishes.

"I established his approval to help you with your demon. Now you've decided for some reason that it wasn't a demon after all, and is apparently your daughter visiting the house in her coma. No, it's definitely not something I can simply act upon alone.

"I can't foretell how he'll respond. Whether he will give permission for further intervention. But I must warn you, something so unprecedented is unlikely to gain his support." He sat back in his large chair in a self-satisfied motion. He clasped his hands across his chest to announce 'subject closed.'

As Glenda took the mantle and angled towards him, he was forced to catch her eye. His obstinacy buckled in the onslaught of determination bombarding him from the eyes of his adversary. She cleared her throat with a disdainful cough.

"Let me tell you what is paramount to me." She leaned even further forward and rested both palms on the huge desk. She looked him straight in the face, almost enjoying seeing the diminishment of his stubbornness, as the glint in his eye quavered for a fraction of a second.

"My daughter was struck from nowhere with a coma. She's been lying, wasting away on a hospital bed in a tiny prison of a room for weeks. Tomorrow morning, the doctors, who haven't got one clue what caused her unconsciousness, want to switch off her life support.

"It is most likely that when they do…" she gulped down a huge wad of emotion and turned it to gritty fury. She stared the priest right in the eye. "When they do, I will have to say goodbye to my daughter."

Father Jenkins was a compassionate, if overburdened, man. It was difficult for him to reconcile his natural compassion with the protocol he knew he had to follow. He opened his mouth to speak, but Glenda's steely gaze intensified. She increased her volume to be sure she wouldn't be interrupted.

"I am, you will appreciate, very keen for a different outcome. When my friends here brought my attention to the possibility Elin's coma might have been caused by the exorcism which you performed, I have to admit, I was a little sceptical."

The priest gave up trying to interrupt when Glenda's volume increased once more in response to his floundering, opening and closing lips. He relaxed. He could let her speak and then give his objections when she'd finished. It was clear she was not to be put off. Glenda continued.

"Since then, I have actually seen her! I've seen the apparition of my daughter, relinquished to the streetlamp outside the house, where you banished her with your ill-timed, ill-advised exorcism. She isn't a demon. Just a girl with paranormal abilities we were previously unaware…"

Father Jenkins could hold his tongue no longer. "I must say, the manifestation of these 'paranormal abilities' as you put it, is highly indicative of a demonic presence."

"Whatever," Glenda raised a dismissive hand. "If you want to save her soul, first you're going to need to put right what you've done." He gasped, taken aback. His culpability seemed ever more possible. Glenda's assault was relentless.

"I fear you are overly concerned with procedure, and not nearly enough with the plight of my daughter. A plight, I have no doubt she's suffering as a direct result of your incompetent meddling. I've no time for you to ask your bishop, and frankly, I couldn't care less what he has to say.

"If you won't see your way to helping me; of putting right what you did wrong, it will be my mission, for the rest of my life, to make sure your bishop, your congregation, every newspaper, internet post and anything else I can think of will know. And if Elin doesn't pull through, I will consider you a murderer. I'll make your life a living misery."

"Is that a threat?"

"It's a promise. No matter how arrogant and foolish you may be, you cannot deny the possibility I'm right. That we are right. We've seen and heard her for God's sake. There's no doubt."

She stopped, silent; waiting for the impact of her insults, threats and misery to seep in. He shuffled uncomfortably in his seat.

"Well, I suppose I don't have a choice. If I'm responsible, which I still very much doubt, I wouldn't want it on my conscience." It wasn't admission of guilt, but that wasn't necessary. He was coming to help. Glenda had succeeded where the others had failed.

Bronwyn used her uni Wi-Fi password (the service encompassed most of the city centre) and searched for images of Elin Treharne on the University network. Not the most flattering image, but she still looked unquestionably stunning.

"Jon, come yere a minute," she called from across the room. He looked straight over, wiped his hands on a bar towel and proceeded to bound over like a puppy relieved to be back in its owner's good books after some doggy misdemeanour.

"You called?" he said, a moment of doubt that Bronwyn had really meant him. She'd never shown him attention before, apart from to put him down.

"Do you know this girl?" she thrust the picture of Elin towards him. There was no need for him to answer. As the colour drained from his rubbery features, leaving him more than reminiscent of a Spitting Image John Major, it was palpably obvious.

"I'll take that as a yes," Bronwyn said. Jon tried to gather his senses.

"Wh… Wh… Why do you want to know?"

"Oh, no reason. She was a friend. I'm trying to track her down and wondered if she'd been in here, that's all."

He darted a look to Aeron, wrestling whether to mention when he had most recently seen her, reaching out like a banshee towards him across the bar. The innocuous purpose behind the inquiry prompted him to lie.

"No. She might have been in. But I don't thinks so. I would've remembered," he said with a Lotharios wink.

Bronwyn didn't want to alert him to her true motive, but not mentioning his frightened reaction to the picture would seem suspicious.

"Why did you flinch when I showed you, then, Jon?" It was almost possible to hear the cogs of Jon's lying brain turning, attempting to find something plausible.

"When you thrust your hand towards me, I really thought you might hit me."

"Did you, Jon? Aw, sorry," she offered, and sat back, showing there was nothing more she wanted from him.

"Is that it, then?" he asked, eyebrows raised.

"You can bring us another couple of beers," Aeron hiccupped, decidedly sloshed.

"Sure. No worries," he said, walking away.

Bronwyn leaned conspiratorially in to Aeron.

"We've got to get him to the house. We have to get him in front of Elin!"

"Why?" Aeron nearly choked on his beer.

"It might jog her memory, remind her why she feels safe in our house. *He* could be the reason!"

"Won't he think it's odd? We've not invited him before."

"Leave it to me." She called out for him to come over again. He looked nervous. As he began his approach, Bronwyn leaned in again. "Just follow my lead," she whispered.

Jon plonked two more beers on the table.

"Sorry. Were you waiting long?"

"Don't worry about that, presh. You wanna sit down. Take the weight off your feet for a minute." Jon looked around, deciding if the busy bar could spare him.

As soon as he sat, Bronwyn placed her unshod foot on his thigh, provocatively near his crotch. She moved it back and forth seductively. As Jon squirmed uncomfortably, it patently had the desired effect.

"Sorry I made you jump earlier," she said, staring at him with deep doe eyes, her foot still thrusting, her top arranged to show just the right amount of titillating cleavage. Aeron watched, eyes wide in horror and disbelief.

"I'd love to make it up to you, presh." Jon glanced nervously at his large subordinate. "Don' worry about Aeron," she gushed, and then added in a loud stage whisper, "he likes to watch." It was too much for Jon. When Bronwyn made it plain it was a now or never offer, it was obvious which choice Jon wanted to take.

"I'm ever-so tipsy, you see? I'll probably pass out later," she said with an exaggerated wink.

"You sure about this, Aeron?"

It took all his strength to swallow back the bile that had risen in his throat. Bronwyn had better know what she was doing. "Yeah, sure." And then, the three of them left. Bronwyn arm in arm with both the men, just to keep up the pretence.

Elin was bored. They knew she was here. They knew who she was, but they still acted as though she was something to fear. And so she'd been left on her own, trapped in the dingy lounge all day. Even her mum and dad had gone. She struggled to stay calm, although the relief being back in the safe haven this house seemed to afford her was a huge comfort.

It wasn't a nice place to be. When she lived here she rarely spent time in this room. It was just a way to get to the kitchen. Beginning her student life eating at the table, she then, like the rest of the housemates, took her meals to her bedroom. Debating exploring the house to relieve her boredom, she decided it would be intrusive. It also wasn't worth the risk of getting stuck. Stay here, in the lounge, where everyone knows where she is.

An unexpected optimism rose within her and she smiled. Hope was in the air. Knowing she had made contact; that the people who loved her most were doing everything they could to save her, gave her a lightness and she smiled a heartfelt smile.

Suddenly, her peace and boredom were broken with the bang of the front door bursting open. Her heart exploded into action at the anticipation of company who may have the answer to her salvation.

With an air of disappointment, she realised it wasn't her mum and dad. She could tell before she even heard them speak. It was the wrong sort of noise, too bustling. And then she heard a voice she was sure she recognised, and it disquieted her.

"Why are we going in here? Shouldn't we go straight to your bedroom? We don't want to be seen."

"Don't you worry about that, lover-boy," the raucous cry of the girl declared, shoving the door open with her foot. She led him in by his tie before pushing him onto the couch. Elin gasped, horrified. What was she doing? Why would she do this when she has a boyfriend?

But then he appeared too. Closing the door, he stood in front of it, blocking the exit like a club bouncer. The girl stood up shaking her head, apparently in an effort to sober up. She cleared her throat to speak.

"Elin? Are you here?"

Stunned to be addressed, she rushed to give a sign and wobbled the curtains. "We've brought you something," the girl announced, waving her arm towards the couch. Elin peered at the offering unsure what to expect. And then she recognised him.

A sudden terror spewed forth as an excruciating scream. She knew him. She knew who he was; his voice, his weasily face from the pub. But now he was in her house!

Shaking, her whole body, or its ethereal representation, convulsed as she tried to control the horror raging within her. Glaring at him from high on the ceiling, shuddering violently and uncontrollably, emotion, stuffed down, dormant for months, erupted forcefully to the surface. And, from the terrified faces blinking up at her, was there for all to see.

Her poor body racked with the sheer power of distress and panic coursing through her unearthly veins. Clutching her head in her hands, she tugged at her hair and screamed, "No!"

Breathless, she glowered at him. As he cowered in her fearsome presence, her anguish was overpowered, slowly at first, and then overwhelmingly by the next level of her emotion: rage.

A power she had never known surged through her. The horrified looks on the faces below told her it looked as it felt. Memories of exactly why she hated the man on the couch were hazy. Sudden, excruciating flashbacks lanced her thoughts—him standing over her, his breath on her neck, the terror choking her.

From nowhere, she lunged. Striking him shocked her. She hadn't known she was capable, but it was so much more satisfying than merely scaring him. As she saw the deep scratch reddening on his grey pallor, her wrath exploded.

With a screeching roar and flailing arms, razor-sharp talons thrashed at his clammy face, gouging skin from flesh in a vicious frenzy she felt powerless to stop. She hated him, and he would know what that meant.

# Chapter Forty-five

To ensure Father Jenkins' cooperation, Glenda made sure he joined them in their car. It was a squash, but he didn't complain. Travelling in uneasy silence, they arrived at the house a few minutes later. Still silent, they filed up the uneven path and steep steps, Father Jenkins sandwiched either end of the line by Neil, Matthew and Sylvie in the front with the Treharne's bringing up the rear.

Before they even reached the door, the screams emanating from within made them shudder. They shared a look of terror.

"What on earth..." Neil hadn't expected to be scared. Father Jenkins filled with fresh purpose to his enforced visit. The screams were surely the phantom squeals of a demon.

Neil's initial reluctance to open the door turned to paralysis. Father Jenkins forced his way past Sylvie and Matthew, both happy to let him. The key turned, and the stocky bulk of the priest barged through like a police raid.

Without the rotting wooden barrier, the sound of the screams filled the air, echoing from every surface, filling them with dread. "It's only Elin," Neil whispered under his breath. "No need to be scared."

When, after a mighty scream of anger the shrieking paused, other sounds reached their heightened senses. They hurried en masse along the cramped corridor. The priest rattled the handle, but the door was firmly closed. From beyond, they were sure they could hear voices.

"Oh my God. Oh my f…ing God!" Bronwyn's Welsh lilt filtered faintly through the door. It sounded as though she was crying.

"What on earth is going on?" Emyr demanded. Pitiful sobs found their way to the collective ears straining to listen.

"I'm sorry. I'm sorry. I'm sorry!"

"Who's that?" Emyr asked again. Neil and Matthew shrugged. It wasn't Aeron's voice.

What they might witness when they prized open the door they were terrified to imagine.

Bang, bang. "Open up," the priest commanded, in his element now, hammering hard on the flexing wood. No-one opened the door, but when he turned the handle again, it swung open. They crowded together at the doorway, unwilling to walk into the unknown prospect.

The spectacle revealed by the opening door was incomprehensible. Father Jenkins gasped and stepped back.

Bronwyn and Aeron were stood, faces etched in horror, staring at a dark mist which hovered over the cowering figure of a man on the floor. He lay foetal, repeating over and over how sorry he was.

The misty shape was perceivable as a girl, and to those who knew her, as Elin Treharne. Her form spectral, but distinct. Her outline stood breathing heavily like Al Capone having dished out retribution to a traitorous underling.

"Stop. Now, Demon!" Father Jenkins commanded. Her gaze fell upon the group, and seeing them for the first time, she shrank back shamefully.

The figure on the floor took its opportunity and rolled out of Elin's reach. When they saw him clearly, there were more gasps. Everyone, except the priest, recognised Jon, but barely. His bloody face and torn clothes did well to disguise him.

Pushing himself up with what little strength he could muster, he stumbled to the floor and forced himself up again. With a huge sob, he barged through the gap which opened in the crowd. He ran, lurching down the hall and out through the front door.

When they looked back in the room, Elin had gone.

# Chapter Forty-six

Elin recoiled from the crowd watching her ferocious outburst. Especially her parents. She didn't know where the fury had come from. It wasn't like her, but she hated him. And she didn't understand why. She attempted to give it consideration but couldn't bear to. A shudder rocked her, and she gave up.

Unaware of going anywhere she was surprised at a new scene opening before her, like a stage reset at the theatre.

Her enemy was no longer present. The rest of them: her mum, dad, the hippie woman, the small one, the fat one, the older looking one and the girl, sat in the familiar position for a séance. The priest was there too. Holding a large crucifix, muttering under his breath and splashing holy water around the room.

Smoke trails from incense sticks burning on the window sill combined with flickering light from various candles to give an eerie glow.

Everyone's lips moved saying the same thing, but she couldn't hear what. A compulsion made her listen hard to the hippie woman. Discerning her name a few times, she struggled to keep her concentration.

The room blurred and she shook herself to refocus. But when she did, it metamorphosised into another scene altogether. The more she tried, the more it swirled and changed until, eventually, she began to recognise familiar objects. The back of a chair. A glass. Then with a sudden gush of energy, she catapulted into the scene completely.

She sat sipping at a long drink at the bar in The Railway, a tugging at her psyche implied it should be significant. It should mean something. But she couldn't for the life of her remember what.

"Top you up there, sweetheart?" It was the smarmy barman. She thought she might be waiting to meet someone. Who it was, she couldn't recall.

"Yeah. Okay. Vodka and lemonade again, please," she asked politely. She placed a five pound note on the counter to pay for it. The drink was duly poured, but the note wasn't taken. She tapped it and pushed it further towards him but he still didn't take it.

"That one's on me," he said with a wink.

"Thanks, but no thanks," Elin replied, not wanting to encourage him. The money remained untouched. Elin left it there, and hopped from the barstool with her drink to go to a table away from the unwanted attention from the creepy little barman.

As she sat sipping the vodka, she still couldn't remember who she was meeting. Whoever it was, she'd have to cry off she considered, suddenly feeling terribly unwell.

Standing up to leave, her chair crashed to the floor behind her. She apologised, but didn't know to whom. The room became hazy and difficult to decipher. When she reached the street, lights of cars passing were impossible to navigate. A car's horn honked loudly as she took a hesitant step onto the road from the safety of the pavement.

"Come on. I'll help you," a familiar and unwelcome voice whispered in her ear. It felt wrong, oh, so wrong. She shoved him away and darted across the road. Not stopping to see if he followed, she strained to recall the way.

Remembering the entire journey escaped her, but she was sure it wasn't long. Each time she came across a turning, it was with relief she grasped a hesitant inkling of which direction to head. The more correct choices she made, the more confident she became.

The promise of deliverance made her hurry more as she walked towards the streetlamp she always used as a landmark for picking out her path from the row of identical looking terraced houses. It seemed to have a particular significance but she didn't have time to wonder why. She had to get inside, into the safety of the house.

The footsteps reverberated hideously behind her. She could see the lamppost only a few metres ahead. Nearly there, she urged. Dare she look back? Her neck stiffened, threatening to paralyse her. Trembling, a certainty of doom clutched her heart. A powerlessness to prevent a horrific inevitability.

The path lay just ahead, she could almost touch it. Catching her sleeve on the hedge, she lost valuable seconds as she fought to free herself from the simple tangle which so perplexed her addled faculties.

The activity forced her gaze to the direction of her pursuer. The shadowy figure swaggered towards her, echoing footsteps becoming ever louder.

She freed herself from the shrubbery and stumbled up the path. The uneven steps proved almost impossible to negotiate, but then she was there, at the door. Where were her keys? She patted herself furiously with fumbling fingers. Where were they? Rooting with one hand, banging the door with the other, she cried out hysterically for help.

The keys dropped from her pocket to the floor in her hurry to retrieve them. As she stooped to pick them up, still banging on the door, the figure loomed over her.

"It doesn't look like anyone's in. Here. Let me help you." She screamed, wriggling away. Soon the door opened and she was being shoved inside. "Come on. Don't mess around. Go in the house. It's what you wanted, isn't it?"

"No. Get away from me," but even she couldn't recognise the garbled warbling escaping her dry lips. With all her force, she wrestled, desperate to be free from his grasp. The place she'd wanted to get to so desperately moments before—the place that seemed to offer sanctuary—she knew now would be the end of her.

As she fought, she felt her strength, and her will, ebb away. The manifestation of a shiny blade at her throat convinced her she had no choice. Her bodily control too impaired to fight off her attacker, she blacked out.

The next images entering her mind were spasmodic and traumatic: the sensation of being dragged, his voice, goading, "you know you want it, you little cock-tease! Lay still!" Determined to be as far from still as possible, Elin tried to writhe fiercely, but couldn't even feel if she was moving.

A vicious slap, and the sensation of cold steel pushing into her throat flared the next memory. His grotesque face pressed against hers. The hot stench of his cigarette breath. The pungent aroma of sweaty sex. And immense pain as her cramping, dry, unaroused genitals were forced to accommodate his.

She sobbed, pushing against him, every fibre fighting against the ultimate intimate intrusion. Resisting the repugnant motion of her body rocking back and fore to the rhythm of the sickening violation. Her mind tried to take her away. Picturing her mum and dad and sister brought no respite, instead shaming her into despair.

Why was she here? Why couldn't she stop him? She gritted her teeth and endured. Each desecrating thrust sending her further into an abhorrent abyss.

Another flash of consciousness and she lay alone on her bedroom floor, still unable to move; incapable even to curl into a ball to comfort herself. Paralysed with fear and humiliation. Unaware how long she'd lain, she could feel herself coming round. Still powerless, she somehow found the strength to open her eyes.

It was dark. A faint glow shone from her alarm clock. It looked different from her perspective on the floor. She wondered if any of her housemates were home. If anyone had come in who might discover her.

Torn between crying for help and wanting to hide, her mind struggled to make a plan. Couldn't she get into bed and disappear under her duvet covers? Pretend it hadn't happened? Her hand was forced when she still couldn't move, and found she cried out instinctively.

A swift movement, and a face loomed from the darkness, stopping inches from her own. She squeezed her eyes tight again and did her best to wriggle out of reach. Arms shook by her sides as she trembled in terror. What would happen to her now? She couldn't cope with any more.

The group huddled around the table in the séance heard everything. In a voice, a mixture of Elin's and her own, Sylvie channelled Elin's trauma and the rest had listened.

"I knew it!" Bronwyn exclaimed, catching Aeron's eye and squeezing his hand. "I'm so sorry," she added, glimpsing the ashen face atop Glenda's torte body.

"So, that little shit we let run away through the front door; who I felt guilty had been attacked by the spirit of my daughter, he…," Emyr fell silent, unable to continue his repulsive thought.

The priest wandered about the room, doing his best to ignore the séance, which he'd made clear he didn't approve of—"it's just this type of thing that got you into this mess", he'd rebuked. He busied himself with his own rituals, which, in-between muttering, occasionally entailed him shouting out phrases such as: "Be gone Demon. Leave Elin. Let her have her body."

Neil glanced at Matthew and Josh who'd been roused to join the others sometime during the cacophony when he'd momentarily removed his surround-sound headphones. "What now?" he asked.

"He can't get away with it!" Glenda growled.

"I don't think he has," ventured Matthew, but stopped abruptly with a dagger stare from Glenda.

"If you think that is enough." She shook her head slowly from side to side. "He'll go away for this, and think himself lucky he's not dead!"

Mumbled murmurs of agreement resounded. Sylvie, sat with eyes firmly closed again, let out a sudden gasp. Silence echoed as she gained the full attention of the group.

Even Father Jenkins, working his way around rosary beads in his hand and muttering under his breath, stopped and listened. Remaining motionless, her lips moved as though about to speak. The ongoing silence became painful to endure.

"What?" Emyr demanded. "What on earth is it now?"

She couldn't get away. The paralysing effects of whatever had been slipped into her drink combined with the stiffness of being forced to lie motionless conspired to leave her utterly helpless.

She daren't open her eyes again. Defenceless, she didn't want to see what he was going to do to her. With her eyes tight shut, she forced terrifying images of him away. A sob forced its way from her throat, exploding and echoing around the room.

What would he do? Had he not done enough? He was going to kill her. She knew it. Force of life-sustaining will allowed her a brief surge of strength. With her arms raised inches from her sides, she didn't trust them to offer much protection, but was determined to inflict whatever damage she could to the disgusting monster holding her in this drug induced prison.

Encouraged by her attempt, she knew she must use all her senses to make an effective strike. Perceiving his proximity from the shadows on her closed eyelids, and the warmth on her face from his, she took a final gulp of courage and opened her eyes.

"Elin? Oh my God! Elin!"

A wondrous euphoria washed over her as she gazed into the incredulous, tear-stained face of her sister. Her arms had reached the full extent of their range of motion which was scarcely enough to clutch at Alis's sides. But the feeling of love arced between them as they both broke down in purging sobs.

Sylvie gasped one more time, eyes darting in all directions behind their lids. Her mouth slowly formed the upward bow of a smile. When she opened them again, her eyes twinkled with delight. The group waited with expectancy and baited breath. "She's gone," she announced.

At the same moment, a shrill, American style long ring-tone resonated in the hallway. It took a while to recognise what it was, so immersed had they been in their paranormal world.

Recognition finally struck Emyr, who realised he must have removed his jacket and hung it by the front door. He hurried down the corridor and fumbled in his pocket for his phone. It stopped ringing, reverting to answerphone after its set number of rings.

Examining the screen, scrutinising the 'missed calls,' it burst into life again. Before it had displayed the caller, he thrust it to his ear and almost shouted hello.

"Dad? She's awake! You have to get back here. Elin has woken up!"

# Epilogue

Neil arrived at the hospital and parked. He had been so many times in the weeks since Elin's recovery he'd lost count. Elin had moved from the High Dependency Unit to a regular ward where most of the other patients were in their eighties.

She'd struck up firm friendships with several of them, and they cooed whenever Neil visited.

"Oh, your boyfriend's here, cariad." Elin always smiled politely and never bothered correcting them, persuading Neil in the part of his mind that harboured such fantasies, that her willingness to have him described so, meant something. His logical brain knew without a doubt she was just being kind.

He learned in the weeks Elin's formerly motionless body began to cope with moving again under the strict care of the hospital's team of physiotherapists, that as well as being the most incredibly beautiful girl he'd ever seen, she was also the most intelligent, kind and funny one, too.

After the emotional family reunion, Neil's part in saving Elin was bigged up. It could have been argued that it was Bronwyn who saved her. But recalling how Neil had seen her at the window, and set in motion the events which led to the lifesaving discoveries; and that the rest of the group, Glenda and Emyr included, thoroughly approved of the pair spending time together, it had been agreed: Neil was her saviour.

Elin thanked him profusely, and now, she assured him his support and encouragement with her Physio was really helping too.

He blushed at the attention from the old ladies, smiling at him behind all-seeing, twinkling eyes.

"Come on, Neil," Elin invited. "You can help me to the day room. We can have something to eat."

Neil looked enquiringly.

"Yes. I'm allowed to eat now. Just something light. Maybe some toast."

He felt sorry for her needing help to slowly hobble along the corridor. She'd improved loads since being bed-bound, to taking her first tentative steps, to now, walking with support. His sorrow faded at the thrill that once again, she had elected to use his arm for support rather than the Zimmer frame the Physio's had provided. He could fool himself they were on a date, walking arm in arm.

Elin ate toast, which one of the nurses had happily provided, while Neil chomped on a ham sandwich from the vending machine. They dissected, for the hundredth time, the events which led them here. They'd resigned themselves to not ever understanding fully, but they couldn't help but try.

"And you've never had any psychic ability?" Neil confirmed, chewing on the crust of his sandwich. Elin's delightful, delicate blonde hair shimmered as she shook her head.

"I sensed things at Erw Lon—my mum and dad's house. And I knew it worried my mum. But with our new perspective, I suppose we have to consider it might not be a ghost. Just the previous owner having a dream!"

"I hope I don't go anywhere in my dreams. I have pretty weird ones!" Neil frowned. Elin laughed. It was a delight to see.

"I know what you mean. I'm sure I don't travel every time. Just when there's unfinished business."

Neil looked thoughtful, unsure whether to broach the subject on his mind. He decided he should.

"Speaking of unfinished business… Jon," Elin flinched at the name. Neil got to the point quickly. "They've found plenty of other witnesses. Loads of girls have come forward after some inquiries. You were by no means the only one.

"Because of the large amounts of drugs he forced on you and the others, they didn't remember enough to make a complaint. And like you, they felt guilty. Ashamed, like they should have done something to stop him."

"I re-lived it. I know there's nothing I could have done." Elin closed her eyes, the memories a scab over a sceptic wound. A tear glistened in the corner of her eye. Shaking her head, she swallowed it down. "They've found the knife," she announced, a positive smile forced on her pretty face. "A policewoman came a few days ago. I think he's going down for a long time."

"He's not at The Railway anymore," Neil reported. "One of his near victims and her huge brother—he put him in hospital when he stepped out of line with his sister. Obviously nothing like he did to you or he'd have killed him—they're managing the pub now. Looks like it'll be permanent."

Elin munched her toast thoughtfully. "I'm glad. I'm not looking forward to testifying in court, but I'm glad he's not going to get away with it."

"I haven't seen him since you mauled him. I wonder how much damage you did."

The damage was mainly superficial, but he'd been severely traumatised by Elin's revenge. Scabs had formed on wounds all over his face, it wasn't clear yet if some of them might scar.

But Jon's life would never be the same again. Apart from the physical pain, and the distress of the peculiar circumstance in which he'd sustained his injuries, during the seeking of witnesses his likeness had been plastered in all the newspapers and even shown on television.

More than a few victims had come forward, along with dozens of damning character witnesses. A class action for compensation was being sought by lawyers for the victims. Most were unwilling to enter into it, not wanting to give any indication that what he did was made okay simply by throwing money at them.

"But you're owed more than most," Emyr prompted his daughter. "You became attached to that house purely because of the trauma he caused you. It's not the same for you. He put your life at risk twice."

Elin had given up being angry with her dad. She knew he only had her best interests at heart. He'd argued that nothing would change what happened. If anything faintly positive could come from it, then she was owed it.

Of course she was. And when she'd learned how much she might be able to claim, she had been tempted. She would never accept anything from him personally. But the criminal injuries compensation the police were encouraging her to take seemed somehow separate. Compensation from them for their failure to prevent Jon's abuse of women, rather than post-abuse remittance which sounded like prostitution.

After a lot of consideration, she decided not to accept any compensation from wherever the source. Anything she bought: a holiday to put it behind her, some nice clothes, or a car or whatever else, she feared would only serve to remind her of her lengthy ordeal. She just wanted to try to forget.

"I'm not taking any money, Dad. I've told you. Please don't go on," she said calmly, but with no hint she would ever change her mind. He smiled warmly. He admired her so much, and deep down, he knew she was making the right choice.

**Six weeks later…**

Elin laid her nicest outfits on the bed. Her dad patted her on the head and left her in peace. It was lovely to be home again. At her parents' home in any case. She hadn't made plans for the future yet, but apart from still needing a stick to walk for the time being, she felt better than she had in months.

And, tonight, she had a date. Well, kind of. Neil had been such a sweetheart, coming in most days for companionship; and it was obvious the debt of gratitude her mum and dad seemed to consider they owed him. When he'd asked her if he could take her out to dinner to celebrate her return home, she hadn't the heart to refuse.

Now, she had to admit to quite looking forward to it. He was certainly good company, and after her ordeal, she couldn't wish for a less threatening individual. She didn't want to encourage him too much, but opted for a classic LBD. She trusted Neil to behave himself and it had been such a long, long time since she'd had the opportunity.

She didn't wear a lot of make-up, but what she wore, was applied expertly, accentuating her best features (which was all of them.) Seeing herself looking so well was a real comfort. By the time she heard wheels on the gravel of the long drive of Erw Lon, she felt fantastic. Her mother's soft tones called gently from the foot of the stairs that Neil had arrived to take her out.

Glenda had become deeply spiritual since nearly losing her eldest daughter. She talked regularly to the spirit who resided in the hallway who wasn't a dreamer, but the ghost of the lady who'd lived there before them. She'd succumbed to frailty after a long illness and fallen to her death on the staircase. Her new friend, Sylvie had told her.) Having offered her love, and welcomed her to their home, they'd found comfort in occasionally feeling her presence.

Glenda ceased her own deliberate dream-travelling to the old Treharne family home. Knowing she was being seen, she didn't want to scare anyone. She wondered if everyone had the same power—to travel to places they felt particularly connected, or if it was the Treharne women's unique ability.

Sylvie hadn't heard of anything like it before, but thought it unlikely they'd be the only two women in the world it happened to. They pondered, dreamily, the possibilities and implications, but for now were just thrilled everything was okay again.

Ambling from her room, Elin sensed the ghost of the old lady smiling at her. She turned instinctively but wasn't surprised when she was no longer there. She thought she heard a faint whisper, "You deserve to be happy, my dear," but then she was distracted by the adoring gaze rising from the hallway.

As she descended the stairs, Neil opened and closed his mouth a few times before uttering a simple, "Wow," as she reached him. He was taller than she remembered, and as he stumbled taking her arm, she stifled a chuckle, noticing his several inch high Cuban Heels.

She was glad she hadn't worn a heel herself. Her poor mobility, not just deference to Neil's insecurities, had prompted a flat pump, but she was still inches taller.

Glenda and Emyr both appeared in the hallway to see them off. It felt like prom night. As Emyr held the door open and they stepped out, a shiny black Jaguar sat in the driveway. "It's my dad's," Neil said sheepishly. When he caught sight of the huge grin on Elin's face, he was pleased Collin had insisted on him borrowing it.

He opened her door like a true gentleman before settling himself behind the wheel of the executive saloon car.

"Where are you taking me?" Elin asked with a wink. The tan leather squeaking as she crossed her legs.

He fumbled with the electric seat adjustment for a perplexing moment, turning with a grimace to his evening's date. "Somewhere nice," he promised.

As his face reddened, Elin reached across and placed a reassuring hand on his thigh. "It's alright, Neil. There's no hurry." As he gazed at that perfect smile, he relaxed. He remembered how to access the seat's memory. It whirred into action raising him to the perfect position to commence their journey.

After an initial awkwardness, they chatted comfortably as Neil steered the beast around the tight bends from Llandovery to nearby Lampeter. A smile played on his lips imagining them in a movie scene. Him the hero saving a damsel in distress. His smile soured picturing how unsuited he was to the role. He shrugged it off, determined to enjoy his good fortune.

The Jaguar's fat wheels crunched on the stones as Neil steered into the sweeping drive of an enormous Georgian mansion. It was a wonderful scene, stepping out of the car onto the shingles with the girl of his dreams, surrounded by the stunning splendour of the Cambrian Mountains.

Elin took Neil's arm and left her stick in the car. The date he'd fantasised of when he'd helped her in the hospital was now a fabulous reality.

Smartly dressed front-of-house staff greeted them and showed them to an intimate table. Neil blushed as he caught sight of the buck-toothed midget walking arm in arm with the exquisite vision that was the reflection of the two of them. Elin saw it too and felt immensely proud to be with her kind and funny date.

Their conversation turned to plans for the future when Neil's face reddened. He took a gulp of mineral water (he wouldn't dream of drinking and driving.)

"I've been offered some interesting work. A group of hotels in Gran Canaria want me to set up their computer network. It'll take most of the summer and it pays pretty well."

"I'll miss you," Elin pronounced between dainty mouthfuls. She'd come to rely heavily on his friendship, and had presumed tonight's wonderful date would be the first of many.

"Well…" he tugged at his collar. "I can bring someone with me. It's all free. Food is included. And we can have separate beds. Separate rooms if you like. But it'd be amazing if you'd come with me…" Neil was almost puce now.

He wished he had a camera as the most beautiful girl he'd ever seen, leaned in, pulled him close and kissed him full on the lips.

"I'd love to," she said.

## The End

**We hope you have enjoyed this book**

If you would be happy to leave a few words on Amazon or Goodreads by way of a review, or even just a star rating, that will be invaluable in helping other readers to find it, as well as helping the author to be more discoverable.

If you're happy to help, please follow the link.

Take me to Amazon...

Thank you.

*Remember the link to a free short story mentioned at the beginning of the book?*

Join the author's reader group for updates on new releases etc. and receive *No1 hot new release in short stories*, '***Frankenstein's Hamster***' absolutely free.

Take me to my FREE book!

# About the Author

Michael grew up in the leafy suburbs of Hertfordshire in the eighties. His earliest school memories from his first parent's evening were being told "You have to be a writer"; advice Michael didn't take for another thirty-five years, despite a burning desire.

Instead, he forged a career in direct sales, travelling the length and breadth of Southern England selling fitted kitchens, bedrooms, double-glazing and conservatories, before running his own water-filter business (with an army of over four hundred water filter salesmen and women) and then a conservatory sales and building company.

All that came to an end when Michael became a carer for a family member and moved to Wales, where he finally found the time and inspiration to write.

Michael now indulges his passion in the beautiful Pembrokeshire Coast National Park where he lives, walks and works with his wife, four children and dogs.

If you'd like to contact Michael for any reason, he would be delighted to hear from you and endeavours to answer all messages whenever possible.

mailto:info@michaelchristophercarter.co.uk
https://www.facebook.com/michaelchristophercarter/
https://twitter.com/MCCarterAuthor
https://www.michaelchristophercarter.co.uk

More books from Michael

## Frankenstein's hamster

Monsters can be small... And furry

Harvey Collins is a seventeen year-old prodigy gifted with a scientific mind that even has Oxford University excited.
When his sister's Christmas present of an adorable hamster falls foul of their alcoholic rodent-phobic father, Harvey is the best person to give him a new lease of life.
Using what's left of the hamster and parts of a rat and even himself, Harvey soon develops a pet like no other. Bestowed with remarkable intelligence and a thirst for revenge, Harvey's hamster is a monster in waiting.
Will anyone make it out alive?

*Released just in time for Christmas, this short novella packs in Carter's renowned depth of characters and a thrill-a-minute read in a small package ideal for a car-journey to visit the relatives!*http://getbook.at/FrankensteinKindle

Or get a copy absolutely free by joining Michael's Reader Group (where you'll also get news of new releases) https://www.michaelchristophercarter.co.uk/no-1-hot-new-release-free

**Blood is Thicker Than Water**

*What is wrong with the water in Goreston's Holy Well?*

When the vicar of a small Welsh community disappears
after two little girls are murdered, Reverend Bertie
Brimble steps into the breach.
His family are horrified at the danger he's putting his
own daughter in. Especially as she looks startlingly like
the other victims.
They do everything they can to keep her safe until Bertie
himself begins behaving strangely, battling the worst
possible desires.

And he's not the only one...

A terrible fate awaits anyone who drinks from
Goreston's Holy well
Can Bertie uncover the truth about what's in the water
before it's too late?

"Still reeling from the twists...

"Kept me thinking long after I'd finished reading..."

"The epitome of a great writer…"

*Blood is Thicker Than Water is a remarkably thought-
provoking horror tale from Wales's master of the
supernatural.*

## The Nightmare of Eliot Armstrong

*Can you stop a nightmare coming true?*

Eliot Armstrong, swarthy, handsome, head of history at
Radcliff Comprehensive is jolted awake every morning;
tortured by horrific, indecipherable images of a road
accident.

Piecing the disturbing visions together day by day, he's
horrified when he recognises one of the cars… his wife
Imogen's.

Is it a precognition of his wife's fate?

Or is it a subconscious metaphor for the danger his
marriage is in from his man-eating colleague, Uma
Yazbeck?

He must do everything in his power to save his wife, and
his marriage. But for Eliot, his nightmare is only just
beginning…


*Do you like thrillers with plenty of twists?*

Get this paranormal noir thriller today

**http://viewbook.at/nightmare**

**Destructive Interference**
*– The Devastation of Matthew Morrissey*

*Choices will never be the same again...*

**When Matthew Morrissey takes an innocent stroll to his local convenience store to buy batteries for his daughter's Christmas present**, he doesn't know it will ruin his life.

But, when he returns home, **everything has changed...** There are strangers in his home, his neighbours deny ever knowing him and he ends up attracting the attention of Bristol's finest.

Matthew has a theory about what is happening to him and who is to blame. But first, he has to escape.

Can he solve the mystery and save his family, or has he lost them forever?

Buy yours today. You can be sure it won't be like anything you've read before.
**http://mybook.to/Destructive**

**An Extraordinary Haunting**

*The Christmas holidays can't come soon enough...*

Swansea student, Neil Hedges is counting the days until
he can leave his terrifying student digs and go home for
Christmas.
For weeks he's suffered terrifying noises in the middle
of the night and things moving which shouldn't. It's all
becoming clear: someone or *something* wants him out!
When a psychic friend of the family confirms his worst
fears, Neil and his fellow students can't bear to go back.

But nothing is as it seems, and when beautiful former
housemate, Elin Treharne, is plagued by nightmares of
her one-time home; nightmares which reveal a
disturbing and life-threatening truth, even she doesn't
realise the peril she's in...
Only Neil can work it out and save her before it's too
late.
But Neil can't cope...

*If you're looking for a paranormal thriller beyond the
norm,
you've found it.*
**Get this twisting Christmas thriller today.**

**http://getbook.at/Extraordinary**

**You don't have to be DEAD to work here**

**... But it helps**

**You hear your name, but no-one is there...**

**Night after night after night, growing more
and more gruesome in its demands, a voice from the
darkness.**

*What would you do?*

**Angharad's simple life is about to take a sinister
twist...**

Since retiring from working in a care home, Angharad is
very much self-sufficient: growing her own vegetables,
eating eggs from her hens, drinking milk from her goat
and even water from her own spring flowing at the
bottom of her garden in rural South-West Wales. In
many ways, it seems ideal.
But who is it calling out her name in the dark when no-
one is there? And what could they possibly want?
Angharad doesn't know, but she must find out.
Will she uncover the truth before it costs her, her life?

*An intriguing and thought provoking short novel from
Wales's master of the paranormal.*
<u>Open up the supernatural world of Michael
Christopher Carter with this title today...</u>

# The HUM

*If you're paranoid,*
*does that mean they're not coming to get you?*

A strange humming noise, which seems to have no
source, is tormenting the villagers of Nuthampstead,
England, in 1989...

To the Ellis family, recently moved from the valleys of
Wales, it has a sinister significance. They don't like to
talk about it.

But Carys Ellis is only six, and she has to tell someone
about the terrifying visitors to her room in the middle of
the night when her family would not, and could not be
roused.

And that's only the beginning of Carys's plight. Her
mother is a long-term sufferer of a number of mental
health problems. Diagnosed with bipolar disorder, manic
depression, and borderline disorder, she's a drugged up
mess.

And Carys seems to be heading the same way . . .

Twelve years later, beautiful loner, Carys, is pregnant.
She's never had a boyfriend; never had a one-night
stand; she's never had any intimate contact with anyone
to explain her condition.

Not anyone human anyway.

Plagued by the dreadful humming all her life, Carys is
convinced the noise precedes close encounters of the
fourth kind; and that the baby inside her is not of this

world.

She can't tell anyone. Her mum couldn't cope, and her dad's been relocated from Cambridge Constabulary to a quiet Welsh village after a nervous breakdown leaving Carys struggling with her own demons.

Can she protect her baby from its extra-terrestrial creators, or will they whisk him away for some unknown purpose?

Will the demons who torment her get to him first?

Or, is she just a little crazy...?

*Michael Christopher Carter's stunning portrayal of one family's struggle against mental illness and other-worldly threats is a masterpiece.*

*Described as "Life changing," this thoroughly well-researched novel is a must read for anyone curious about what exists both out in the cosmos and within our own minds.*

Get this book today and prepare to have your eyes opened...

**http://viewbook.at/TheHUM**